TERRY PRATCHETT

DiGGERS

THE SECOND BOOK OF THE NOMES

CORGI BOOKS

Diggers

In the Beginning . . .

. . . Arnold Bros (est. 1905) created the Store.

At least, that was the belief of thousands of nomes who for many generations* had lived under the floorboards of Arnold Bros (est. 1905), an old and respected department store.

The Store had become their world. A world with a roof and walls.

Wind and Rain were ancient legends. So were Day and Night. Now there were sprinkler systems and air conditioners, and their small crowded lives ticked to the clock of Opening Time and Closing Time. The seasons of their year were January Sales, Spring Into Spring Fashions, Summer Bargains and Christmas Fayre. Led by the Abbot and priesthood of the Stationeri, they worshipped – in a polite, easy-going sort of way, so as not to upset him – Arnold Bros (est. 1905), who they believed had created everything, i.e. the Store and all the contents therein.

Some families of nomes had grown rich and powerful and took the names – more or less – of the Store departments they lived under . . . the Del Icatessen, the Ironmongri, the Haberdasheri.

And into the Store, on the back of a lorry, came the last nomes to live Outside. They knew what wind and rain were, all right. That's why they'd tried to leave them behind.

Among them was Masklin, rat-hunter, and Granny

---

* Nome generations, that is. Nomes live ten times faster than humans. To them, ten years is a long lifetime.

Morkie and Grimma, although they were women and didn't really count. And, of course, there was the Thing.

No one quite understood the Thing. Masklin's people had handed it down for centuries; it was very important, that was all they knew. When it came near the electricity in the Store it was able to talk. It *said* it was a thinking machine from a ship which, thousands of years before, had brought the nomes from a far Store, or possibly star. It also said it could hear electricity talk, and one of the things the electricity was saying was that the Store would be demolished in three weeks.

It was Masklin who suggested that the nomes leave the Store on a lorry. He found, oddly enough, that actually working out how you could drive a giant lorry was the easiest part. The hardest part was getting people to believe that they could do it.

He wasn't the leader. He'd have liked to be a leader. A leader could stick his chin out and do brave things. What Masklin had to do was argue and persuade and, sometimes, lie very slightly. He found it was often easier to get people to do things if you let them think it was their idea.

Ideas! That was the tricky bit, all right. And there were lots of ideas that they needed. They needed to learn to work together. They needed to learn to read. They needed to think that female nomes were, well, nearly as intelligent as males (although everyone knew that really this was ridiculous and that if females were encouraged to think too much their brains overheated).

Anyway, it all worked. The lorry did leave the Store just before it mysteriously burned down and, hardly damaging anything very much, was driven out into the country.

The nomes found an abandoned quarry tucked into a hillside, and moved into the ruined buildings. And then, they knew, everything was going to be All Right.

There was going to be, they'd heard, a Bright New Dawn.

Of course, most nomes had never seen a dawn, bright or otherwise, and if they had they would have known that the trouble with bright new dawns is that they're usually followed by cloudy days. With scattered showers.

Six months passed . . .

This is the story of the Winter.

This is the Great Battle.

This is the story of the awakening of Jekub, the Dragon in the Hill, with eyes like great eyes and a voice like a great voice and teeth like great teeth.

But the story didn't end there.

It didn't start there, either.

The sky blew a gale. The sky blew a fury. The wind became a wall sweeping across the country, a giant stamping on the land. Small trees bent, big trees broke. The last leaves of autumn whirred through the air like lost bullets.

The rubbish heap by the gravel pits was deserted. The seagulls that patrolled it had found shelter somewhere, but it was still full of movement.

The wind tore into the heap as though it had something particular against old detergent boxes and leftover shoes. Tins rolled into the ruts and clanked miserably, while lighter bits of rubbish flew up and joined the riot in the sky.

Still the wind burrowed. Papers rustled for a while, then got caught and blasted away.

Finally, one piece that had been flapping for hours tore free and flew up into the booming air. It looked like a large white bird with oblong wings.

Watch it tumble . . .

It gets caught on a fence, but very briefly. Half of it tears off and now, that much lighter, it pinwheels across the furrows of the field beyond . . .

It is just gathering speed when a hedge looms up and snaps it out of the air like a fly.

> I. *And in that time were Strange Happenings: the Air moved harshly, the Warmth of the Sky grew Less, on some mornings the tops of puddles grew Hard and Cold.*
>
> II. *And the nomes said unto one another, What is this Thing?*
>
> From The Book of Nome, *Quarries 1, v.I–II*

'Winter,' said Masklin firmly. 'It's called winter.'

Abbot Gurder frowned at him.

'You never said it would be like *this*,' he said. 'It's so *cold*.'

'Call this cold?' said Granny Morkie. 'Cold? This ain't cold. You think this is cold? You wait till it gets really cold!' She was enjoying this, Masklin noticed; Granny Morkie always enjoyed doom, it was what kept her going. 'It'll be really cold then, when it gets cold. You get *real* frosts and, and water comes down out of the sky in frozen bits!' She leaned back triumphantly. 'What d'you think to that, then? Eh?'

'You don't have to use baby talk to us,' sighed Gurder. 'We *can* read, you know. We know what snow is.'

'Yes,' said Dorcas. 'There used to be cards with pictures on, back in the Store. Every time Christmas Fayre came around. We know about snow. It's glittery.'

'You get robins,' agreed Gurder.

'There's, er, actually there's a bit more to it than that,' Masklin began.

Dorcas waved him into silence. 'I don't think we need to worry,' he said. 'We're well dug in, the food stores are looking satisfactory, and we know where to go to get more if we need it. Unless anyone's got anything else to raise, why don't we close the meeting?'

Everything was going well. Or, at least, not very badly.

Oh, there was still plenty of squabbling and rows between the various families, but that was nomish nature for you. That's why they'd set up the Council, which seemed to be working.

Nomes liked arguing. At least the Council of Drivers meant they could argue without hardly ever hitting one another.

Funny thing, though. Back in the Store the great departmental families had run things. But now all the families were mixed up and, anyway, there were no departments in a quarry. But by instinct, almost, nomes liked hierarchies. The world had always been neatly divided between those who told people what to do, and those who did it. So, in a strange way, a new set of leaders were emerging.

The Drivers.

It depended on where you had been during the Long Drive. If you were one of the ones who had been in the lorry cab, then you were a Driver. All the rest were just Passengers. No one talked about it much. It wasn't official or anything. It was just that the bulk of nomekind felt that anyone who could get the Truck all the way here was the sort of person who knew what they were doing.

Being a Driver wasn't necessarily much fun.

Last year, before they'd found the Store, Masklin had to hunt all day. Now he only hunted when he felt like it;

the younger Store nomes liked hunting and apparently it wasn't *right* for a Driver to do it. They mined potatoes and there'd been a big harvest of corn from a nearby field, even after the machines had been round. Masklin would have preferred them to grow their own food, but the nomes didn't seem to have the knack of making seeds grow in the rock-hard ground of the quarry. But they were getting fed, that was the main thing.

Around him he could feel thousands of nomes living their lives. Raising families. *Settling down.*

He wandered back to his own burrow, down under one of the derelict quarry sheds. After a while he reached a decision and pulled the Thing out of its own hole in the wall.

None of its lights were on. They wouldn't do that until it was close to electricity wires, when it would light up and be able to talk. There were some in the quarry, and Dorcas had got them working. Masklin hadn't taken the Thing to them, though. The solid black box had a way of talking that always made him unsettled.

He was pretty certain it could hear, though.

'Old Torrit died last week,' he said after a while. 'We were a bit sad but, after all, he was very old and he just died. I mean, nothing ate him first or ran him over or anything.'

Masklin's little tribe had once lived in a motorway embankment beside rolling countryside which was full of things that were hungry for fresh nome. The idea that you could die simply of not being alive any more was a new one to them.

'So we buried him up on the edge of the potato field, too deep for the plough. The Store nomes haven't got the hang of burial yet, I think. They think he's going to sprout, or something. I think they're mixing it up with what you do with seeds. Of course, they don't know about growing things. Because of living in the Store, you see. It's all new to them. They're always complaining about eating food that comes out of the ground; they think it's not natural. And they think the rain is a sprinkler system. I think *they* think the whole world is just a bigger store. Um.'

He stared at the unresponsive cube for a while, scraping his mind for other things to say.

'Anyway, that means Granny Morkie is the oldest nome,' he said eventually. 'And *that* means she's entitled to a place on the Council even though she's a woman. Abbot Gurder objected to that but we said, all right, you tell her, and he wouldn't, so she is. Um.'

He looked at his fingernails. The Thing had a way of listening that was quite off-putting.

'Everyone's worried about the winter. Um. But we've got masses of potatoes stored up, and it's quite warm down here. They've got some funny ideas, though. In the Store they said that when it was Christmas Fayre time there was this thing that came called Santer Claws. I just hope it hasn't followed us, that's all. Um.'

He scratched an ear.

'All in all, everything's going right. Um.'

He leaned closer.

'You know what that means? If you think everything's going right, something's going wrong that you haven't heard about yet. That's what I say. Um.'

The black cube managed to look sympathetic.

'Everyone says I worry too much. I don't think it's *possible* to worry too much. Um.'

He thought some more.

'Um. I think that's about all the news for now.' He lifted the Thing up and put it back in its hole.

He'd wondered whether to tell it about his argument with Grimma, but that was, well, personal.

It was all that reading books, that was what it was. He

shouldn't have let her learn to read, filling her head with stuff she didn't need to know. Gurder was right, women's brains *did* overheat. Grimma's seemed to be boiling hot the whole time, these days.

He'd gone and said, look, now everything was settled down more, it was time they got married like the Store nomes did, with the Abbot muttering words and everything.

And she'd said, she wasn't sure.

So he'd said, it doesn't work like that, you get told, you get married, that's how it's done.

And she'd said, not any more.

He'd complained to Granny Morkie. You'd have expected some support there, he thought. She was a great one for tradition, was Granny. He'd said: Granny, Grimma isn't doing what I tell her.

And *she'd* said: Good luck to her. Wish I'd thought of not doin' what I was told when I was a gel.

Then he'd complained to Gurder who said, yes, it was very wrong, girls should do what they were instructed. And Masklin had said, right then, you tell her. And Gurder had said, well, er, she's got a real temper on her, perhaps it would be better to leave it a bit and these were, after all, changing times . . .

Changing times. Well, that was true enough. Masklin had done most of the changing. He'd had to make people think in different ways to leave the Store. Changing was necessary. Change was right. He was all in favour of change.

What he was dead against was things not staying the same.

His spear was leaning in the corner. What a pathetic thing it was . . . now. Just a bit of flint held on to the shaft with a twist of binder twine. They'd brought saws and things from the Store. They could use metal these days.

He stared at the spear for some time. Then he picked it up and went out for a long, serious think about things and his position in them. Or, as other people would have put it, a good sulk.

The old quarry was about halfway up the hillside. There was a steep turf slope above it, which in turn became a riot of bramble and hawthorn thicket. There were fields beyond.

Below the quarry a lane wound down through scrubby hedges and joined the main road. Beyond that there was the railway, another name for two long lines of metal on big wooden blocks. Things like very long trucks went along it sometimes, all joined together.

The nomes had not got the railway fully worked out yet. But it was obviously dangerous, because they could see a lane that crossed it and, whenever the railway moving thing was coming, two gates came down over the road.

The nomes knew what gates were for. You saw them on fields, to stop things getting out. It stood to reason, therefore, that the gates were to stop the railway from escaping from its rails and rushing around on the roads.

Then there were more fields, some gravel pits – good for fishing, for the nomes who wanted fish – and then there was the airport.

Masklin had spent hours in the summer watching the planes. They drove along the ground, he noticed, and then went up sharply, like a bird, and got smaller and smaller and disappeared.

That was the *big* worry. Masklin sat on his favourite stone, in the rain that was starting to fall, and started to worry about it. So many things were worrying him these days he had to stack them up, but below all of them was this big one.

They should be going where the planes went. That was what the Thing had told him, when it was still speaking to him. The nomes had come from the sky. Up above the sky, in fact, which was a bit hard to understand, because surely the only thing above the sky was more sky. And they should go back. It was their . . . something beginning with D. Density. Their density. Worlds of their own, they once had. And somehow they'd got stuck here. But – this was the worrying part – the ship thing, the aeroplane that flew through the really high sky, between the stars, was still up there somewhere. The first nomes had left it behind when they came down here in a smaller ship, and it had crashed, and they hadn't been able to get back.

And he was the only one that knew.

The old Abbot, the one before Gurder, he had known. Grimma and Dorcas and Gurder all knew some of it, but they had busy minds and they were practical people and there was so much to organize these days.

It was just that everyone was settling down. We're going to turn this into our little world, just like in the Store, Masklin realized. They thought the roof was the sky, and we think the sky is the roof.

We'll just stay and . . .

There was a truck coming up the quarry road. It was such an unusual sight that Masklin realized he had been watching it for a while without really seeing it at all.

'There was no one on watch! Why wasn't there anyone on watch? I said there should always be someone on watch!'

Half a dozen nomes scurried through the dying bracken towards the quarry gate.

'It was Sacco's turn,' muttered Angalo.

'No, it wasn't!' hissed Sacco. 'You remember, yesterday you asked me to swap because – '

'I don't care whose turn it was!' shouted Masklin. 'There was no one there! And there should have been! Right?'

'Sorry, Masklin.'

'Yeah. Sorry, Masklin.'

They scrambled up a bank and flattened themselves behind a tuft of dried grass.

It was a small truck, as far as trucks went. A human had already climbed out of it and was doing something to the gates leading into the quarry.

'It's a Land Rover,' said Angalo smugly. He'd spent a long time in the Store reading everything he could about vehicles, before the Long Drive. He liked them. 'It's not really a truck, it's more to carry humans over –'

'That human is sticking something on the gate,' said Masklin.

'On *our* gate,' said Sacco disapprovingly.

'Bit odd,' said Angalo. The man sleepwalked, in the slow, ponderous way that humans did, back to the vehicle. Eventually it backed around and roared off.

'All the way up here just to stick a bit of paper on the gate,' said Angalo, as the nomes stood up. 'That's humans for you.'

Masklin frowned. Humans were big and stupid, that was true enough, but there was something unstoppable about them and they seemed to be controlled by bits of paper. Back in the Store a piece of paper had said the Store was going to be demolished and, sure enough, it *had* been demolished. You couldn't trust humans with bits of paper.

He pointed to the rusty wire netting, an easy climb for an agile nome.

'Sacco,' he said, 'you'd better fetch it down.'

Miles away, *another* piece of paper fluttered on the hedge. Spots of rain pattered across its sun-bleached words, soaking the paper until it was heavy and soggy and . . .

. . . tore.

It flopped on to the grass, free. A breeze made it rustle.

2

III. *But there came a Sign, and people said, What is it that this means?*

IV. *And it was not good.*

From The Book of Nome, *Signs, Chap. 1, v.III–IV*

Gurder shuffled on hands and knees across the paper which had been taken down from the gate.

'Of course I can read it,' he said. 'I know what every word means.'

'Well, then?' said Masklin.

Gurder looked embarrassed. 'It's what every sentence means that's giving me trouble,' he said. 'It says here . . . where was it . . . yes, it says here the quarry is going to be re-opened. What does that mean? It's open already, any fool knows that. You can see for miles.'

The other nomes crowded around. You certainly could see for miles. That was the terrible part. On three sides the quarry had decent high cliff walls, but on the fourth side . . . well, you got into the habit of not looking in that direction. There was too much of nothing, which made you feel even smaller and more vulnerable than you were already.

Even if the meaning of the paper wasn't clear, it certainly looked unpleasant.

'The quarry's a hole in the ground,' said Dorcas. 'You can't open a hole unless it's been filled in. Stands to reason.'

'A quarry's a place you get stone from,' said Grimma. 'Humans do it. They dig a hole and they use the stone for making, well, roads and things.'

'I expect you read that, did you?' said Gurder sourly. He suspected Grimma of lack of respect for authority. It was also incredibly annoying that, against all the obvious deficiencies of her sex, she was better at reading than he was.

'I did, actually,' said Grimma, tossing her head.

'But, you see,' said Masklin patiently, 'there aren't any more stones here, Grimma. That's why there's a hole.'

'Good point,' said Gurder, sternly.

Then he'll make the hole bigger!' snapped Grimma. 'Look at those cliffs up there — ' they obediently looked, ' — they're made of stone! Look here — ' every head swivelled down to where her foot was tapping impatiently at the paper, '— it says it's for a motorway extension! That's a road! He's going to make the quarry bigger! Our quarry! That's what it says he's going to do!'

There was a long silence.

Then Dorcas said: 'Who is?'

'Order! He's put his name on it,' said Grimma.

'She's right, you know,' said Masklin. 'Look. It says: "To be re-opened, by Order".'

The nomes shuffled their feet. Order. It didn't sound a promising name. Anyone called Order would probably be capable of anything.

Gurder stood up and brushed the dust off his robe.

'It's only a piece of paper, when all's said and done,' he said sullenly.

'But the human came up here,' said Masklin. 'They've never come up here before.'

'Dunno about that,' said Dorcas. 'I mean, all the quarry buildings. The old workshops. The doorways and so on. I mean, they're for humans. Always worried me, that has. Where humans have been before, they tend to go again. They're rascals for that.'

There was another crowded silence, the kind that gets made by lots of people thinking unhappy thoughts.

'Do you mean,' said a nome slowly, 'that we've come all this way, we've worked so hard to make a place to live in, and now it's going to be taken away?'

'I don't think we should get too disturbed right at this time — ' Gurder began.

'We've got families here,' said another nome. Masklin realized that it was Angalo. He'd been married in the spring to a young lady from the Del Icatessen family, and they'd already got a fine pair of youngsters, two months old and talking already.

'And we were going to have another go at planting seeds,' said another nome. 'We've spent ages clearing that ground behind the big sheds. You *know* that.'

Gurder raised his hand imploringly.

'We don't know anything,' he said. 'We mustn't start getting upset until we've found out what's going on.'

'And *then* can we get upset?' said another nome sourly. Masklin recognized Nisodemus, one of the Stationeri and Gurder's own assistant. He'd never liked the young nome, and the young nome had never liked anyone, as far as Masklin could see.

'I've never, um, been happy with the *feel* of this place, um, I *knew* there was going to be trouble — ' Nisodemus complained.

'Now, now, Nisodemus,' said Gurder. 'There's no cause to go talking like that. We'll have another meeting of the Council,' he added. 'That's what we'll do.'

The crumpled newspaper lay beside the road. Occasionally a breeze would blow it randomly along the verge while, a few inches away, the traffic thundered past.

A stronger gust hit it at the same time as a particularly

large truck roared by, dragging a tail of whirling air. The paper shot up over the road, spread out like a sail, and rose on the wind.

The Quarry Council was in session, in the space under the floor of the old quarry office.

Other nomes had crowded in and the rest of the tribe milled around outside.

'Look,' said Angalo, 'there's a big old barn up on the hill, the other side of the potato field. It wouldn't hurt to take some stores up there. Make it ready, you know. Just in case. Then if anything *does* happen, we've got somewhere to go.'

'The quarry buildings don't have spaces under the floors, except in the canteen and the office,' said Dorcas gloomily. 'It's not like the Store. There aren't many places to hide. We need the sheds. If humans come here, we'll have to leave.'

'So the barn will be a good idea, won't it?' repeated Angalo.

'There's a man on a tractor who goes up there sometimes,' said Masklin.

'We could keep out of his way. Anyway,' said Angalo, looking around at the rows of faces, 'maybe the humans will go away again. P'raps they'll just take their stone and go. And we can come back. We could send someone to spy on them every day.'

'It seems to me you've been thinking about this barn for some time,' said Dorcas.

'Me and Masklin talked about it one day when we were hunting up there,' said Angalo. 'Didn't we, Masklin?'

'Hmm?' said Masklin, who was staring into space.

'You remember, we went up there and I said that'd be a useful place if ever we needed it, and you said yes.'

'Hmm,' said Masklin.

'Yes, but there's this Winter thing coming,' said one of the nomes. 'You know. Cold. Glitter on everythin'.'

'Robins,' another nome put in.

'Yeah,' said the first nome uncertainly. 'Them, too. Not a good time to go movin' around, with robins zoomin' about.'

'Nothing wrong with robins,' said Granny Morkie, who had nodded off for a moment. 'My dad used to say there's good eatin' on a robin, if you catched one.' She beamed at them, proudly.

This comment had the same effect on everyone's train of thought as a brick wall built across the line. Eventually Gurder said: 'I still say we shouldn't get too excited right at this moment. We should wait and trust in Arnold Bros (est. 1905)'s guidance.'

There was more silence. Then Angalo said, very quietly: 'Fat lot of good that'll do us.'

There was silence again. But this time it was a thick, heavy silence, and it got thicker and heavier and more menacing, like a storm cloud building up over a mountain, until the first flash of lightning would come as a relief.

It came.

'What did you say?' said Gurder, slowly.

'Only what everyone's been thinking,' said Angalo. Many of the nomes started to stare at their feet.

'And what do you mean by that?' said Gurder.

'Where *is* Arnold Bros (est. 1905), then?' said Angalo. '*How* did he help us get out of the Store? Exactly, I mean? He didn't, did he.' Angalo's voice shook a bit, as if even he was terrified to hear himself talking like this. '*We* did it. By learning things. We did it all ourselves. We learned to read books, *your* books, and we found things out and we did things for ourselves . . .'

Gurder jumped to his feet, white with fury. Beside him Nisodemus put his hand over his mouth and looked too shocked to speak.

'Arnold Bros (est. 1905) goes wherever nomes go!' Gurder shouted.

Angalo swayed backwards, but his father had been one of the toughest nomes in the Store and he didn't give in easily.

'You just made that up!' he snorted. 'I'm not saying that there wasn't, well, *something* in the Store, but that was the Store and this is here and all we've got is *us*! The trouble is, you Stationeri were so powerful in the Store you just can't bear to give it up!'

Now Masklin stood up.

'Just a moment, you two – ' he began.

'So that's all it is, is it?' growled Gurder, ignoring him. 'That's the Haberdasheri for you! You always were too proud! Too arrogant by half! Drive a lorry a little way and we think we know it all, do we? Perhaps we're getting what we deserve, eh?'

' – this isn't the time or place for this sort of thing – ' Masklin went on.

'That's just a silly threat! Why can't you accept it, you old fool. Arnold Bros doesn't exist! Use the brains Arnold Bros gave you, why don't you?'

'If you don't both shut up I'll bang your heads together!'

That seemed to work.

'Right,' said Masklin, in a more normal voice. 'Now, I think it would be a very good idea if everyone went and got on with – with whatever it was they were getting on with. Because this is no way to make complicated decisions. We all need to think for a bit.'

The nomes filed out, relieved that it was over. Masklin could hear Gurder and Angalo arguing outside.

'Not you two,' he warned.

'Now *look* – ' said Gurder.

'No, you look, the pair of you!' said Masklin. 'Here we are, maybe a big problem looming up, and you start arguing! You both ought to know better! Can't you see you're upsetting people?'

'Well, it's important,' muttered Angalo.

'*What we should do now*,' said Masklin sharply, 'is have another look at this barn. Can't say I'm happy with the idea, but it might be useful to have a bolt-hole. Anyway, it'll keep people occupied, and that'll stop them worrying. How about it?'

'I suppose so,' said Gurder, with bad grace. 'But – '

'No more buts,' said Masklin. 'You're acting like idiots. People look up to the pair of you, so you'll set an example, do you hear?'

They glowered at one another, but they both nodded.

'Right, then,' said Masklin. 'Now, we'll all go out, and people'll see you've made up, and that'll stop them fretting. *Then* we can start planning.'

'But Arnold Bros (est. 1905) *is* important,' said Gurder.

'I dare say,' said Masklin, as they came out into the daylight of the quarry. The wind was dropping again, leaving the sky a deep cold blue.

'There's no "dare say" about it,' said Gurder.

'Listen,' said Masklin, 'I don't know whether Arnold Bros exists, or was in the Store, or just lives in our heads or whatever. What I *do* know is that he isn't just going to drop out of the sky.'

All three of them glanced up when he said this. The Store nomes shuddered just a bit. It still took a certain courage to look up at the endless sky when you'd been used to nice friendly floorboards, but it was traditional, when you referred to Arnold Bros, to look up. Up was where Management and Accounts had been, back in the Store.

'Funny you should say that. There's something up there,' said Angalo.

Something white and vaguely rectangular was drifting gently through the air, and growing bigger.

'It's just a bit of paper,' said Gurder. 'Something the wind's blown off the dump.'

It was definitely a lot bigger now, and turned gently in the air as it tumbled into the quarry.

'I think,' said Masklin slowly, as its shadow raced towards him across the ground, 'that we'd better stand back a bit — '

It dropped on him.

It was, of course, only paper. But nomes are small and it had fallen quite some way, so the force was enough to knock him over.

What was more surprising were the words he saw as he fell backwards. They were: Arnold Bros.

3

> I. *And they Sought for a Better Sign from Arnold Bros (est. 1905), and there was a Sign;*
>
> II. *And some spake up saying, Well, all right, but it is really nothing but a Co incidence;*
>
> III. *But others said, Even a Co incidence can be a Sign.*
>
> *From* The Book of Nome, *Signs, Chap. 2, v.I–III*

Masklin had always kept an open mind on the subject of Arnold Bros (est. 1905). When you thought about it, the Store had been pretty impressive, what with the moving staircases and so on, and if Arnold Bros (est. 1905) hadn't created it, who had? After all, that only left humans. Not that he considered humans to be as stupid as most nomes thought. They might be big and slow but there was a sort of gormless unstoppability about them. They could certainly be taught to do simple tasks.

On the other hand, the world was *miles* across and full of complicated things. It seemed to be asking a lot of Arnold Bros (est. 1905) to create the whole thing.

So Masklin had decided not to decide anything about Arnold Bros (est. 1905), in the hope that if there *was* an Arnold Bros (est. 1905) and he found out about Masklin, he wouldn't mind much.

The trouble with having an open mind, of course, is that people will insist on coming along and trying to put things in it.

The faded newspaper from the sky had been carefully spread out on the floor of one of the old sheds.

It was covered in words. Most of them even Masklin could understand, but even Grimma had to admit she couldn't guess at what they were supposed to mean when you read them all in one go. SCHOOL SLAMS SHOCK PROBE, for example, was a bit of a mystery. So was FURY OVER RATES REBEL. So was PLAY SUPER BINGO IN YOUR SOARAWAY BLACKBURY EVENING POST & GAZETTE. But they were mysteries that would have to wait.

What all eyes were staring at was the quite small area of words, about nome-sized, under the word PEOPLE.

'That means people,' said Grimma.

'Really?' said Masklin.

'And the lettering underneath it says: 'Fun-loving, globe-trotting millionaire playboy Richard Arnold will be jetting to the Florida sunshine next week to witness the launch of Arnsat 1, the first communi – ' she hesitated, ' – cations sat . . . ellite built by Arnco Inter . . . national Group. This leap into the future comes only a few months after the dest . . . ruction by fire of – '

The nomes, who'd been silently reading along with her, shivered.

' – Arnold Bros, the store here in Blackbury which was the first of the Arnold chain and the basis of the multi-million trad . . . ing group. It was founded in 1905 by Alderman Frank W. Arnold and his brother Arthur. Grand . . . son Richard, 39, who will – ' Her voice faded to a whisper.

'Grandson Richard, 39,' repeated Gurder, his face bright with triumph. 'What d'you think of *that*, eh?'

'What does globe-trotting mean?' said Masklin.

'Well, globe means ball, and trotting is a sort of slow running,' said Grimma. 'So he runs slowly on a ball. Globe-trotting.'

'This is a message from Arnold Bros,' said Gurder ponderously. 'It's been sent to us. A message.'

'A message meant, um, for us!' said Nisodemus, who was standing just behind Gurder. He held up his hands. 'Yea, all the way from – '

'Yes, yes, Nisodemus,' said Gurder. 'Do be quiet, there's a good chap.' He gave Masklin an embarrassed look.

'Doesn't sound very likely, running slowly. I mean, you'd fall off. If it was a ball, is what I'm saying,' said Masklin.

They stared at The Picture again. It was made up of tiny dots. They showed a smiling face. It had teeth and a beard.

'It stands to reason,' said Gurder, more confidently. 'Arnold Bros (est. 1905) has sent Grandson, 39, to – to – '

'And these two names who founded the Store,' said Masklin. 'I don't understand that. I thought Arnold Bros (est. 1905) created the Store.'

'Then these two people founded it,' said Gurder. 'That makes sense. It was a big Store. It'd be easy to find, even if you weren't looking for it.' He looked slightly uneasy. 'Losted and founded,' he said, half to himself. 'That makes sense. Yes.'

'O–kay,' said Dorcas. 'So let's just see where we've got to. The message is, isn't it, that Grandson, 39, is in Florida, wherever that is – '

'Going to *be* in Florida,' said Grimma.

'It's a type of coloured juice,' volunteered a nome. 'I know, 'cos one day when we went over to the dump, there was this old carton, and it said "Florida Orange Juice". I read it,' he added proudly.

'Going to *be* in this orange-coloured juice, so I'm given to understand,' said Dorcas doubtfully, 'running slowly on a ball and jetting, whatever that is. And liking it, apparently.'

The nomes fell silent while they thought about this.

'Holy utterances are often difficult to understand,' said Gurder gravely.

'This must be a *powerful* holy one,' said Dorcas.

'*I* think it's just a coincidence,' said Angalo loftily. 'This is just a story about a human being, like in some of the books we read.'

'And how many humans could even stand on a ball, let along run slowly on it?' demanded Gurder.

'All *right*,' said Angalo, 'but what are we going to *do*, then?'

Gurder's mouth opened and shut a few times. 'Why, it's obvious,' he said uncertainly.

'Tell us, then?' said Angalo sourly.

'Well, er. It's, er, obvious. We must go to, er, the place where the orange juice is – '

'Yes?' said Angalo.

'And, er, and find Grandson, 39, which should be easy, you see, because we've got this picture – '

'Yes?' said Angalo.

Gurder gave him a haughty look. 'Remember the commandment that Arnold Bros (est. 1905) put up in the Store,' he said. 'Did it not say, *If You Do Not See What You Require, Please Ask?*'

The nomes nodded. Many of them had seen it. And the other commandments: *Everything Must Go*, and, by the Moving Stairs, *Dogs and Pushchairs Must be Carried*. They were the words of Arnold Bros (est. 1905). You couldn't really argue with them . . . But on the other hand, well, that had been the Store, and this was here.

'And?' said Angalo.

Gurder began to sweat. 'Well, er, and then we ask him to let us be left alone in the quarry.'

There was an awkward silence.

Then Angalo said, 'That sounds about the most half-baked – '

'What does jetting mean?' said Grimma. 'Is it anything to do with jet?'

'A jet is a kind of aircraft,' said Angalo, the transport expert.

'So jetting means to go like an aircraft. Or in an aircraft?' said Grimma.

Everyone turned to Masklin, whose fascination with the airport was well known to one and all.

He wasn't there.

Masklin pulled the Thing from its niche in the wall and padded back out into the open. The Thing didn't have to be attached to any wires. It was enough to put it near them.

There was electricity in the old manager's office. He ran across the empty alley between the tumbledown buildings and squeezed his way in through a crack in the sagging door.

Then he placed the box in the middle of the floor and waited.

It always took some while for the Thing to wake up. Its lights flickered at random and it made odd beeping noises. Masklin supposed it was the machine's equivalent of a nome getting up in the morning.

Eventually it said, *'Who is there?'*

'It's me,' said Masklin, 'Masklin. Look, I need to know what the words "communications satellite" mean. I've heard you use the word "satellite" before. You said the moon is one, didn't you?'

'Yes. But communications satellites are artificial moons. They are used for communications. Communications means the transferring of information. In this case, by radio and television.'

'What's television?' said Masklin.

'A *means of sending pictures through the air.*'

'Does this happen a lot?'

'*All the time.*'

Masklin made a mental note to look out for any pictures in the air.

'I see,' he lied. 'So these satellites — where are they, exactly?'

'*In the sky.*'

'I don't think I've ever seen one,' said Masklin doubtfully. There was an idea forming in his mind. He wasn't quite sure yet. Bits and pieces of things he'd read and heard were coming together. The important thing was to let them take their own time, and not frighten them away.

'*They are in orbit, many miles up. There are a great many above this planet,*' said the Thing.

'How do you know that?'

'*I can detect them.*'

'Oh.'

Masklin stared at the flickering lights.

'If they are artificial, does that mean they're not real?' he said.

'*They are machines. They are usually built on the planet and then launched into space.*'

The idea was nearly there now. It was rising like a bubble . . .

'Space is where our ship is, you said.'

'*That is correct.*'

Masklin felt the idea explode quietly, like a dandelion clock. 'If we knew where one of these things was going to be flown into space,' he said, speaking quickly before the words had time to escape, 'and we could sort of hang on to the sides or whatever, or maybe drive it like the Truck, and we took you with us, then we could jump off when we got up there and go and find this ship of ours, couldn't we?'

The lights on top of the Thing moved oddly, into patterns Masklin had never seen before. This went on for quite a while before it spoke again. When it did, it sounded almost sad.

'*Do you know how big space is?*' it said.

'No,' said Masklin politely. 'It's pretty big, is it?'

'*Yes. However, it might be possible for me to detect and summon the ship if I was taken above the atmosphere. But do you know what the words "oxygen supply" mean?*'

'No.'

'"*Space suit*"?'

'No.'

'*It is very cold in space.*'

'Well, couldn't we sort of jump around a bit to keep warm?' said Masklin desperately.

'*I think you do not appreciate what it is that space contains.*'

'What's that, then?'

'*Nothing. It contains nothing. And everything. But there is very little everything and more nothing than you could imagine.*'

'It's still worth a try, though, isn't it?'

'*What you are proposing is an extremely unwise endeavour,*' said the Thing.

'Yes, but, you see,' said Masklin firmly, 'if I don't try, then it's always going to be like this. We're always going to escape, and find somewhere new, and just when we're getting the hang of it all, we'll have to go again. Sooner or later we must find somewhere that we can know really belongs to us. Dorcas is right. Humans get everywhere. Anyway, you were the one who told me that our home was . . . up there somewhere.'

'*This is not the right time. You are ill-prepared.*'

Masklin clenched his fists. 'I'll never be well-prepared! I was born in a hole, Thing! A muddy hole in the ground! How can I ever be well-prepared for anything? That's what being alive *is*, Thing! It's being badly prepared for everything! Because you only get one chance, Thing! You only get one chance and then you die and they don't let you go round again after you've got the hang of it! Do you understand, Thing! So we'll try it *now*! I *order* you to help! You're a machine and you must do what you're told!'

The lights formed a spiral.

'You're learning fast,' said the Thing.

4

III. *And in a voice like Thunder, the Great Masklin said unto the Thing, Now is the Time to go back to our Home in the Sky;*

IV. *Or we will For Ever be Running from Place to Place.*

V. *But None must know what I Intend, or they will say, Ridiculous, Why go to the Sky when we Have Problems Right Here?*

VI. *Because that is how People are.*

From The Book of Nome, *Quarries, Chap. 2, v.III–VI*

Gurder and Angalo were having a blazing row when Masklin got back.

He didn't try to interrupt. He just put the Thing down on the floor and sat down next to it, and watched them.

Funny how people needed to argue. The whole secret was not to listen to what the other person was saying, Masklin had noticed.

Gurder and Angalo had really got the hang of *that*. The trouble was that neither of them was entirely certain he was right, and the funny thing was that people who weren't *entirely* certain they were right always argued much louder than other people, as if the main person they were trying to convince was themselves. Gurder was not certain, not *entirely* certain, that Arnold Bros (est. 1905) really existed, and Angalo wasn't entirely certain that he didn't.

Eventually Angalo noticed Masklin.

'You tell him, Masklin,' he said. 'He wants to go and find Grandson, 39!'

'Do you? Where do you think we should look?' Masklin asked Gurder.

'The airport,' said Gurder. 'You know that. Jetting. In a jet. That's what he'll do.'

'But we *know* the airport!' said Angalo. 'I've been right up to the fence several times! Humans go in and out of it all day! Grandson, 39, looks just like them! He could have gone already. He could be in the juice by now! You can't believe words that just drop out of the sky!' He turned to Masklin again. 'Masklin's a steady lad,' he said, 'he'll tell you. You tell him, Masklin,' he said. 'You listen to him, Gurder. He thinks about things, Masklin does. At a time like this — '

'Let's go to the airport,' said Masklin.

'There,' said Angalo, 'I told you, Masklin isn't the kind of nome — what?'

'Let's go to the airport and watch.'

Angalo's mouth opened and shut silently.

'But . . . but . . .' he managed.

'It must be worth a try,' said Masklin.

'But it's all just a coincidence!' said Angalo.

Masklin shrugged. 'Then we'll come back. I'm not suggesting we *all* go. Just a few of us.'

'But supposing something happens while we're gone?'

'It'll happen anyway, then. There's thousands of us. Getting people to the old barn won't be difficult, if we need to do it. It's not like the Long Drive.'

Angalo hesitated.

'Then *I'll* go,' he said. 'Just to prove to you how, how superstitious you're being.'

'Good,' said Masklin.

'Provided Gurder comes, of course,' Angalo added.

'What?' said Gurder.

'Well, you *are* the Abbot,' said Angalo sarcastically. 'If we're going to talk to Grandson, 39, then it'd better be you who does it. I mean, he probably won't want to listen to anyone else.'

'Aha!' shouted Gurder. 'You think I won't come! It'd be worth it just to see your face — '

'That's settled, then,' said Masklin calmly. 'And now, I think we'd better see about keeping a special watch on the road. And some teams had better go to the old barn. And it would be a good idea to see what people can carry. Just in case, you know.'

Grimma was waiting for him outside. She didn't look happy.

'I know you,' she said. 'I know the kind of expression you have when you're getting people to do things they don't want to do. What are you planning?'

They strolled into the shadow of a rusting sheet of corrugated iron. Masklin occasionally squinted upwards. This morning he'd thought the sky was just a blue thing with clouds. Now it was something that was full of words and invisible pictures and machines whizzing around. Why was it that the more you found out, the less you really *knew*?

Eventually he said, 'I can't tell you. I'm not quite sure myself.'

'It's to do with the Thing, isn't it?'

'Yes. Look, if I'm away for, er, a little bit longer than — '

She stuck her hands on her hips. 'I'm not stupid, you know,' she said. 'Orange-coloured juice, indeed! I've read nearly every book we brought out of the Store. Florida is a, a *place*. Just like the quarry. Probably even bigger. And it's a long way away. You have to go across a lot of water to get there.'

'I think it might even be further away than we came on

the Long Drive,' said Masklin quietly. 'I know, because one day when we went to look at the airport I saw water on the other side, by the road. It looked as though it went on for ever.'

'I told you,' said Grimma smugly. 'It was probably an ocean.'

'There was a sign by it,' said Masklin. 'Can't remember everything on it, I'm not as good at the reading as you. One of the words was res . . . er . . . voir, I think.'

'There you are, then.'

'But it must be worth a try.' Masklin scowled. 'There's only one place where we can ever be safe, and that's where we belong,' he said. 'Otherwise we'll always have to keep running away.'

'Well, I don't like it,' said Grimma.

'But *you* said you didn't like running away,' said Masklin. 'There isn't an alternative, is there? Let me just try something. If it doesn't work, then we'll come back.'

'But supposing something goes wrong? Supposing you don't come back? I'll . . .' Grimma hesitated.

'Yes?' said Masklin hopefully.

'I'll have a terrible job explaining things to people,' she said firmly. 'It's a silly idea. I don't want to have anything to do with it.'

'Oh.' Masklin looked disappointed but defiant. 'Well, I'm going to try anyway. Sorry.'

5

V. *And he said, What are these frogs of which you speak?*

VI. *And she said, You wouldn't understand.*

VII. *And he said, You are right.*

From The Book of Nome, *Strange Frogs, Chap. 1, v.V–VII*

There was a busy night . . .

It would be a journey of several hours to the barn. Parties went on to mark the path and generally prepare the way, besides watching out for foxes. Not that they were often seen, these days; a fox might be quite happy to attack a solitary nome, but thirty well-armed, enthusiastic hunters were a different proposition and it would be a very stupid fox indeed that even showed an interest. The few that did live near the quarry tended to wander off hurriedly in the opposite direction whenever they saw a nome. They'd learned that nomes meant trouble.

It had been a hard lesson for some of them. Not long after the nomes moved into the quarry a fox was surprised and delighted to come across a couple of unwary berry-gatherers, which it ate. It was even more surprised that night when two hundred grim-faced nomes tracked it to its earth, lit a fire in the entrance, and speared it to death when it ran out, eyes streaming.

There are a lot of animals that would like to dine off nome, Masklin had said. They'd better learn: it's us or them. And they'd better learn right now that it's going to be *them*. No animal is going to get a taste for nome. Not any more.

Cats were a lot brighter. No cats came anywhere near the quarry.

'Of course it might all be nothing to worry about,' said Angalo nervously, around dawn. 'We might never have to do it.'

'Just when we were beginning to get settled down, too,' said Dorcas. 'Still, I reckon that if we keep a proper lookout we can have everyone on the move in five minutes. And we'll start moving some food stores up there this morning. No harm in that. Then they'll be there if we need them.'

Nomes sometimes went as far as the airport. There was a rubbish dump on the way, which was a prime source of bits of cloth and wire, and the flooded gravel pits further on were handy if anyone had the patience to fish. It was a pleasant enough day's journey, largely along badger tracks. There was a main road to be crossed, or rather, to be burrowed under; for some reason pipes had been carefully put underneath it just where the track needed to cross it. Presumably the badgers had done it. They certainly used it a lot.

Masklin found Grimma in her school-hole under one of the old sheds, supervizing a class in writing. She glared at him, told the children to get on with it – and would Nicco Haberdasheri like to share the joke with the rest of the class? No? Then he could jolly well get on with things – and came out into the passage.

'I've just called to say we're off,' said Masklin, twiddling his hat in his hands. 'There's a load of nomes going over to the dump, so we'll have company the rest of the way. Er.'

'Electricity,' said Grimma, vaguely.

'What?'

'There's no electricity at the old barn,' said Grimma. 'You remember what that meant? On moonless nights there was nothing to do but stay in the burrow. I don't want to go back to that.'

'Well, maybe we were better nomes for it,' mumbled Masklin. 'We didn't have all the things we've got today, but we were – '

'Cold, frightened, ignorant and hungry!' snapped Grimma. 'You know that. You try telling Granny Morkie about the Good Old Days and see what she says.'

'We had each other,' said Masklin.

Grimma examined her hands.

'We were just the same age and living in the same hole,' she said vaguely. She looked up. 'But it's all different now! There's . . . well, there's the frogs, for one thing.'

Masklin looked blank. And, for once, Grimma looked unsure.

'I read about them in a book,' she said. 'There's this place, you see. Called Southamerica. And there's these hills where it's hot and rains all the time, and in the rain forests there are these very tall trees and right in the top branches of the trees there are these like great big flowers called bromeliads and water gets into the flowers and makes little pools and there's a type of frog that lays eggs in the pools and tadpoles hatch and grow into new frogs and these little frogs live their whole lives in the flowers right at the top of the trees and don't even know about the ground and the world is full of things like that and now I know about them and I'm never ever going to be able to see them and then *you*,' she gulped for breath, 'want me to come and live with you in a hole and wash your socks!'

Masklin ran this sentence through his head again, in case it made any sense when you listened to it a second time.

'But I don't wear socks,' he pointed out.

This was apparently not the right thing to say. Grimma prodded him in the stomach.

'Masklin,' she said, 'you're a good nome and bright enough in your way, but there aren't any answers up in the sky. You need to have your feet on the ground, not your head in the air!'

She swept away, and shut the door behind her.

Masklin felt his ears growing hot.

'I can do both!' Masklin shouted after her. 'At the same time!'

He thought about it and added, 'So can everyone!'

He stamped off along the tunnel. Bright enough in his way! Gurder *was* right, universal education was not a good idea. He'd never understand women, he thought. Even if he lived to be ten.

Gurder had turned over the leadership of the Stationeri to Nisodemus. Masklin felt less than happy about this. It wasn't that Nisodemus was stupid. Quite the reverse. He was clever in a bubbling, sideways way that Masklin distrusted; he always seemed to be bottling up excitement about something, and when he spoke the words always rushed out, with Nisodemus putting 'ums' in the flow of words so that he could catch his breath without anyone having the chance to interrupt him. He made Masklin uneasy. He mentioned this to Gurder.

'Nisodemus might be a bit over-enthusiastic,' said Gurder, 'but his heart's in the right place.'

'What about his head?'

'Listen,' said Gurder. 'We know each other well enough, don't we? We understand one another, wouldn't you say?'

'Yes. Why?'

'Then I'll let you make the decisions that affect all nomes' bodies,' said Gurder, his voice just one step away from being threatening, 'and you'll let me make the decisions that affect all nomes' souls. Fair enough?'

And so they set off.

The goodbyes, the last-minute messages, the organization and, because they were nomes, the hundred little arguments, are not important.

They set off.

Life at the quarry began to get back to something like normal. No more trucks came up to the gate. Dorcas sent a couple of his more agile young assistant engineers up the wire netting, just in case, to stuff the rusty padlock full of mud. He also ordered a team of nomes to twist wire round and round the gates as well.

'Not that it'd hold them very long,' he said. 'Not if they were determined.'

The Council, or what was left of it now, nodded wisely although frankly none of them understood or cared much about mechanical things.

The truck came back the same afternoon. The two nomes watching the lane hurried back into the quarry to report. The driver had fiddled with the padlock for a while, pulled at the wire, and then driven off.

'And it said something,' said Sacco.

'Yes, it said something. Sacco heard it,' said his partner, Nooty Kiddies Klothes. She was a plump young nome who wore trousers and was good at engineering and had actually volunteered to be a guard instead of staying at home learning how to cook; things were really changing in the quarry.

'I heard it say something,' said Sacco helpfully, in case the point hadn't sunk in.

'That's right,' said Nooty. 'We both heard it, didn't we, Sacco?'

'And what was it?' said Dorcas encouragingly. I don't really deserve this sort of thing, he thought. Not at my time of life. I'd rather be in my workshop, trying to invent radio.

'It said – ,' Sacco took a deep breath, his eyes bulged, and he attempted the foghorn mooing that was human sound: ' "Bbblllloooooooodddddyyyee kkiiidddddddssss!" '

Dorcas looked at the others.

'Anyone got any ideas?' he said. 'It almost seems to mean something, doesn't it? I tell you, if only we could understand them . . .'

'This must have been one of the stupid ones,' said Nooty. 'It was trying to get in!'

'Then it'll come back,' said Dorcas gloomily. He shook his head.

'All right, you two,' he said. 'Well done. Get back on watch. Thank you.'

He watched them go off hand in hand, and then he wandered away across the quarry, heading for the old manager's office.

I've seen Christmas Fayre come around six times, he thought. Six whatd'youcallems – years. And almost one more, I think, although it's hard to be sure out here. No one puts up any signs to say what's happening, and the heating just gets turned down. Seven years old. Just about the time when a nome ought to be taking it easy. And I'm out here, where there aren't any proper walls to the world, and the water goes cold and hard as glass some mornings, and the ventilation and heating systems are quite shockingly out of control. Of course – he pulled himself together a bit – as a scientist I find all these phenomena extremely interesting. It would just be nicer to find them extremely interesting from somewhere nice and snug, inside.

Ah, inside. That was the place to be. Most of the older nomes suffered from the fear of the Outside, but no one liked to talk about it much. It wasn't too bad in the quarry with its great walls of rock. If you didn't look up too much, and avoided the fourth side with its terribly huge views across the countryside, you could almost believe you were back in the Store. Even so, most of the older nomes preferred to stay in the sheds, or in the cosy gloom under the floorboards. That way you avoided this horrible *exposed* feeling, the dreadful sensation that the sky was watching you.

The children seemed to quite like the Outside, though. They weren't really used to anything else. They could just about remember the Store, but it didn't mean much to them. They belonged Outside. They were used to it. And the young men who went out hunting and gathering . . . well, young men liked to show how brave they were, didn't they? Especially in front of other young men. And young women.

Of course, Dorcas thought, as a scientist and rational thinking nome I know we weren't really intended to live under floorboards the whole time. It's just that, as a nome who is probably seven years old and feeling a bit creaky, I've got to admit I'd find it sort of comforting to have a few of the good old signs around the place. *Amazing Reductions*, perhaps, or just a little sign saying, *Mammoth Sale Starts Tomorrow*. It wouldn't hurt, and I'm sure I'd feel happier. Which is, of course, totally ridiculous, when you look at it rationally.

It's just like Arnold Bros (est. 1905), he thought sadly. I'm pretty sure he doesn't exist in the way I was taught he did, when I was young. But when you saw things like *If You Do Not See What You Require, Please Ask* on the walls, you felt that everything was somehow *all right*.

He thought: these are very wrong thoughts for a rational thinking nome.

There was a crack in the woodwork by the door of the manager's office. Dorcas slipped into the familiar gloom under the floor and padded along until he found the switch.

He was rather proud of this idea. There was a big red bell on the outside wall of the office, presumably so that humans could hear the telephone ring when the quarry was noisy. Dorcas had changed the wiring so that he could make it ring whenever he liked.

He pressed the switch.

Nomes came running from all corners of the quarry. Dorcas waited as the underfloor space filled up, and then dragged up an empty matchbox to stand on.

'The human has been back,' he announced. 'It didn't get in, but it'll keep trying.'

'What about your wire?' said one of the nomes.

'I'm afraid there are such things as wire cutters.'

'So much for your theory about, um, humans being intelligent. An *intelligent* human would know enough not to go, um, where it wasn't wanted,' said Nisodemus sourly.

Dorcas liked to see eagerness in a young nome, but Nisodemus vibrated with a peculiarly hungry kind of eagerness that was unpleasant to see. He gave him as sharp a look as he dared.

'Humans out here might be different from the ones in the Store,' he snapped. 'Anyway — '

'Order must have sent it,' said Nisodemus. 'It's a judgement, um, on us!'

'None of that. It's just a human,' said Dorcas. Nisodemus glared at him as he went on, 'Now, we really should be sending some of the women and children to the — '

There was the sound of running feet outside and the gate guards piled in through the crack.

'It's back! It's back!' panted Sacco. 'The human's back!'

'All right, all right,' said Dorcas. 'Don't worry about it, it can't — '

'No! No! No!' yelled Sacco, jumping up and down. 'It's got a pair of cutter things! It's cut the wire *and* the chain that holds the gates shut and it – !'

They didn't hear the rest of it.

They didn't need to.

The sound of an engine coming closer said it all.

It grew so loud that the shed shook, and then it stopped suddenly, leaving a nasty kind of silence that was worse than the noise. There was the crump of a metal door slamming. Then the rattle and squeak of the shed door.

Then footsteps. The boards overhead buckled and dropped little clouds of dust as great thumping steps wandered around the office.

The nomes stood in absolute silence. They moved nothing except their eyes, but *they* moved in perfect time to the footsteps, marking the position, flicking backwards and forwards as the human crossed the room above. A baby started to whimper.

There was some clicking, and then the muffled sound of a human voice making its usual incomprehensible noises. This went on for some time.

Then the footsteps left the office again. The nomes could hear them crunching around outside, and then more noises. Nasty, clinking metal noises.

A small nome said, 'Mum, I want the lavatory, Mum – '

'Shh!'

'I really *mean* it, Mum!'

'Will you be quiet!'

All the nomes stood stock still as the noises went on around them. Well, nearly all. One small nome hopped from one foot to the other, going very red in the face.

Eventually the noise stopped. There was the thunk of a truck door closing, the growl of its engine, and the motor noise died away.

Dorcas said, very quietly, 'I think perhaps we can relax now.'

Hundred of nomes breathed a sigh of relief.

'*Mum!*'

'Yes, all right, off you go.'

And after the sigh of relief, the outbreak of babble. One voice rose above the rest.

'It was never like this in the Store!' said Nisodemus, climbing on to a half-brick. 'I ask you, fellow nomes, is this what we were led, um, to expect?'

There was a mumble chorus of 'noes' and 'yesses' as Nisodemus went on: 'A year ago we were safe in the Store. Do you remember what it was like at Christmas Fayre? Do you remember what it was like in the Food Hall? Anyone remember, um, roast beef and turkey?'

There were one or two embarrassed cheers. Nisodemus looked triumphant. 'And here we are at the same time of year – well, *they* tell us it's the same time of year,' he said, sarcastically, ' – and what we're expected to eat are knobbly things actually grown in *dirt*! Um. And the meat isn't proper meat at all, it's just dead animals cut up! Actual dead animals, actually cut up! Is this what you want your, um, children to get used to? Digging up their food? And *now* they tell us we might even have to go to some barn that hasn't even got proper floorboards for us to live under as Arnold Bros (est. 1905) intended. Where next, we ask ourselves? Out in a field somewhere? Um. And do you know what is the worst thing about all of this? I'll tell you.' He pointed a finger at Dorcas. 'The people who seem to be giving us all the orders now are the very people who, um, got us into this trouble in the first place!'

'Now just you hold on – ' Dorcas began.

'You all know I'm right!' shouted Nisodemus. 'Think about it, nomes! Why in the name of Arnold Bros (est. 1905) did we have to leave the Store?'

There were a few more vague cheers and several arguments broke out among the audience.

'Don't be stupid,' said Dorcas. 'The Store was going to be demolished!'

'We don't know that!' shouted Nisodemus.

'Of course we do!' roared Dorcas. 'Masklin and Gurder saw — '

'*And where are they now, eh?*'

'They've gone to — well, they've gone to —' Dorcas began. He wasn't much good at this, he knew. Why did it have to be him? He preferred messing around with wires and bolts and things. Bolts didn't keep shouting at you.

'Yes, they've gone!' Nisodemus lowered his voice to a sort of angry hiss. 'Think about it, you nomes! Use your, um, brains! In the Store we knew where we were, things worked, everything was exactly as Arnold Bros (est. 1905) decreed. And suddenly we're out here. Remember how you used to despise Outsiders? Well, the Outsiders are us! Um. And now it's all panic again, and it always will be — until we mend our ways and Arnold Bros (est. 1905) graciously allows us back into the Store as better, wiser nomes!'

'Let's just get this clear,' said a nome. 'Are you saying that the Abbot *lied* to us?'

'I'm not saying anything like that,' said Nisodemus, sniffing. 'I'm just presenting you with the facts. Um. That's all I'm doing.'

'But, but, but the Abbot has gone to get help,' said a lady nome uncertainly. 'And, and, after all, I'm *sure* the Store was demolished. I mean, we wouldn't have gone to all this trouble otherwise, would we? Er.' She looked desperate.

'I know this, though,' said the nome beside her. 'Say what you like, but I don't fancy this old barn everyone's talking about. There's not even any electric there.'

'Yes, and it's in the middle of – ' another nome began, and then lowered his voice, ' – you know. Things. You know what I'm talking about.'

'Yeah,' said an elderly nome. '*Things*. I've seen 'em. My lad took me blackberryin' a month or two back, up above the quarry, and I seen 'em.'

'I don't mind seeing them a long way off,' said the worried lady nome. 'It's the thought of being in the middle of them that makes me come over all shaky.'

They don't even like to say the words *open fields*, thought Dorcas. I know how they feel.

'It's snug enough here, I'll grant you,' said the first nome, 'but all this stuff you get outside, what d'you call it, begins with an N – '

'Nature?' said Dorcas weakly. Nisodemus was smiling madly, his eyes sparkling.

'That's right,' said the nome. 'Well, it's not natural. And there's a sight too much of it. 'S not like a proper world at all. You've only got to look at it. The floor's all rough, 'n' it should be flat. There's hardly any walls. All them little starry lights that comes out at night, well, they're not much help, are they? And now these humans go where they please, and there's no proper Regulations like there was in the Store.'

'That's why Arnold Bros Established the Store in 1905,' said Nisodemus. 'A *proper* place for, um, nomes to live.'

Dorcas gently grabbed Sacco's ear and pulled the young nome towards him.

'Do you know where Grimma is?' he whispered.

'Isn't she here?'

'I'm quite sure she isn't,' said Dorcas. 'She'd have had something very sharp to say by now if she was. She may have stayed in the school-hole with the children when the bell went. It's just as well.'

Nisodemus has got something on his mind, he

thought. I'm not certain what it is, but it smells bad.

And it got worse as the day wore on, especially since it began to rain. A nasty, freezing sort of rain. Sleet, according to Granny Morkie. It was soggy, not really water but not quite ice. Rain with bones.

Somehow it seemed to find its way into places where ordinary rain hadn't managed to get. Dorcas organized younger nomes to digging drainage trenches and rigged up a few of the big light bulbs for heat. The older nomes sat hunched around them, sneezing and grumbling.

Granny Morkie did her best to cheer them up. Dorcas began to really wish the old woman wouldn't do that.

'This ain't nothing,' she said. 'I remember the Great Flood. Made our hole cave right in, we was cold and drenched for days!' She cackled and rocked backwards and forwards. 'Like drownded rats, we was! Not a dry stitch on, you know, and no fire for a week. Talk about laugh!'

The Store nomes stared at her, and shivered.

'And you don't want to go worrying about crossing them open fields,' she went on, conversationally. 'Nine times out o' ten you don't get et by anything.'

'Oh, dear,' said a lady nome, faintly.

'Yes, I've been out in fields hundreds o' times. It's a doddle if you stay close to the hedge and keep your eyes open. You hardly ever have to run very much,' said Granny.

No one's temper was improved when they learned that the Land Rover had parked right on the patch of ground they were going to plant things in. The nomes had spent ages during the summer hacking the hard ground into something resembling soil. They'd even planted seeds, which hadn't grown. Now there were two great ruts in it, and a new padlock and chain on the gate.

The sleet was already filling the ruts. Oil had

leaked in and formed a rainbow sheen on the surface.

And all the time Nisodemus was reminding people how much better it had been in the Store. They didn't really need much persuading. After all, it *had* been better. Much better.

I mean, thought Dorcas, we can keep warm and there's plenty of food, although there is a limit to the number of ways you can cook rabbit and potatoes. The trouble is, Masklin thought that once we got outside the Store we'd all be digging and building and hunting and facing the future with strong chins and bright smiles. Some of the youngsters are doing well enough, I'll grant you. But us old 'uns are too set in our ways. It's all right for me, I like tinkering with things, I can be useful, but the rest of them, well . . . all they've really got to occupy themselves is grumbling, and they've become really *good* at that.

I wonder what Nisodemus's game is. He's too keen, if you ask me.

I wish Masklin would come back.

Even young Gurder wasn't too bad.

It's been three days now.

At a time like this, he knew he'd feel better if he went and looked at Jekub.

6

I. *For in the Hill was a Dragon, from the days when the World was made.*

II. *But it was old and broken and dying.*

III. *And the Mark of the Dragon was on it.*

IV. *And the Mark was Jekub.*

From The Book of Nome, *Jekub, Chap. 1, v.I–IV*

Jekub.

Jekub was his. His little secret. His *big* secret, really. No one else knew about Jekub, not even Dorcas's assistants.

He'd been pottering around in the big old half-ruined sheds on the other side of the quarry, one day back in the summer. He hadn't really got any aim in mind, except perhaps the possibility of finding a useful bit of wire or something.

So he'd rummaged around in the shadows, straightened up, glanced above him *and there Jekub was.*

With his mouth open.

It had been a terrible few seconds until Dorcas's eyes adjusted to the distance.

After that he'd spent a lot of time with Jekub, poking around, finding out about it. Or *him.* Jekub was definitely a him. A terrible him, perhaps, and old and wounded, like a dragon that had come here for one last final sleep.

Or perhaps it was like one of those big animals Grimma had showed him in a book once. Diner soars.

But Jekub didn't grumble, and he didn't keep on asking Dorcas why he hadn't got around to inventing radio *yet*. Dorcas had spent many a peaceful hour getting to know Jekub. He was someone to talk to. He was the best kind of person to talk to, in fact, because you didn't have to listen to him back.

Dorcas shook his head. There was no time for that sort of thing now. Everything was going wrong.

Instead, he went to find Grimma. She seemed to have her head screwed on right, even if she was a girl.

The school-hole was under the floor of the old shed with 'Canteen' on the door. It was Grimma's personal world. She'd invented schools for children, on the basis that since reading and writing were quite difficult it was best to get them over with early.

The library was also kept there.

In those last hectic hours the nomes had managed to rescue about thirty books from the Store. Some were very useful – *Gardening All the Year Round* was well-thumbed, and Dorcas knew *Essential Theory for the Amateur Engineer* almost by heart – but some were, well, difficult, and not opened much.

Grimma was standing in front of one of these when he wandered in. She was biting her thumb, which she always did when she was concentrating.

He had to admire the way she read. Not only was Grimma the best reader among the nomes, she also had an amazing ability to understand what she was reading.

'Nisodemus is causing trouble,' he said, sitting down on a bench.

'I know,' said Grimma vaguely. 'I've heard.' She grabbed the edge of the page in both hands, and turned it over with a grunt of effort.

'I don't know what he's got to gain,' said Dorcas.

'Power,' said Grimma. 'We've got a *power vacuum*, you see.'

'I don't think we have,' said Dorcas uncertainly. 'I've never seen one here. There were plenty in the Store. *Sixty-Nine Ninety-Five with Range of Attachments for Round-the-House Cleanliness,*' he added, remembering with a sigh the familiar signs.

'No, it's not a thing like that,' said Grimma. 'It's what you get when no one's in charge. I've been reading about them.'

'*I'm* in charge, aren't I?' said Dorcas plaintively.

'No,' said Grimma, 'because no one really listens to you.'

'Oh. Thank you very much.'

'It's not your fault. People like Masklin and Angalo and Gurder can make people listen to them, but you don't seem to keep their attention.'

'Oh.'

'But you can make nuts and bolts listen to you. Not everyone can do that.'

Dorcas thought about this. He would never have put it like that himself. Was it a compliment? He decided it probably was.

'When people are faced with lots of troubles and they don't know what to do, there's always someone ready to say anything, just to get some power,' said Grimma.

'Never mind. When the others get back I'm sure they'll sort it all out,' said Gurder, more cheerfully than he felt.

'Yes, they'll – ' Grimma began, and then stopped. After a while Dorcas realized that her shoulders were shaking.

'Is there anything the matter?' he said.

'It's been more than three whole days!' sobbed

Grimma. 'No one's ever been away that long before! Something must have happened to them!'

'Er,' said Dorcas, 'well, they *were* going to look for Grandson, 39, and we can't be sure that — '

'And I was so nasty to him before he went! I told him about the frogs and all he could think of was socks!'

Dorcas couldn't quite see how frogs had got involved. When he sat and talked to Jekub, frogs were never dragged into the conversation.

'Er?' he said.

Grimma, in between sobs, told him about the frogs.

'And I'm sure he didn't even begin to understand what I meant,' she mumbled. 'And you won't either.'

'Oh, I don't know,' said Dorcas. 'You mean that the world was once so simple, and suddenly it's full of amazingly interesting things that you'll never ever get to the end of as long as you live. Like biology. Or climatology. I mean, before all you Outsiders came, I was just tinkering with things and I really didn't know anything about the world.'

He stared at his feet. 'I'm still very ignorant,' he said, 'but at least I'm ignorant about really important things. Like what the sun is, and why it rains. That's what you're talking about.'

She sniffed, and smiled a bit, but not too much because if there is one thing worse than someone who doesn't understand you it's someone who understands perfectly, before you've had a chance to have a good pout about not being understood.

'The thing *is*,' she said, 'that he still thinks I'm the person he used to know when we all lived in the old hole in the bank. You know, running around. Cooking things. Bandaging up people when they'd been hur-hur-hur — '

'Now then, now then,' said Dorcas. He was always at a loss when people acted like this. When machines

57

went funny you just oiled them or prodded them or, if nothing else worked, hit them with a hammer. Nomes didn't respond well to this treatment.

'Supposing he never comes back?' she said, dabbing at her eyes.

'Of course he'll come back,' said Dorcas reassuringly. 'What could have happened to him, after all?'

'He could have been eaten or run over or trodden on or blown away or fallen down a hole or trapped,' said Grimma.

'Er, yes,' said Dorcas. 'Apart from that, I meant.'

'But I shall pull myself together,' said Grimma, sticking out her chin. 'When he *does* come back, he won't be able to say, "Oh, I see everything's gone to pieces while I've been away".'

'Jolly good,' said Dorcas. 'That's the spirit. Keep yourself occupied, that's what I always say. What's the book called?'

'It's *A Treasury of Proverbs and Quotations*,' said Grimma.

'Oh. Anything useful in it?'

'That,' said Grimma distantly, 'depends.'

'Oh. What's Proverbs mean?'

'Not sure. Some of them don't make much sense. Do you know, humans think the world was made by a sort of big human?'

'Get away?'

'It took a week.'

'I expect it had some help, then,' said Dorcas. 'You know. With the heavy stuff.' Dorcas thought of Jekub. You could do a lot in a week, with Jekub helping.

'No. All by himself, apparently.'

'Hmm.' Dorcas considered this. Certainly bits of the world were rough, and things like grass seemed simple enough. But from what he'd heard it all broke down every year and had to be started up again in the spring, and – 'I don't know,' he said. 'Only humans could believe something like that. There's a good few months' work, if I'm any judge.'

Grimma turned the page. 'Masklin used to believe – I mean, Masklin *believes* – that humans are much brighter than we think.' She looked thoughtful. 'I really wish we could study them properly,' she said. 'I'm sure we could learn a – '

For the second time, the alarm bell rang out across the quarry.

This time, the hand on the switch belonged to Nisodemus.

7

> II. *And Nisodemus said, You are betrayed, People of the Store;*
>
> III. *Falsely you were led into This Outside of Rain and Cold and Sleet and Humans and Order, and Yet it Will become Worse;*
>
> IV. *For there will be Sleet and Snow, and Hunger in the Land;*
>
> V. *And There will come Robins;*
>
> VI. *Um.*
>
> VII. *Yet those that brought you here, where are they Now?*
>
> VIII. *They said, We go to seek Grandson, 39, but tribulation abounds on every side and no help comes. You are betrayed into the hands of Winter.*
>
> IX. *It is time to put aside things of the Outside . . .*
>
> From The Book of Nome, *Complaints v.II–IX*

'Yes. Well. That's hard to do, isn't it?' said a nome uneasily. 'I mean, we *are* Outside.'

'But I have a *plan*,' said Nisodemus.

'Ah,' said the nomes, in unison. Plans were the thing. Plans were what was needed. You knew where you were, with a plan.

Grimma and Dorcas, almost the last to arrive, sidled their way into the crowd. The old engineer was going to push his way to the front, but Grimma restrained him.

'Look at the others up there,' she whispered.

There were quite a few nomes behind Nisodemus. Many of them Dorcas recognized as Stationeri, but there were a few others from some of the great departmental families. They weren't looking at Nisodemus as he spoke, but at the crowd. Their eyes flickered back and forth, as though they were searching for something.

'I don't like the look of this,' said Grimma quietly. 'The big families never used to get on too well with the Stationeri, so why are they up there now?'

'Grubby pieces of work, some of them,' said Dorcas.

Some of the Stationeri had been particularly upset about common, everyday nomes learning to read. They said it gave people ideas, Dorcas gathered, which were not a good thing unless they were the right kind of ideas. And some of the great families hadn't been too happy about nomes being able to go where they pleased, without having to ask permission.

They're all up there, he thought. The nomes who haven't done so well since the Drive. They all lost a little power.

Nisodemus was explaining his plan.

As he listened, Dorcas's mouth slowly dropped open.

It was magnificent in its way, that plan. It was like a machine where every single bit was perfectly made, but had been put together by a one-handed nome in the dark. It was crammed full of good ideas which you couldn't sensibly argue with, but they had been turned upside down. The trouble was, they were *still* ones you couldn't sensibly argue with, because the basically good idea was still in there somewhere . . .

Nisodemus wanted to rebuild the Store.

The nomes stood in horrified admiration as the Stationeri explained that yes, Abbot Gurder *had* been right: when they left the Store they had taken Arnold Bros (est. 1905) with them *inside their heads*. And, if they could show him that they really *cared* about the Store,

61

he would come out again and put a stop to all these problems and re-establish the Store here, in this green unpleasant land.

That was how it all arrived in Dorcas's head, anyway. He'd long ago decided that if you spent all your time listening to what people actually *said*, you'd never have time to work out what they *meant*.

But it wouldn't mean building the whole Store, said Nisodemus, his eyes shining like two bright black marbles. They could change the quarry in other ways. Go back to living in proper departments instead of any old how all over the place. Put up some signs. Get back to the Good Old Ways. Make Arnold Bros (est. 1905) feel at home. Build the Store *inside their heads*.

Nomes didn't often go mad. Dorcas vaguely recalled an elderly nome who had once decided that he was a teapot, but he'd changed his mind after a few days.

Nisodemus, though, had definitely been getting too much fresh air.

It was obvious that one or two other nomes thought so too.

'I don't quite see,' said one of them, 'how Arnold Bros (est. 1905) is going to stop these humans. No offence meant.'

'Did humans interfere with us when we were in the Store?' demanded Nisodemus.

'Well, no, because — '

'Then trust in Arnold Bros (est. 1905)!'

'But that didn't stop the Store being demolished, did it?' said a voice. 'When it came to it, you all trusted Masklin and Gurder and the Truck. And yourselves! Nisodemus is always telling you how clever you are. Try and *be* clever, then!'

Dorcas realized it was Grimma. He'd never seen anyone so angry.

She pushed her way through the apprehensive nomes

until she was face to face, or at least, since Nisodemus was standing on something and she wasn't, face to chest. He was one of those people who liked standing on things.

'What will actually *happen*, then?' she shouted. 'When you've built the Store, what will *happen*? Humans came into the Store, you know!'

Nisodemus's mouth opened and shut for a while. Then he said, 'But they obeyed the Regulations! Yes! Um! That's what they did! And things were better then!'

She glared at him.

'You don't really think people are going to accept that, do you?' she said.

There was silence.

'You've got to admit,' said an elderly nome, very slowly, 'things *were* better then.'

The nomes shuffled their feet.

That was all you could hear.

Just people, shuffling their feet.

'They just accepted it!' said Grimma. 'Just like that! No one's bothered about the Council any more! They just do what he tells them!'

Now she was in Dorcas's workspace under a bench in the old quarry garage. My little sanctuary, he always called it. My little nook. Bits of wire and tin were scattered everywhere. The wall was covered with scrawls done with a bit of pencil lead.

Dorcas sat and twiddled a bit of wire aimlessly.

'You're being hard on people,' he said quietly. 'You shouldn't yell at them like that. They've been through a lot. They get all confused if you shout at them. The Council was all right for when times were good – ' He shrugged. 'And without Masklin and Gurder and Angalo, well, it hardly seems worthwhile.'

'But after all that's happened!' She waved her arms. 'To act so *stupidly*, just because he's offered them – '

'A bit of comfort,' said Dorcas. He shook his head. You couldn't explain things like this to people like Grimma. Nice girl, bright head on her, but she kept thinking that everyone else was as passionate about things as she was. All people *really* wanted, Dorcas considered, was to be left alone. The world was quite difficult enough as it was without people going around trying to make it better all the time.

Masklin had understood that. He knew the way to make people do what you wanted was to make them think it was their idea. If there was one thing that got right up a nome's nose, it was someone saying, 'Here is a really sensible idea. Why are you too *stupid* to understand?'

It wasn't that people *were* stupid. It was just that people were people.

'Come on,' he said wearily. 'Let's go and see how the signs are getting on.'

The whole of the floor of one of the big sheds had been turned over to the making of the signs. Or rather, the Signs. Another thing Nisodemus was good at was giving words capital letters. You could *hear* him doing it.

Dorcas had to admit that the Signs were a pretty good idea, though. He felt guilty about thinking this.

He'd thought that when Nisodemus had summoned him and asked if there was any paint in the quarry, only now the quarry was being called the New Store.

'Um,' Dorcas had said, 'there's some old tins. White and red, mainly. Under one of the benches. We might be able to lever the tops off.'

'Then do it. It is very important. Um. We must make Signs,' said the Stationeri.

'Signs. Right,' said Dorcas. 'Cheer the place up a bit, you mean?'

'No!'

'Sorry, sorry, I just thought – '

64

'Signs for the gate!'

Dorcas scratched his chin. 'The gate?' he said.

'Humans obey Signs,' said Nisodemus, calming down. 'We know that. Did they not obey the Signs in the Store?'

'Most of 'em,' agreed Dorcas. *Dogs and Pushchairs Must Be Carried* had always puzzled him. Lots of humans didn't carry either of them.

'Signs make humans do things,' said Nisodemus, 'or stop doing things. So get to work, good Dorcas. Signs. Um. Signs that say *No*.'

Dorcas had given this a lot of thought as teams of nomes sweated to pry the lids off the paint-streaked tins. They still had *The Highway Code* from the Truck, and there were plenty of signs in there. And he could remember some of the signs from the Store.

Then there was a stroke of luck. Normally the nomes stayed at floor level, but Dorcas had taken to sending his young assistants on to the big desk in the manager's office occasionally, where there were useful scraps of paper. Now he needed to work out what the signs should say.

Sacco and Nooty came back with the news.

They'd found more signs. A great big grubby notice pinned to the wall, covered with signs.

'Masses of them,' Sacco said, coming back out of breath. 'And you know what, sir? You know what? I read what it said on the notice and it said, *Health and Safety at Work*, it said, *Obey These Signs*, it said, and it said, *'They Are There For Your Protection.'*

'That's what it said?' said Dorcas.

'*For Your Protection*,' Sacco repeated.

'Can you get it down?'

'There's a coat-hook next to it,' said Nooty enthusiastically. 'I bet we could sling a hook up and then pull it over towards the window, and then — '

'Yes, yes, you're good at that sort of thing,' said

Dorcas. Nooty could climb like a squirrel. 'I expect Nisodemus will be very pleased,' he added.

Nisodemus was, especially with the bit that said *For Your Protection*. It showed, he said, that, um, Arnold Bros (est. 1905) was on their side.

Every bit of board and rusty sheet of metal had to be pressed into service. The nomes went at it cheerfully enough, though, happy to be doing something.

Next morning the sun rose to see a variety of signs hanging, not always squarely, on the battered quarry gate.

They had been very thorough. The signs said: *No Etnry. Exit This Way. Dagner — Hard Hat Area. Blastign In Progres. All Lories Report To Wieghbridge. Slipery when Wet. This Till Closed. Lift Out Fo Order. Beware of Flaling Rocks. Road Floooded.*

And, one that Dorcas had found in a book and was rather proud of: *Unexploded Bom.*

Just to be on the safe side, though, and without telling Nisodemus, he found some more chain and, in one of the greasy old toolboxes in Jekub's shed, a padlock nearly as big as he was. It took four nomes to carry it.

The chain was massive. Some of the nomes found Dorcas painstakingly levering it along across the quarry floor, one link at a time. He didn't seem to want to tell them where he found it.

The truck turned up around noon. The nomes waiting in the hedge by the side of the lane saw the driver get out, look at the signs, and . . .

No, that wasn't right. Humans couldn't do that sort of thing. It couldn't be true. But twenty nomes, peering out from the undergrowth, saw it happen.

The human disobeyed the signs.

Not only that, it pulled some of them off the gate and threw them away.

They watched in astonishment. Even *Unexploded Bom*

was whirled into the bushes, nearly knocking young Sacco from his perch.

The new chain, though, caused the human a few problems. It rattled it once or twice, peered in through the wire mesh of the gate, stamped around for a bit, and then drove off.

The nomes in the bushes cheered, but not too happily. If humans weren't going to do what was expected of them, nothing was right in the world.

'I reckon that's it,' said Dorcas, when they got back. 'I don't like the idea any more than anyone else, but we've got to move. I know humans. That chain won't stop them if they really want to get in.'

'I absolutely forbid anyone to leave!' said Nisodemus.

'But you see, metal can be cut through – ' Dorcas began, in a reasonable tone of voice.

'Silence!' shouted Nisodemus. 'It's your fault, you old fool! Um! You put the chain on the gate!'

'Well, you see, it was to stop the – pardon?' said Dorcas.

'If you *hadn't* put the chain on the gate, the signs *would* have stopped the human,' said Nisodemus. 'But you can't expect Arnold Bros (est. 1905) to help us if we show we don't trust him!'

'Um,' said Dorcas. What he was thinking was: mad. A mad nome. A dangerously mad nome. We're not talking about teapots here. He backed out of Nisodemus's presence and was glad to get out into the bitingly cold air.

Everything's going wrong, he thought. I was left in charge, and now it's all going wrong. We haven't got any proper plans, Masklin hasn't come back, and it's all going wrong.

If humans come into the quarry, they'll find us.

Something cold landed on his head. He brushed at it irritably.

I'll have a word with some of the younger nomes, he

thought. Maybe going to the barn isn't such a bad idea; we could keep our eyes shut on the way. Or something.

Something else, cold and soft, settled on his neck.

Oh, why are people so *complicated*?

He looked up, and realized that he couldn't see the other side of the quarry. The air was full of white specks that got thicker as he watched.

He stared at it in horror.

It was snowing.

8

VII. *And Grimma said, We have two choices.*

VIII. *We can run, or we hide.*

IX. *And they said, Which shall we do?*

X. *She said, We shall Fight.*

From The Book of Nome, *Quarries, Chap. 3, v.VII–X*

It wasn't much of a fall, just one of those nippy little sprinklings that come early in the winter to make it absolutely clear that it is, well, the winter. That's what Granny Morkie said.

She'd never been very interested in the Council anyway. She liked to spend her time with the other old people, exchanging grumbles and, as she put it, cheerin' them up and takin' them out o' themselves.

She strutted around in the snow as if it belonged to her.

The other old nomes watched her in horrified silence.

' 'Corse, this is nothing to some of 'em,' she said. 'I mind we've had snow, we couldn't walk round in it, we had to dig tunnels! Talk about laugh!'

'Er, madam,' said a very old nome, gravely, 'does it always drop out of the sky like this?'

' 'Corse! Sometimes it gets blown along by the wind. You get great big heaps!'

'We thought it — you see, on the cards — that is, in the Store — well, we though it just sort of appeared on things,' said the old nome. 'In a rather jolly and festive way,' he added, looking embarrassed.

They watched it pile up. Over the quarry the clouds hung like overstuffed mattresses.

'At least it means we won't have to go to that horrid barn place,' said a nome.

'That's right,' said Granny Morkie. 'You could catch your death, going out in this.' She looked cheerful.

The old nomes grumbled among themselves, and scanned the sky anxiously for the first signs of robins or reindeer.

The snow closed the quarry in. You couldn't see out across the fields.

Dorcas sat in his workshop and stared at the snow piling up against the grubby window, giving the shed a dull grey light.

'Well,' he said quietly, 'we wanted to be shut away. And now we are. We can't run away, and we can't hide. We ought to have gone when Masklin left.'

He heard footsteps behind him. It was Grimma. She spent a long time near the gate these days, but the snow had driven her indoors at last.

'He wouldn't be able to come,' she said. 'Not in the snow.'

'Yeah. Right,' said Dorcas uncertainly.

'It's been eight days now.'

'Yes. Quite a long time.'

'What were you saying when I came in?' she said.

'I was just talking to myself. Does this snow stuff stay for a long time?'

'Granny says it does, sometimes. Weeks and weeks, she says.'

'Oh.'

'When the humans come back, they'll be here for good,' said Grimma.

'Yes,' said Dorcas sadly. 'Yes, I think you're right.'

'How many of us would be able to . . . you know . . . go on living here?'

'A couple of dozen, perhaps. If they don't eat much, and lie low during the day. There's no Food Hall, you see.' He sighed. 'And there won't be much hunting. Not with humans around the quarry the whole time. All the game up in the thickets will run away.'

'But there's thousands of us!'

Dorcas shrugged.

'It's hard enough for me to walk through this snow,' he said. 'There's hundreds of older nomes who'll never do it. And young ones, come to that.'

'So we've got to stay, just like Nisodemus wants,' said Grimma.

'Yes. Stay and hope. Perhaps the snow will be gone. We could make a run for the thickets or something,' he said vaguely.

'We could stay and fight,' said Grimma.

Dorcas growled. 'Oh, that's easy. We fight all the time. Bicker, bicker, bicker. That's nomish nature for you.'

'I mean, fight the humans. Fight for the quarry.'

There was a long pause.

Then Dorcas said, 'What, us? Fight *humans*?'

'Yes.'

'But they're *humans*!'

'Yes.'

'But they're so much bigger than we are!' said Dorcas desperately.

'Then they'll make better targets,' said Grimma, her eyes alight. 'And we're faster than them, and smarter than them, and we know they exist and we have,' she added, 'the element of surprise.'

'The what?' said Dorcas, totally lost.

'The element of surprise. They don't know we're here,' she explained.

71

He gave her a sidelong glance.

'You've been reading strange books again,' he said.

'Well, it's better than sitting around wringing our hands and saying, "Oh dear, oh dear, the humans are coming and we shall all be squashed." '

'That's all very well,' said Dorcas, 'but what are you suggesting? Bashing them over the head would be really tricky, take it from me.'

'Not their heads,' said Grimma.

Dorcas stared at her. Fight humans? It was such a novel idea it was hard to get your mind around it.

But . . . well, there was that book, wasn't there? The one Masklin had found in the Store, the one that had given him the idea for driving the Truck. What was it? *Gulliver's Travels*? And there'd been this picture of a human lying down, with what looked like nomes tying it up with hundreds of ropes. Not even the oldest nomes could remember it ever happening. It must have been a long time ago.

A snag struck him.

'Hang on a minute, he said. 'If we start fighting humans — ' his voice tailed off.

'Yes?' said Grimma impatiently.

'They'll start fighting us, won't they? I know they're not very bright, but it'll dawn on them that something's happening and they'll fight back. Retaliation, that's called.'

'That's right,' said Grimma. 'And that's why it's vitally important we retaliate right at the start.'

Dorcas thought about this. It seemed a logical idea.

'But only in self-defence,' he said. 'Only in self-defence. Even with humans. I don't want there to be any unnecessary suffering.'

'I suppose so,' she said.

'You really think we could fight humans?'

'Oh, yes.'

'So . . . how?'

Grimma bit her lip. 'Hmm,' she said, 'Young Sacco and his friends. Can you trust them?'

'They're keen lads. And lasses, one or two of them.' He smiled. 'Always ready for something new.'

'Right. Then we shall need some nails . . .'

'You've really been thinking hard, haven't you?' said Dorcas. He was almost in awe. Grimma was often bad-tempered. He thought perhaps it was because her mind worked very fast, sometimes, and she was impatient with people who weren't keeping up. But now she was furious. You could begin to feel sorry for any humans who got in her way.

'I've been doing a lot of reading,' she said.

'Er, yes. Yes, I can see,' said Dorcas. 'But, er, I wonder if it wouldn't be more sensible to – '

'We're not going to run away again,' she said flatly. 'We shall fight them in the lane. We shall fight them at the gates. We shall fight them in the quarry. And we shall never surrender.'

'What does "surrender" mean?' said Dorcas, desperately.

'We don't know the meaning of surrender,' said Grimma.

'Well, *I* don't,' said Dorcas.

Grimma leaned against the wall.

'Do you want to hear something strange?' she said.

Dorcas thought about it.

'I don't mind,' he said.

'There's books about us.'

'Like *Gulliver*, you mean?'

'No. That was about a human. About us, I mean. Ordinary-sized people, like us. But wearing all green suits and with little knobbly stalks on their heads. Sometimes humans put out bowls of milk for us and we do all the housework for them. And they have wings, like

73

bees. That's what gets put in books about us. They call us pixies. It's in a book called *Fairy Tales for Little Folk.*'

'I don't think the wings would work,' said Dorcas doubtfully. 'I don't think you could get the lifting power.'

'And they think we live in mushrooms,' Grimma finished.

'Hmm? Doesn't sound very practical to me,' said Dorcas.

'And they think we repair shoes.'

'That's a bit more like it,' said Dorcas. 'Good solid work.'

'And the book said we paint the flowers to make them pretty colours,' said Grimma.

Dorcas stared at her.

'Nah,' he said eventually. 'I've looked at the colours on flowers. They're definitely built-in.'

'We're real,' said Grimma. 'We do real things. Why do you think that sort of thing goes in books?'

'Search me,' said Dorcas. 'I only read manuals. It's not a proper book, I've always said, unless it's got lists and part numbers in it.'

'If ever humans do catch us, that's what we'll become,' said Grimma. 'Sweet little people, painting flowers. They won't let us be anything else. They'll turn us into *little* people.' She sighed. 'Do you ever get the feeling you'll never know everything you ought to know?'

'Oh, yes. All the time.'

Grimma frowned.

'*I* know one thing,' she said. 'When Masklin comes back, he's going to have somewhere to come back to.'

'Oh,' said Dorcas.

'Oh,' he repeated. 'Oh. I see.'

It was bitterly cold in Jekub's lair. Other nomes never

74

came in, because it was drafty and stunk unpleasantly. That suited Dorcas fine.

He padded across the floor and under the huge tarpaulin where Jekub lived. It took quite a long time to climb up to his preferred perch on the monster, even using the bits of wood and string he'd painstakingly tied to it . . . *him*.

He sat down and waited until he got his breath back.

'I only want to help people,' he said quietly. 'Like giving them things like electricity and making their lives better. But they never say thank you, you know. They wanted me to paint signs, so I painted signs. Now Grimma wants to fight humans. She's got lots of ideas out of books. I know she's doing it to help forget about Masklin but no good will come of it, you mark my words. But if I don't help, things will only be even worse. I don't want *anybody* to get hurt. People like us can't be repaired as easily as people like you.'

He drummed his heels on Jekub's — what would it be? — Jekub's neck, probably.

'It's all right for you,' he said. 'Sleeping quietly here all the time. Having a nice rest . . .'

He stared at Jekub for a long while.

Then, very quietly, he said, 'I wonder . . . ?'

Five long minutes went past. Dorcas appeared and reappeared amongst the complicated shadows, muttering to himself, saying things like, 'That's dead, that's no good, we need a new battery,' and 'Seems OK, nothing that a good clean couldn't put right,' and 'Hmm, not much in your tank . . .'

Finally he walked out from under the dusty cloth and rubbed his hands together.

Everyone has a purpose in life, he thought. It's what keeps them going.

Nisodemus wants things to be as they were. Grimma wants Masklin back. And Masklin . . . no one knows exactly what it is that Masklin wants, except that it's very big.

But they all have this *purpose*. If you have a purpose in life, you can feel six inches tall.

And now I've found one.

Gosh.

The human came back later and he did not come alone. There was the small truck and a much larger lorry, with the words 'Blackbury Stone & Gravel PLC' painted on the side. Its tyres turned the thin coating of snow into glistening mud.

It jolted up the lane, slowed down as it came out into the open area in front of the quarry gates, and stopped.

It wasn't a very good stop. The back of the vehicle swung around and nearly hit the hedge. The engine coughed into silence. There was the sound of hissing. And, very slowly, the lorry sank.

Two humans got out. They walked around the lorry, looking at each tyre in turn.

'They're only flat at the bottom,' whispered Grimma, in their hiding place in the bushes.

'Don't worry about it,' hissed Dorcas. 'The thing about tyres is, the flat bit always sinks to the bottom. Amazing what you can do with a few nails, isn't it?'

The smaller truck stopped behind the lorry. Two humans got out of that, too, and joined the others. One of them was holding the longest pair of pliers Dorcas had ever seen. While the rest of the humans bent down by one of the flat tyres it strolled up to the gate, fiddled the teeth of the pliers on to the padlock, and squeezed.

It was an effort, even for a human. But there was a snap loud enough to be heard in the bushes, and then a long-drawn-out clinking noise as the chain fell away.

Dorcas groaned. He'd had great hopes of that chain. It was Jekub's; at least, it was in a big yellow box bolted to part of Jekub, so presumably it had belonged to Jekub. But it had been the padlock that had broken, not the chain. Dorcas felt oddly proud about that.

'I don't understand it,' Grimma muttered. 'They can see they're not wanted, so why are they so stupid?'

'It's not as if there isn't masses of stone around,' agreed Sacco.

The human pulled at the gate and swung it enough to allow itself inside.

'It's going to the manager's office,' said Sacco. 'It's going to make noises in the telephone.'

'No, it's not,' Dorcas prophesied.

'But it will be ringing up Order,' said Sacco. 'It'll be saying – in Human, I mean – it'll be saying, "Some Of Our Wheels Have Gone Flat." '

'No,' said Dorcas, 'it'll be saying, "Why Doesn't the Telephone Work?" '

'Why doesn't the telephone work?' said Nooty.

'Because I know what wires to cut,' said Dorcas. 'Look, it's coming back out.'

They watched it walk around the sheds. The snow had covered the nomes' sad attempts at cultivation. There were plenty of nome tracks, though, like little bird trails in the snow. The human didn't notice them. Humans hardly ever noticed anything.

'Tripwires,' said Grimma.

'What?' said Dorcas.

'Tripwires. We should put tripwires down. The bigger they are,' said Grimma, 'the harder they fall.'

'Not on us, I hope,' said Dorcas.

'No. We could put more nails down,' said Grimma.

'Good grief.'

The humans clustered around the stricken lorry. Then they appeared to reach a decision and walked back to the Land Rover. They got in. It couldn't go forward, but reversed slowly down the lane, turned around in a field gateway, and headed back to the main road. The lorry was left alone.

Dorcas breathed out.

'I was afraid one of them would stay,' he said.

'They'll come back,' said Grimma. 'You've always said it. Humans'll come back and mend the wheels or whatever it is they do.'

'Then we'd better get on with it,' said Dorcas. 'Come on, you lot.'

He stood up and trotted towards the lane. To Sacco's surprise, Dorcas was whistling under his breath.

'Now, the important thing is to make sure they can't move it,' he said, as they ran to keep up. 'If they can't move it, it means it stays blocking the lane. And if it stays blocking the lane, they can't get any more machines in.'

'Good thinking,' said Grimma, in a slightly puzzled voice.

'We must immobilize it,' said Dorcas. 'We'll take out the battery first. No electricity, no go.'

'Right,' said Sacco.

'It's a big square thing,' said Dorcas, 'it'll need eight of you at least. Don't drop it, whatever you do.'

'Why not?' said Grimma. 'We want to smash it, don't we?'

'Er. Er. Er,' said Dorcas urgently, like a motor trying to get started. 'No, because, because, because it could be dangerous. Yes. Dangerous. Yes. Because, because, because of the acid and whatnot. You must take it out very carefully, and I'll find somewhere safe to put it. Yes. Very safe. Off you go now. Two nomes to a spanner.'

They trotted off.

'What else can we do?' said Grimma.

'We'd better drain the fuel out,' said Dorcas firmly, as they walked under the shadow of the lorry. It was much smaller than the one that had brought them out of the

Store, but still quite big enough. He wandered around until he was under the enormous swelling bulk of the fuel tank.

Four of the young nomes had dragged an empty can out of the bushes. Dorcas called them over and pointed to the tank above them.

'There'll be a nut on there somewhere,' he said. 'It'll be to let the fuel out. Get a spanner round it. Make sure the can's underneath it first!'

They nodded enthusiastically and got to work. Nomes are good climbers and remarkably strong for their size.

'And try not to spill any, please!' Dorcas shouted up after them.

'I don't see why that matters,' said Grimma, behind him. 'All we want to do is get it out of the lorry. Where it *goes* doesn't matter, does it?'

She gave him another thoughtful look. Dorcas blinked back at her, his mind racing.

'Ah,' he said. 'Ah. Ah. Because. Becausebecausebecause. Ah. Because it's dangerous stuff. We don't want it polluting things, do we? Best to put it carefully in a can and – '

'Keep it safe?' said Grimma suspiciously.

'Right! Right,' said Dorcas, who was starting to sweat. 'Good idea. Now let's just go over here – '

There was sudden rush of air and a thump from right behind them. The lorry's battery landed where they had been standing.

'Sorry, Dorcas,' Sacco called down. 'It was a lot heavier than we thought. It got away from us.'

'You idiots!' Grimma shouted.

'Yes, you idiots!' shouted Dorcas. 'You might have damaged it! Just you come down here right now and get it into the hedge, quickly!'

'He might have damaged *us*!' said Grimma.

'Yes. Yes. Yes, that's what I meant, of course,' said

Dorcas vaguely. 'You wouldn't mind organizing them a bit, would you? They're good boys, but always a bit too enthusiastic, if you know what I mean.'

He wandered off into the shadow, his head tilted backwards.

'Well!' said Grimma. She looked around at Sacco and his friends, who were sheepishly climbing down again.

'Don't just stand there,' she said. 'Get it into the hedge. Hasn't Dorcas told you about using levers? Very important things. It's amazing what you can do with levers. We used them a lot on the Long Drive – '

Her voice trailed off. She turned and looked at the distant figure of Dorcas and her eyes narrowed.

The cunning old devil is up to something, she thought.

'Oh, just get on with it,' she said, and ran after Dorcas.

He was standing under the truck's engine, staring intently into the masses of rusting pipework. As she came up she distinctly heard him say, 'Now, what else do we need?'

'How do you mean, need?' said Grimma quietly.

'Oh, to help Jek – ' Dorcas stopped, and turned around slowly. 'I mean, what else do we need to *do* to make the thing totally immobile,' he said stonily. 'That was what I meant.'

'You're not planning to drive this truck, are you?' said Grimma.

'Don't be silly. Where'd we go? It'd never get across the fields to the barn.'

'Well. All right, then.'

'I just want to have a look around it. Time spent collecting knowledge is never wasted,' said Dorcas primly. He stepped out into the light on the other side of the truck and looked up.

'Well, well,' he said.

'What is it?'

'They left the door open. I suppose they thought it was all right because they'd be coming back.'

Grimma followed his gaze. The truck's door *was* slightly ajar.

Dorcas looked around at the hedge behind them.

'Help me find a big enough stick,' he said. 'I reckon we could climb up there and have a look around.'

'A look around? What do you expect to find?'

'You never know till you've looked,' said Dorcas philosophically. He peered back underneath the truck.

'How are you all doing under there? We need a hand here.'

Sacco staggered up. 'We managed to get the battery thing behind the hedge,' he said, 'and the can's nearly full. Smells horrible. There's still lots coming out.'

'Can you get the screw back in?'

'Nooty tried and she got all covered in yuk.'

'Let it go on the road, then,' said Dorcas.

'Hang on, you said that would be dangerous,' said Grimma. 'It's dangerous until you've filled the can up, is it, and then not dangerous at all?'

'Look, you wanted me to stop the lorry and I've stopped the lorry,' said Dorcas. 'So just shut up, will you?'

Grimma looked at him in horror.

'What did you say?' she said.

Dorcas swallowed. Oh, well. If you were going to get shouted at, you might as well get your money's worth.

'I said just shut up,' he said quietly. 'I don't want to be rude, but you do go on at people. I'm sorry, but that's how it is. I'm helping you. I'm not asking you to help me, but at least you can let me get on with things instead of badgering me the whole time. And you never say please or thank you, either. People are a bit like machines,' he added solemnly, while her face went redder, 'and words like please and thank you are just like grease. They make

81

them work better. Is that all right?' He turned to the
boys, who were looking very embarrassed.

'Find a stick long enough to reach up to the cab,' he
said. 'Please.'

They fell over themselves to obey.

9

It was pretty much like the cab of the truck that had brought them from the Store. It brought back old memories.

'Wow!' said Sacco. 'And we all drove one of these?'

'Seven hundred of us,' said Dorcas proudly. 'Your dad was one of them. You were in the back with your mothers. All you lads were.'

'I'm not a lad,' said Nooty.

'Sorry,' said Dorcas. 'Slip of the tongue. In my day girls stayed at home most of the time. Not that I've got anything at all against them getting out and about a bit now,' he added hurriedly, not wanting another Grimma on his hands. 'I'm not against that at all.'

'I wish I'd been older on the Drive,' said Nooty. 'It must have been *amazing.*'

'It terrified the life out of me,' said Dorcas.

The others wandered around the cab like tourists in a cathedral, gawping. Nooty tried to press a pedal.

'Amazing,' she said, under her breath.

'Sacco, you get up there and take those keys out,' said Dorcas. 'The rest of you, no lallygagging. Those humans could be back any time. Nooty, stop making those brrrm-brrrm noises. I'm sure nice girls shouldn't make those kind of noises,' he added lamely.

Sacco swarmed up the steering-wheel post and wrestled the keys out of the ignition while the rest of the boys poked around in the cab.

Grimma wasn't with them. She hadn't wanted to come up into the cab. She'd gone very quiet, in fact. She'd stayed down in the lane with a sullen look on her face.

But it had needed saying, Dorcas told himself.

He looked around the cab. Let's see, he thought . . . we've got the battery, we've got the fuel, was there anything else Jekub needed?

'Come on, everyone,' he called, 'let's be getting out of here. Nooty, stop trying to *move* things all the time. It'd take all of you to shift the gear lever. Come on, before the humans come back.'

He made his way to the door, and heard a click behind him.

'I said come on — *What do you think you're doing?*'

The young nomes stared at him, wide-eyed.

'We're seeing if we can move the gear lever, Dorcas,' said Nooty. 'If you press this knob you can — '

'*Don't press the knob! Don't press the knob!*'

The first inkling Grimma had that something was going wrong was a nasty little crunching sound and a change in the light.

The truck was moving. Not very fast, because the two front tyres were flat. But the lane was steep. It was moving all right, and just because it had started off slowly didn't mean there wasn't something huge and unstoppable about it.

She stared at it in horror.

The lane ran between high banks all the way down to the big road — and the railway.

'*I said don't press it! Did I say press it? I said don't press it!*'

The terrified nomes stared at him, their open mouths a row of 'O's.

'*It's not the gear lever! It's the handbrake, you idiots!*'

Now they could all hear the crunching noise and feel the slight vibration.

'Er,' said Sacco, his voice shaking, 'what's a handbrake, Dorcas?'

'It keeps it stopped on hills and things! Don't just stand there! Help me push it back up!'

The cab was, very gently, beginning to sway from side to side. The lorry was definitely moving. The handbrake wasn't. Dorcas heaved on it until blue and purple spots flashed in front of his eyes.

'I just gave the knob on the end a push!' Nooty babbled. 'I only wanted to see what it did!'

'Yes, yes, all right . . .' Dorcas stared around. What he needed was a lever. What he needed was about fifty nomes. What he needed most of all was not to be here.

He staggered across the bouncing floor to the doorway and cautiously peered out. The hedge was moving past quite gently, as if it wasn't in a particular hurry to get anywhere, but the surface of the lane already had a blurred look.

We could probably jump, he thought. And if we're lucky, we won't break anything. If we're even luckier, we'll avoid the wheels. How lucky do I feel, right at this minute?

Not very.

Sacco joined him.

'Perhaps if we took a good running jump — ' he began.

There was a thump as the lorry hit the bank, heeled over, and then bounced back on to the lane.

The nomes struggled to their feet.

'On the other hand, perhaps not a good idea,' said Sacco. 'What shall we do now, Dorcas?'

'Just hang on,' said Dorcas. 'I think the banks will keep it on the lane and I suppose it'll just roll to a halt eventually.' He sat down suddenly as the truck bounced off the bank again. 'You wanted to know what a truck ride was like. Well, now you know.'

There was another thump. The branch of a tree caught the door, swung it open and then, with a terrible metallic noise, ripped it off.

'Was it like this?' shouted Nooty, above the noise. To Dorcas's amazement, now that the immediate danger was over, she seemed to be quite enjoying it. We're bringing up new nomes, he thought. They're not so scared of things as we were. They know about a bigger world.

He coughed.

'Well, apart from it being in the dark, and we could see where we were going, yes,' he said. 'I think we all ought to hang on to something. Just in case it gets bumpy.'

The lorry rolled down the lane and on to the main road. A car skidded into the hedge to avoid it; another lorry managed to stop at the end of four long streaks of scorched rubber on the wet road.

None of the nomes in the cab noticed this at the time. All they felt was another thump as the lorry bounced gently off the far side of the road and down the lane that ran towards the railway. Where, with red lights flashing, the barriers were coming down.

Sacco peered out of the stricken doorway.

'We've just crossed over a road,' he said.

'Ah,' said Dorcas.

'I just saw a car run into the back of another

car and a lorry ended up going sideways,' Sacco went on.

'Ah. Lucky we got over, then,' said Dorcas. 'There's some dangerous drivers around.'

The gritty sound of the flat tyres rolling over gravel gradually slowed down. There was the snap of something breaking behind the lorry, a couple of bumps, and then another thump that brought them to a halt.

They heard a low, booming noise.

Nomes hear things differently to humans, and the shrill clanging of the level-crossing's warning alarms sounded, to them, like the mournful tolling of an ancient bell.

'We've stopped,' said Dorcas. He thought: we could have pressed the brake pedal. We could have looked for something to press it with and pressed it. I must be getting too old. Oh, well. 'Come on, no hanging around. We can jump out. You youngsters can, anyway.'

'Why? What are you going to do?' said Sacco.

'I'm going to wait until you've all jumped out, and then I'm going to tell you to catch me,' said Dorcas pleasantly. 'I'm not as young as I was. Now, off you go.'

They got down awkwardly, hanging on to the edge of the sill and dropping on to the road.

Dorcas lowered himself gingerly on to the brink and sat with his legs dangling over the drop.

It looked a long way down.

Below him, Nooty prodded Sacco respectfully on the arm.

'Er. Sacco,' she said, nervously.

'What is it?'

'Look at that metal rail thing over there.'

'Well, what about it?'

'There's another one over *there*,' said Nooty, pointing.

'Yes, I can see,' said Sacco testily. 'What about them? They're not doing anything.'

'We're right in between them,' said Nooty. 'I just thought I should, you know, point it out. And there's that bell thing ringing.'

'Yes, I can hear it,' said Sacco irritably. 'I wish it would stop.'

'I just wondered why it was.'

Sacco shrugged. 'Who knows why anything happens?' he said. 'Come *on*, Dorcas. *Please*. We haven't got all day.'

'I'm just composing myself,' said Dorcas quietly.

Nooty wandered miserably away from the group and looked down at one of the rails. It was bright and shiny.

And it seemed to be singing.

She bent closer. Yes, it was certainly making a faint humming sound. Which was odd. Bits of metal didn't normally make any noise at all. Not by themselves, anyway.

She looked up at the lorry.

As she stared at the lorry stuck between the flashing lights and the shiny rails, the world seemed to change slightly and a horrible idea formed in her head.

'Sacco!' she quavered. 'Sacco, we're right on the railway line, Sacco!'

Something a long way off made a deep, mournful noise. *Two* deep, mournful noises, one a little deeper and more mournful than the other.

Dee-dah.

Dee-dah.

From the gateway of the quarry Grimma had a good view of the road all the way to the airport. She saw the train, and the truck.

The train had seen the truck too. It suddenly started to make the long-drawn-out screaming noise of bits of

88

metal in distress. By the time it actually *hit* the thing, it seemed to be going quite slowly. It even managed to stay on the rails.

Bits of truck spun away in every direction, like a firework.

IO

> I. *Nisodemus said unto them, Do you doubt that I can stop the power of Order?*
>
> II. *And they said, Um . . .*
>
> From The Book of Nome, *Chases v.I–II*

Other nomes came running across the quarry floor, with Nisodemus in the lead, and piled up in a crowd around the gate.

'What happened? What happened?'

'I saw everything,' said a middle-aged nome. 'I was on watch, and I saw Dorcas and some of the boys go into the truck. And then it rolled away down the hill and then it went over the road and then it stopped right on the railway and then . . . and then . . .'

'I forbade all meddling with these infernal machines,' said Nisodemus. 'And I said we were to stop, um, putting people on watch, didn't I? The watch Arnold Bros (est. 1905) maintains should be enough for humble nomes!'

'Yes . . . well . . . Dorcas said he thought it wouldn't do any harm if we gave him a hand, sort of thing,' said the nome nervously. 'And he said –'

'I gave *orders*!' screamed Nisodemus. 'You will all obey me! Did I not stop the lorry by the power of Arnold Bros (est. 1905)?'

'No,' said Grimma quietly. 'No, you didn't. Dorcas did. He put nails down in the road.'

There was a huge, horrified silence. In the middle of it Nisodemus went slowly white with rage.

'Liar!' he shouted.

'No,' said Grimma, meekly. 'He really did. He really did all sorts of things to help us, and we never said please or thank you and now he's dead.'

There were sirens along the road below and a lot of excitement around the stationary train. Blue lights flashed.

The nomes shifted uneasily. One of them said, 'He's not really dead, though, is he? Not *really*. I expect he jumped out at the last minute. A clever person like him.'

Grimma looked helplessly at the crowd. She saw Nooty's parents in the crowd. They were a quiet, patient couple. She'd hardly ever spoken to them. Now their faces were grey and lined with worry. She gave in.

'Yes,' she said. 'Perhaps they got out.'

'Bound to have done,' muttered another nome, trying to look cheerful. 'Dorcas isn't the type to go around dying all the time. Not when we need him.'

Grimma nodded.

'And now,' she went on, 'I think even humans will be wondering what's happening here. They'll soon work out where the lorry came from and they'll be coming up here and I think they might be very angry.'

But Nisodemus licked his lips and said, 'We won't be afraid. We will confront them and defy them. Um. We will treat them with scorn. We don't need Dorcas, we need nothing except faith in Arnold Bros (est. 1905). Nails, indeed!'

'If you start out now,' said Grimma, 'you should all be able to get to the barn, even through what's left of the snow. I don't think the quarry will be a very safe place to be, quite soon.'

There was something about the way she said it

which made people nervous. Normally Grimma shouted or argued, but this time she spoke quite calmly. It wasn't like her at all.

'Go on,' she said. 'You'll have to start now. You'll have to take as much food and stuff as possible. Go on.'

'No!' shouted Nisodemus. 'No one is to move! Do you think Arnold Bros (est. 1905) will let you down? Um, I will protect you from the humans!'

Down below, a car with a flashing blue light on top of it pulled away from the excitement around the train, crossed the main road and headed slowly up the lane.

'I will call upon the power of Arnold Bros (est. 1905) to *smite* the humans!' shouted Nisodemus.

The nomes looked unhappy. Arnold Bros had never smitten anyone in the Store. He'd just founded it, and seen to it that nomes lived comfortable and not very strenuous lives in it, and apart from putting the signs on the walls hadn't really interfered very much. Now, suddenly, he was going around being angry and upset all the time, and smiting people. It was very bewildering.

'I will stand here and defy the dreadful minions of Order!' Nisodemus yelled. 'I will teach them a lesson they won't forget.'

The rest of the nomes said nothing. If Nisodemus wanted to stand in front of a car then that was all right by them.

'We will *all* defy them!' he shouted.

'Er . . . what?' said a nome.

'Brothers, let us stand here resolute and show Order that we are united in opposition! Um. If you truly believe in Arnold Bros (est. 1905), no harm will come to you!'

The flashing light was well up the lane now. Soon it would be crossing the wide patch in front of the gates, where the great chain hung uselessly from the broken padlock.

Grimma opened her mouth to say: Don't be stupid,

you idiots, Arnold Bros (est. 1905) doesn't want you to stand in front of cars. I've *seen* what happens to nomes who stand in front of cars. Your relatives have to bury you in an envelope.

She was about to say all that, and decided not to. For months and months people had been telling nomes what to do. Perhaps it was time to stop.

She saw a number of worried faces in the crowd turn towards her, and someone said, 'What shall we *do*, Grimma?'

'Yeah,' said another nome, 'she's a Driver, they always know what to do.'

She smiled at them. It wasn't a very happy smile.

'Do whatever you think best,' she said.

There was a chorus of indrawn breaths.

'Well, yeah,' said a nome, 'but, well, Nisodemus says we can stop this thing just by believing we can. Is that true, or what?'

'I don't know,' said Grimma. 'You might be able to. I know I can't.'

She turned and walked off quickly towards the sheds.

'Stand firm,' commanded Nisodemus. He hadn't been listening to the worried discussions behind him. Perhaps he wasn't able to listen to anything now, except for little voices deep inside his head.

' "Do whatever you think best",' muttered a nome. 'What sort of help is that?'

They stood in their hundreds, watching the car coming closer. Nisodemus stood slightly ahead of the crowd, holding his hands in the air.

The only sound was the crunch of tyres on gravel.

If a bird had looked down on the quarry in the next few seconds it would have been amazed.

Well, probably it wouldn't. Birds are somewhat stupid creatures and have a hard enough job even coming to terms with the ordinary, let alone the extraordinary. But if it had been an unusually intelligent bird – an escaped mynah bird, perhaps, or a parrot that had been blown several thousand miles off course by very strong winds – it would have thought:

Oh. There is a wide hole in the hill, with little old rusty sheds in it, and a fence in front of it.

And there is a car with a blue light on the top of it just going through a gate in the fence.

And there are little black dots on the ground ahead of it. One dot standing very still, right in the path of the thing, and the others, the others –

Breaking away and running. Running for their lives.

They never did find Nisodemus again, even though a party of strong-stomached nomes went back much later and searched through the ruts and the mud.

So a rumour grew up that perhaps, at the last minute, he had jumped up and caught hold of part of the car and had clambered on to it somehow. And then he'd waited there, too ashamed to face other nomes, until the car went back to wherever it came from, and had got off, and was living out the rest of his life quietly and without any fuss. He had been a good nome in his way, they said. Whatever else you might say about him, he believed in things and he did what he thought was proper, so it was only right that he'd been spared and was still out there in the world, somewhere.

This was what they told one another, and what they wrote down in *The Book of Nome*.

What nomes might have thought in those private moments before they went to sleep . . . well, that was private.

Humans clomped slowly around the train and what remained of the truck. Lots of other vehicles had turned up at what was, for humans, great speed. Many of them had blue lights on top.

The nomes had learned to be worried by things with flashing blue lights on top.

The Land Rover belonging to the quarry men was there as well. One of the quarry men was pointing to the wrecked truck and shouting at the others. He'd opened the smashed engine compartment, and was pointing to where the battery wasn't.

Beside the railway the breeze rustled the long grass. And some of the long grass rustled without any wind at all.

Dorcas had been right. Where humans went once, they went again. The quarry belonged to them. Three trucks were parked outside the sheds and humans were everywhere. Some were repairing the fence. Some were taking boxes and drums off the lorries. One was even in the manager's office, tidying up.

The nomes crouched where they could, listening fearfully to the sounds above them. There weren't many hiding places for two thousand nomes, small though they were.

It was a very long day. In the shadows under some of the sheds, in the darkness behind crates, in some cases even on the dusty rafters under the tin roofs, the nomes passed it as best they could.

There were escapes so narrow a postcard couldn't have got through them. Old Munby Confectioneri and most of his family were left blinking in the light when a human moved the tatty old box they were cowering behind. Only a quick dash to the shelter of a stack of tins saved them. And, of course, the fact that humans never really looked hard at what they were doing.

That wasn't the worst bit, though.

The worst bit was much worse.

The nomes sat in the noisy darkness, not daring even to speak, and felt their world vanishing. Not because the humans hated nomes. *Because they didn't notice them.*

There was Dorcas's electricity, for example. He'd spent a long time twisting bits of wire together and finding a safe way to steal electricity from the fusebox. A human pulled them out without thinking, twiddled inside with a screwdriver, and put up a new box with a lock on it. Then it mended the telephone.

The Store nomes needed electricity. They couldn't remember a time when they had been without it. It was a natural thing, like air. And now theirs was a world of endless darkness.

And still the terror when on. The rough floorboards shook overhead, raining dust and splinters. Metal drums boomed like thunder. There was the continual sound of hammering. The humans were back, and they meant to stay.

They did go eventually, though. When the daylight drained from the winter sky, like steel growing cold, some of the humans got into their vehicles and drove off down the lane.

They did one puzzling thing before they left. Nomes had to scramble over one another to get out of the way when one of the floorboards in the manager's office was pulled up. A huge hand reached down and put a little tray on the packed earth under the floor. Then the darkness came back as the board was replaced.

The nomes sat in the gloom and wondered why on earth the humans, after a day like this, were giving them food.

The tray was piled with flour. It wasn't much, compared to Store food, but to nomes who had spent all day hungry and miserable it smelled *good*.

A couple of younger ones crawled closer. It was the most tantalizing smell.

One of them took a handful of the stuff.

'Don't eat it!'

Grimma pushed her way through the packed bodies.

'But it smells so – ' one of the nomes warbled.

'Have you ever smelled anything like it before?' she said.

'Well, no – '

'So you don't *know* it's good to eat, do you? Listen. I know about stuff like this. Where we – where I used to live, in the hole . . . there was a place along the road where humans came to eat, and sometimes we'd find stuff like this among the rubbish bins at the back. It kills you if you eat it!'

The nomes stared at the innocent little tray. Food that killed you? That didn't make sense.

'I remember there was some tinned meat we had once in the Store,' said an elderly nome. 'Gave us all a nasty upset, I remember.' He gave Grimma a hopeful look.

She shook her head. 'This isn't like that,' she said. 'We used to find dead rats near it. They didn't die in a very nice way,' she added, shuddering at the memory.

'Oh.'

The nomes stared at the tray again. And there was a thump from overhead.

There was still a human in the quarry.

It was sitting in the old swivel chair in the manager's office, reading a paper.

From a knothole near the floor the nomes watched carefully. There were huge boots, great sweeps of trouser, a mountain range of jacket and, far above, the distant gleam of electric light on a bald head.

After a long while the human put the paper down and reached over to the desk by its side. The watching nomes gazed at a pack of sandwiches bigger than they were, and a Thermos flask that steamed when it was opened and filled the hut with the smell of soup.

They climbed back down and reported to Grimma. She was sitting by the food tray, and had ordered six of the older and more sensible nomes to stand guard around it to keep children away.

'He's not doing anything,' she was told. 'He's just sitting there. We saw him look out of the window once or twice.'

'Then he'll be here all night,' said Grimma. 'I expect the humans are wondering who's causing all this trouble.'

'What shall we *do*?'

Grimma sat with her chin on her hands.

'There's those big old tumbledown sheds across the quarry,' she said, at last. 'We could go there.'

'Dorcas said — Dorcas used to say it was very dangerous in the old sheds,' said a nome cautiously. 'Because of all the old junk and stuff. Very dangerous, he said.'

'More dangerous than here?' said Grimma, with just a trace of her old sarcasm.

'You've got a point.'

'Please, m'm.'

It was one of the younger female nomes. They held Grimma in awe because of the way she shouted at the men and read better than anyone. This one held a baby in her arms, and kept curtsying every time she finished a sentence.

'What is it, Sorrit?' said Grimma.

'Please, m'm, some of the children are very hungry, m'm. There isn't anything wholesome to eat down here, you see.' She gave Grimma a pleading look.

Grimma nodded. The stores were under the other sheds, what was left of them. The main potato store had been found by some of the humans, which was perhaps why the poison had been put down. Anyway, they couldn't light a fire and there was no meat. No one had been doing any proper hunting for *days*, because Arnold Bros (est. 1905) would provide, according to Nisodemus.

'As soon as it gets light I think all the hunters we can spare should go out,' said Grimma.

They considered this. The dawn was a long way away. To a nome, a night was as long as three whole days . . .

'There's plenty of snow,' said a nome. 'That means we've got water.'

'*We* might be able to manage without food, but the children won't,' said Grimma.

'And the old people, too,' said a nome. 'It's going to freeze again tonight. We haven't got the electric and we can't light a fire outside.'

They sat staring glumly at the dirt.

What Grimma was thinking was: they're not bickering. They're not grumbling. Things are so serious they're actually not arguing and blaming each other.

'All right,' she said, 'and what do *you* all think we should do?'

> I. *We will come out of the woodwork.*
> II. *We will come out of the floor.*
> III. *They will wish they had never seen us.*
>
> *From* The Book of Nome, *Humans v.I–III*

The human lowered its newspaper and listened.

There was a rustling in the walls. There was a scratching under the floor.

Its eyes swivelled to the table beside it.

A group of small creatures were dragging its packet of sandwiches across the tabletop. It blinked.

Then it roared and tried to stand up, and it wasn't until it was nearly upright that it found that its feet were tied very firmly to the legs of its chair.

It crashed forward. A crowd of tiny creatures, moving so fast that it could hardly see them, charged out from under the table and wrapped a length of old electricity wire around its outflung arms. Within seconds it was trussed awkwardly, but very firmly, between the furniture.

They saw its great eyes roll. It opened its mouth and mooed at them. Teeth like yellow plates clashed at them.

The wire held.

The sandwiches turned out to be cheese and chutney and the Thermos, once they got the top off, was full of coffee. 'Store food,' the nomes told one another. 'Good Store food, like we used to know.'

They poured into the room from every crack and mouse-hole. There was an electric fire by the table and they sat in solemn rows in front of its glowing red bar, or wandered around the cramped office.

'We done it,' they said, 'just like that *Gullible Travels*. The bigger they come, the harder they fall!'

There was a school of thought that said they should kill the human, whose mad eyes followed them around the floor. This was when they found the box.

It was on one of the shelves. It was yellow. It had a picture of a very unhappy-looking rat on the front. It had the words *SCRAMOFF* in big red lettering, too. On the back . . .

Grimma's forehead wrinkled as she tried to read the smaller words on the back.

'It says, "They Take A Bite, But They Don't Come Back For More!" ' she said. 'And apparently it contains Polydichloromethylinlon-4, whatever that is. "Clears Outhouses Of Troublesome . . ." ' she paused.

'Troublesome what?' said the listening nomes. 'Troublesome what?'

Grimma lowered her voice.

'It says, "Clears Outhouses of Troublesome *Vermin* in a trice!" ' she said. 'It's poison. It's the stuff they put under the floor.'

The silence that followed this was black with rage. The nomes had raised quite a lot of children in the quarry. They had very firm views about poison.

'We should make the human eat it,' said one of them. 'Fill up its mouth with Polypuththeketlon or whatever it is. Troublesome *vermin*.'

'I think they think we're rats,' said Grimma.

'And that would be all right, would it?' said a nome with withering sarcasm. 'Rats are OK. We've never had

101

any trouble with rats. No call to go around giving them poisoned food.'

In fact the nomes got on rather well with the local rats, probably because their leader was Bobo, who had been a pet of Angalo's when they lived in the Store. The two species treated each other with the distant friendliness of creatures who could, at a pinch, eat one another but had decided not to.

'Yeah, the rats'd thank us for getting rid of a human,' he went on.

'No,' said Grimma. 'No. I don't think we should do that. Masklin always said that they're nearly as intelligent as we are. You can't go around poisoning intelligent creatures.'

'*They* tried.'

'They're not nomes. They don't know how to behave,' said Grimma. 'Anyway, be sensible. More humans will come along in the morning. If they find a dead human, there'll be a lot of trouble.'

That was a point. But they had shown themselves to a human. No nome could remember it ever being done before. They'd had to do it, or starve and freeze, but there was no knowing where it would end. *How* it would end was a bit more certain. It would probably end badly.

'Go and put it somewhere where the rats can't get it,' said Grimma.

'I reckon we should just give it a taste — ' said the nome.

'No! Just take the stuff away. We'll stay here the rest of the night and then move out before it's light.'

'Well, all right. If you say so. I just hope we're not sorry about it later, that's all.' The nomes carried the dreadful box away.

Grimma wandered over to where the human lay. It was well trussed up by now, and couldn't move a finger.

It looked just like the picture of Gullible or whoever he was, except the nomes had got hold of what the nomes in those days had never heard of, which was lots of electric wire. It was a lot tougher than rope. And they were a lot angrier. Gullible hadn't been driving a great big lorry around the place and putting down rat poison.

They'd gone through its pockets and piled up the contents in a heap. There'd been a big square of white cloth amongst them, which a group of nomes had managed to tie around the human's mouth after its mooing got on everyone's nerves.

Now they stood around eating fragments of sandwich and watching its eyes.

Humans can't understand nomes. Their voices are too fast and too high, like a bat squeak. It was probably just as well.

'*I* say we should find something sharp and stick it into it,' said a nome. 'In all the soft bits.'

'There's things we could do with matches,' said a lady nome, to Grimma's surprise.

'And nails,' said a middle-aged nome.

The human growled behind its gag and strained at the wires.

'We could pull all its hair out,' said the lady nome. 'And then we could – '

'Do it, then,' said Grimma, coming up behind them. They turned.

'What?'

'Do it, if you want to,' said Grimma. 'There it is, right in front of you. Do what you like.'

'What, *me*?' The lady nome drew back. 'I didn't . . . not *me*. I didn't mean *me*. I meant . . . well, us. Nomekind.'

'There you are, then,' said Grimma. 'And nomekind is only nomes. Besides, it's wrong to hurt prisoners. I read it in a book. It's called the *Geneva Convention*. When

103

you've got people at your mercy, you shouldn't hurt them.'

'Seems like the ideal time to me,' said a nome. 'Hit them when they can't hit back, that's what I say. Anyway, it's not as if humans are the same as real people.' But he shuffled backwards anyway.

'Funny, though, when you see their faces close to,' said the lady nome, putting her head on one side. 'They look a lot like us. Only bigger.'

One of the nomes peered into the human's frightened eyes.

'Hasn't it got a hairy nose?' he said. 'And ears, too.'

'Quite gross,' said the lady.

'You could almost feel sorry for them, with great big noses like that.'

Grimma stared into the human's eyes. I wonder, she thought. They're bigger than us, so there must be room for brains. And they've got great big eyes. Surely they must have seen us once? Masklin said we've been here for thousands of years. In all that time, humans must have seen us.

They must have known we were real people. But in their minds they turned us into pixies. Perhaps they didn't want to have to share the world.

The human was definitely looking at her.

Could we share? she thought. They live in a big long slow world and we live in a small short fast one, and we can't understand each other. They can't even see us unless we stand still like I'm standing now. We move too quickly for them. They don't think we exist.

She stared up into the big frightened eyes.

We've never tried to – what was the word? – *communicate* with them before. Not properly. Not as though they were real people, thinking real thoughts. How can we tell them we're really real and really here?

But perhaps when you're lying down on the floor

and tied up by little people you can hardly see and don't believe in, that's not the best time to start communicating. Perhaps we should try it another time. Not signs, not shouting, just trying to get them to understand us.

Wouldn't it be amazing if we could? They could do the big slow jobs for us and we could do – oh, little fast things. Fiddly things that those great fingers can't do . . . but not paint flowers or mend their shoes . . .

'Grimma? You ought to see this, Grimma,' said a voice behind her.

The nomes were clustered around a white heap on the floor.

Oh, yes. The human had been looking at one of those big sheets of paper . . .

The nomes had spread it out flat on the floor. It looked a lot like the first one they'd seen, except this one was called READ IT FIRST IN YOUR SOARAWAY BLACKBURY EVENING POST & GAZETTE. It had more of the great blocky writing, some of the letters nearly as big as a nome's head.

Grimma shook her own head as she tried to make sense of it. She could understand the books quite well, she considered, but the papers seemed to use a different language. It was full of PROBES and SHOCKS and fuzzy pictures of smiling humans shaking hands with other humans ('TABLERS RAISE £455 FOR HOS-PITAL APPEAL'). It wasn't difficult to work out what each word meant, but when they were put together they either didn't mean anything at all or something quite unbelievable ('CIVIC CENTRE RATES RUMPUS').

'No, this is the bit,' said one of the nomes, 'this page here. Look, some of the words, they're the same as last time, look! *It's about Grandson, 39!*'

Grimma ran the length of a story about somebody slamming somebody's plan for something.

There was indeed a fuzzy picture of Grandson, 39, under the words: 'TV-IN-THE-SKY HITCH.'

She knelt down and stared at the smaller words below it.

'Read it aloud!' they said.

' "Richard Arnold, the Blackbury-based chairman of the Arnco Group, said in Florida today",' she said, ' "that scientists are still trying to r . . . r . . . regain control of Arnsat 1, the multi-million pound com . . . communications sat . . . ellite — " '

The nomes looked at one another.

'Multimillion pound,' they said. 'That's really heavy.'

' "Hopes were high after yesterday's s . . . s . . . successful l . . . lunch in Florida",' Grimma read, uncertainly, ' "that Arnsat 1 would begin test tr . . . tr . . . transmissions today. Instead, it is s . . . sending a stream of strange sig . . . signals. 'It's like some sort of c . . . code,' said Richard, 39 — " '

There was an appreciative murmur from the listeners.

' "It's as if it had a mind of its own",' Grimma read.

There was more stuff about 'teething troubles', whatever that meant, but Grimma didn't bother to read it.

She remembered the way Masklin had talked about the stars, and why they stayed up. And there was the Thing. He'd taken it with him. The Thing could talk to electricity, couldn't it? It could listen to the electricity in wires, and the stuff in the air that Dorcas called 'radio'. If anything could send strange signals, the Thing could. *I may go even further than the Long Drive*, he'd said.

'They're alive,' she said, to no one in particular. 'Masklin and Gurder and Angalo. They got to the Florida place and they're alive.'

She remembered him trying to tell her, sometimes, about the sky and the Thing and where nomes first came from, and she'd never really understood, any more than he'd understood about the little frogs.

'They're alive,' she repeated. 'I know they are. I don't know exactly how or where, but they've got some sort of plan and they're alive.'

The nomes exchanged meaningful glances, and the kind of meaning they were full of was: She's fooling herself, but it'd take a braver nome than *me* to tell her.

Granny Morkie patted her gently on the shoulder.

'Yes, yes,' she said soothingly. 'And thank goodness they had a successful lunch. I bet they needed to get some food inside of them. And if I was you, my girl, I'd get some sleep.'

Grimma dreamed.

It was a confused dream. Dreams nearly always are. They don't come neatly packaged. She dreamed of loud noises and flashing lights. And eyes.

Little, yellow eyes. And Masklin, standing on a branch, climbing through leaves, peering down at little yellow eyes.

I'm seeing what he's doing now, she thought. *He's alive. I always knew he was, of course. But Outer Space has got more leaves than I thought. Or perhaps none of it is real and I'm just dreaming . . .*

Then someone woke her up.

It's never wise to speculate about the meaning of dreams, so she didn't.

It snowed again in the night, on an icy wind. Some of the nomes scouted around the sheds and came back with a few vegetables that had been missed, but it was a pitifully small amount. The tied-up human went to sleep after a while, and snored like someone sawing a thick log with a thin saw.

'The others will come looking for it in the morning,' Grimma warned. 'We mustn't be here then. Perhaps we should –'

She stopped. They all listened.

Something was moving around under the floorboards.

'Is anyone still down there?' Grimma whispered.

The nomes near her shook their heads. No one wanted to be in the chilly space under the floor when there was the warmth and light of the office for the having.

'And it can't be rats,' she said.

Then someone called out, in that half-loud, half-soft way of someone who wants to make themselves heard while at the same time remaining as quiet as possible.

It turned out to be Sacco.

They dragged aside the floorboard the humans had loosened and helped him up. He was covered in mud and swaying with exhaustion.

'I couldn't find anyone!' he gasped. 'I looked everywhere and couldn't find anyone and we saw the trucks come here and I saw the lights on and I thought the humans were still here and I came in and I heard your voices and you've got to come because it's Dorcas!'

'He's alive?' said Grimma.

'If he isn't, he can swear pretty well for a dead person,' said Sacco, sagging to the floor.

'We thought you were all de – ' Grimma began.

'We're all fine except for Dorcas. He hurt himself jumping out of the lorry! Come on, *please*!'

'You don't look in any state to go anywhere,' said Grimma. She stood up. 'You just tell us where he is.'

'We got him halfway up the lane and we got so tired and I left them and came on ahead,' Sacco blurted out. 'They're under the hedge and – ' His eyes fell on the snoring bulk of the human. He stared at Grimma.

'You've captured a *human*?' he said. He stumbled sideways. 'Need a bit of a rest, so tired,' he repeated, vaguely. Then he fell forwards.

Grimma caught him and laid him down as gently as she could.

'Someone put him somewhere warm and see if there's any food left,' she said to the nomes in general. 'And I want some of you to help me look for the others. Come on. This isn't a night for being outside.'

The expression on the faces of some of the nomes said that they definitely agreed with this point of view, and that among the people who shouldn't be out on a night like this was themselves.

'It's snowing quite a lot,' said one of them, uncertainly. 'We'll never find them in all the dark and snow.'

Grimma glared at him.

'We might,' she said. 'We *might* find them in all the dark and snow. We *won't* find them by staying in the light and warm, I know that much.'

Several nomes pushed their way forwards. Grimma recognized Nooty's people, and the parents of some of the lads. Then there was a bit of a commotion from under the table, where the oldest nomes were clustering together to keep warm and have a good moan.

'I'm comin' too,' said Granny Morkie. 'Do me good to have a drop of fresh air. What you all lookin' at me like that for?'

'I think you ought to stay inside, Granny,' said Grimma gently.

'Don't you come the bein'-tactful-to-old-people to me, my gel,' said Granny, prodding her with her stick. 'I bin out in deep snow before you was even thought of.' She turned to the rest of the nomes. 'Nothin' to it if you acts sensible and keeps yellin' out so's everyone knows where everyone is. I went out to help look for my Uncle Joe before I was a year old,' she said, proudly. 'Dreadful snow, that was. It come down sudden, like, when the men were out huntin'. We found nearly all of him, too.'

'Yes, yes, all right, Granny,' said Grimma quickly. She looked at the others. 'Well, *we're* going,' she said.

In the end fifteen of them went, many out of sheer embarrassment.

In the yellow light from the shed windows the snowflakes looked beautiful. By the time they reached the ground they were pretty unpleasant.

The Store nomes really *hated* the Outside snow. There had been snow in the Store, too, sprayed on merchandise around Christmas Fayre time. But it wasn't cold. And snowflakes were huge beautiful things that were hung from the ceilings on bits of thread. *Proper* snowflakes. Not ghastly things which looked all right in the air but turned into freezing wet stuff which was allowed to just lie around on the floor.

It was already as deep as their knees.

'What you do is,' said Granny Morkie, 'you lift your feet up really high and plonk them down. Nothin' to it.'

The light from the shed shone out across the quarry, but the lane was a dark tunnel leading into the night.

'And spread out,' said Grimma. 'But keep together.'

'Spread out and keep together,' they muttered.

A senior nome put his hand up.

'You don't get *robins* at night, do you?' he asked cautiously.

'No, of course not,' said Grimma.

'No, you don't get robins at night, daft,' said Granny Morkie.

They looked relieved.

'No, you get foxes,' Granny added, in a self-satisfied way. 'Great big foxes. They get good and hungry in the cold weather. And maybe you get owls.' She scratched her chin. 'Cunnin' devils, owls. You never hear 'em till they're almost on top o' you.' She banged on the wall with her stick. 'Look sharp, you lot. Best foot forward. Unless you're like my Uncle Joe – a fox got his best foot, 'e 'ad to have a wooden leg, 'e was livid.'

There was something about Granny Morkie cheering people up that always got them moving. Anything was better than being cheered up some more.

The snowflakes were caking up on the dried grasses and ferns on either bank. Every now and again some of it fell off, sometimes on to the lane, often on to the nomes stumbling along it. They prodded the snowy tussocks and peered doubtfully into the gloomy holes under the hedge, while the flakes continued to fall in a soft, crackly silence. Robins, owls and other terrors of the Outside lurked in every shadow.

Eventually the light was left behind and they walked by the glow of the snow itself. Sometimes one of them would call out, softly, and then they'd all listen.

It was very cold.

Granny Morkie stopped suddenly.

'Fox,' she announced. 'I can smell it. Can't mistake a fox. *Rank.*'

They huddled together and stared apprehensively into the darkness.

'Might not still be around, mind,' said Granny. 'Hangs about for a long time, that smell.'

They relaxed a bit.

'Really, Granny,' muttered Grimma.

'I was just tryin' to be a help,' sniffed Granny Morkie. 'You don't want my help, you've only got to say.'

'We're doing this wrong,' said Grimma. 'It's *Dorcas* we're looking for. He wouldn't just be sitting out in the open, would he? He knows about foxes. He'd get the boys to find somewhere sheltered and as safe as possible.'

Nooty's father stepped forward.

'If you look the way the snow falls,' he said hesitantly, 'you can see the air conditioning is blowing it *this* way,' he pointed, 'so it piles up more on this side of things than that side. So they'd want to be as much away from the air conditioning as possible, wouldn't they?'

'It's called the wind, when it's outside,' said Grimma gently. 'But you're right. That means . . .' she stared at the hedges, 'they'd be on the other side of the hedge. In the field, up against the bank. Come on.'

They scrambled up through the masses of dead leaves and dripping twigs and into the field beyond.

It was desolate. A few tufts of dead grass stuck above the endless wilderness of snow. Several of the nomes groaned.

It's the size, Grimma thought. They don't mind the quarry, or the thickets above it, or even the lane, because a lot of it is closed in and you can pretend there are sort of walls around you. It's too *big* for them here.

'Stick close to the hedge,' she said, more cheerfully than she felt. 'There's not so much snow there.'

Oh, Arnold Bros (est. 1905), she thought. Dorcas doesn't believe in you, and I certainly don't believe in you, but if you could just see your way clear to existing just long enough for us to find them, we'd all appreciate it very much. And perhaps if you could stop the snow and see us all safely back to the quarry as well, that would be a big help.

That's daft, she thought. Masklin always said that if there was an Arnold Bros, he was sort of inside our heads, helping us think.

She realized that she was staring at the snow.

Why is there a hole in it? she thought.

12

> IV. *There is Nowhere to go, and we must Leave.*
>
> *From* The Book of Nome, *Exits Chap. 3, v.IV*

'Rabbits, I thought,' she said.

Dorcas patted her hand.

'Well done,' he said weakly.

'We were in the lane after Sacco left,' said Nooty, 'and it was getting really cold and Dorcas said to take him the other side of the hedge and, well, it was me who said you can see rabbits in this field sometimes, and *he* said find a rabbit-hole. So we did. We thought we'd be here all night.'

'Ow,' moaned Dorcas.

'Don't make a fuss, I didn't hurt a bit,' said Granny Morkie, cheerfully, as she examined his leg. 'Nothin' broken, but it's a nasty sprain.'

The Store nomes looked around the burrow with interest and a certain amount of approval. It was nicely closed-in.

'Your ancestors probably lived in holes like this,' said Grimma. 'With shelves and things, of course.'

'Very nice,' said a nome. 'Homely. Almost like being under the floor.'

'Pongs a bit, mind,' said another.

'That'll be the rabbits,' said Dorcas, nodding towards the deeper darkness. 'We've heard them rustling about but they're staying out of our way. Nooty said she thought there was a fox snuffling around a while ago.'

'We'd better get you back as soon as possible,' said Grimma. 'I don't *think* any fox would bother the pack of us. After all, the local ones know who we are. Eat a nome and you die, that's what they've learned.'

The nomes shuffled their feet. It was true, of course. The trouble *was*, they thought, that the person who'd really regret it the most would be the one nome who was eaten. Knowing that the fox might be given a bad time afterwards wouldn't be a lot of consolation.

Besides, they were cold and wet and the burrow, while it wouldn't have sounded a very comfortable proposition back at the quarry, was suddenly much better than the horrible night outside. They'd staggered past a dozen rabbit-holes, calling down into the gloom, before they'd heard Nooty's voice answering them.

'I really don't think we need worry,' said Grimma. 'Foxes learn very quickly. Isn't that so, Granny?'

'Eh?' said Granny Morkie.

'I was telling everyone how foxes learn quickly,' said Grimma desperately.

'Oh, yes. Right enough,' said Granny. 'He'll go a long way out of his way for something he likes to eat, will your average fox. Especially when it's cold weather.'

'I didn't mean that! Why do you have to make everything sound so *bad*?'

'I'm sure I don't mean to,' said Granny Morkie, and sniffed.

'We must get back,' said Dorcas firmly. 'This snow isn't just going to go away, is it? I can get along OK if I've got someone to lean on.'

'We can make you a stretcher,' said Grimma. 'Though goodness knows there isn't much to get back *to*.'

'We saw the humans go up the lane,' said Nooty. 'But we had to go all the way along to the badger tunnel and there were no proper tracks. Then we tried to cut across the fields at the bottom and that was a mistake, they were all ploughed up. We haven't had anything to eat,' she added.

'Don't expect much, then,' said Grimma. 'The humans have taken most of our stores. They think we're rats.'

'Well, that's not so bad,' said Dorcas. 'We used to encourage them to think we were, back in the Store. They used to put traps down. We used to hunt rats in the basement and put them in the traps, when I was a lad.'

'Now they're using poisoned food,' said Grimma.

'That's not good.'

'Come on. Let's get you back.'

The snow was still falling outside, but raggedy fashion, as if the last flakes in stock were being sold off cheaply. There was a line of red light in the east — not the dawn, but the promise of the dawn. It didn't look cheerful. When the sun did rise, it would find itself locked behind bars of cloud.

They broke off some pieces of dead cow parsley stalk to make a rough sort of chair for Dorcas, which four nomes could carry. He'd been right about the shelter of the hedge. The snow wasn't very deep there, but it made up for it by being littered with old leaves, twigs and debris. It was slow going.

It must be great to be a human, Grimma thought, as thorns the length of her hand tore at her dress. Masklin was right, this really is their world. It's the right size for them. They go where they want and do whatever they like. We think we do things for ourselves and all we do is live in odd corners of their world — under their floors, stealing things.

The other nomes trudged along in weary silence. The only sound, apart from the crunch of feet on snow and leaves, was of Granny Morkie eating. She'd found some hawthorn berries on a bush and was chewing her way through one with every sign of enjoyment. She'd offered them around, but the other nomes found them bitter and unpleasant.

'Prob'ly an acquired taste,' she muttered, glaring at Grimma.

It's one we are all going to have to acquire, thought Grimma, ignoring Granny's hurt stare. The only hope we've got is to split up and leave the quarry in little groups, once we get back. Move out into the country, go back to living in old rabbit-holes and eating whatever we can find. Some groups may survive the winter, once the old people have died off.

And it'll be goodbye electricity, goodbye reading, goodbye bananas . . .

But I'll wait at the quarry until Masklin comes back.

'Cheer up, my girl,' said Granny Morkie, trying to be friendly. 'Don't look so gloomy. It may never happen, that's what I always say.'

Even Granny was shocked when Grimma looked at her with a face from which all the colour had drained away. The girl's mouth opened and shut a few times.

Then she folded up, very gently, and collapsed to her knees and started to sob.

It was the most shocking sound they'd heard. Grimma yelled, complained, bullied and commanded. Hearing her cry was *wrong*, as though the whole world had turned upside down.

'All I did was try and cheer her up,' mumbled Granny Morkie.

The embarrassed nomes stood around in a circle. No one dared go near Grimma. Anything might happen. If you tried to pat her on the shoulder and say 'There, there,' anything might happen. She might bite your hand off, or anything.

Dorcas looked at the nomes on either side of him,

sighed, and eased himself up off his makeshift carrier. He limped over to Grimma, catching hold of a thorn twig to steady himself.

'You've found us, we're going back to the quarry, everything's all right,' he said soothingly.

'It isn't! We'll have to move on!' she sobbed. 'You'd have been better off staying in the hole! It's all gone wrong!'

'Well, I would have said – ' Dorcas began.

'We've got no food and we can't stop the humans and we're trapped in the quarry and I've tried to keep everyone together and now it's all gone wrong!'

'We ought to have gone up to that barn right at the start,' said Nooty.

'You still could,' said Grimma. 'All the younger people could. Just get as far away from here as possible!'

'But children couldn't walk it, and old people certainly couldn't manage the snow,' said Dorcas. '*You* know that. You're just despairing.'

'We've tried everything! It's just got worse! We thought it would be a lovely life in the Outside and now it's all falling to bits!'

Dorcas gave her a long, blank look.

'We might as well give up right now,' she said. 'We might as well give up and die right here.'

There was a horrified silence.

It was broken by Dorcas.

'Er,' he said. 'Er. Are you sure? Are you *really* sure?'

The tone of his voice made Grimma look up.

All the nomes were staring.

There was a fox looking down at them.

It was one of those moments when Time itself freezes solid. Grimma could see the yellow-green glow in the fox's eyes and the cloud of its breath. Its tongue lolled out.

It looked surprised.

It was new to these parts and had never seen nomes before. Its not-very-complicated mind was trying to come to terms with the fact that the *shape* of the nomes – two arms, two legs, a head at the top – was a shape it associated with humans and had learnt to avoid, but the size was the size it had always thought of as a mouthful.

The nomes stood rooted in terror. There was no sense in trying to run away. A fox had twice as many legs to run after you. You'd end up dead anyway, but at least you wouldn't end up dead and out of breath as well.

There was a growl.

To the nomes' astonishment, it had come from Grimma.

She snatched Granny Morkie's walking stick, strode forward and whacked the fox across the nose before it could move. It yelped, and blinked stupidly.

'Push off!' she shouted. 'How dare you come here!' She hit it again. It jerked its head away. Grimma took another step forward and caught it a backward thump across the muzzle.

The fox made up its mind. There were definitely rabbits further down the hedge. Rabbits didn't hit back. It was a lot happier about rabbits.

It whined, backed away with its eyes fixed on Grimma, and then darted off into the darkness.

The nomes breathed out.

'*Well*,' said Dorcas.

'I'm sorry, but I just can't *stand* foxes,' said Grimma. 'And Masklin said we should let them know who's boss.'

'I'm not arguing,' said Dorcas.

Grimma looked vaguely at the stick.

'What was I saying before that?' she said.

'You were saying we might as well give up and die right here,' said Granny Morkie helpfully.

Grimma glared at her. 'No, I wasn't,' she said. 'I was

just feeling a bit tired, that's all. Come on. We'll catch our death standing here.'

'Or the other way round,' said Sacco, staring into the fox-haunted darkness.

'That's not funny,' snapped Grimma, striding off.

'I didn't mean it to be,' said Sacco, shivering.

Overhead, quite unnoticed by the nomes, a rather strangely bright star zig-zagged across the sky. It was small, or perhaps it was very big but a long way off. If you looked at it long enough, it might just have appeared disc-shaped. It was causing a lot of messages to be sent through the air, all around the world.

It seemed to be looking for something.

There were flickering lights in the quarry by the time they got back. Another group of nomes was about to set out to look for them. Not with much enthusiasm, admittedly, but they were going to try.

The cheer that went up when it was realized that everyone was safely back almost made Grimma forget that they were safely back to a very unsafe place. She'd read something in the book of proverbs that summed it up perfectly. As far as she could remember, it was something about jumping out of the thing you cook in and into the thing you cooked on. Or something.

Grimma led the rescue party into the office and listened while Sacco, with many interruptions, recounted the adventure from the time Dorcas, out of sudden terror, had jumped out of the truck and had been carried off the rails just before the train arrived. It sounded brave and exciting. And pointless, Grimma thought, but she kept that to herself.

'It wasn't as bad as it looked,' Sacco said. 'I mean, the truck was smashed but the train didn't even come off the rails. We saw it all,' he finished. 'I'm starving.'

He gave them a bright smile, which faded like a sunset.

'There's no food?' he said.

'Even less than that,' said a nome. 'If you've got some bread, we could have a snow sandwich.'

Sacco thought about this.

'There's the rabbits,' he said. 'There were rabbits in the field.'

'And in the dark,' said Dorcas, who appeared to have something on his mind.

'Well, yes,' admitted Sacco.

'And with that fox hanging about,' said Nooty.

Another proverb floated up in Grimma's mind.

'Needs must,' she said, 'when the Devil drives.'

They looked at her in the flickering light of the matches.

'Who's he?' said Nooty.

'Some sort of horrible person that lives under the ground in a hot place, I think,' said Grimma.

'Like the boiler-room in the Store?'

'I suppose so.'

'What sort of vehicle does he drive?' said Sacco, looking interested.

'It just means that sometimes you're forced to do things,' said Grimma testily. 'I don't think he actually *drives* anything.'

'Well, no. There wouldn't be the room down there, for one thing.'

Dorcas coughed. He seemed to be upset about something. Well, everyone was upset, but he was even more upset.

'All right,' he said quietly.

Something about the way he said it made them pay attention.

'You'd all better come with me,' he went on. 'Believe me, I'd rather you didn't have to.'

'Where to?' said Grimma.

'The old sheds. The ones by the cliff,' said Dorcas.

'But they're all tumbled down. And you said they were very dangerous.'

'Oh, they are. They are. There's piles of junk and stuff in tins the children shouldn't touch and stuff like that . . .'

He twiddled his beard nervously.

'But,' he said, 'there's something else. Something I've been sort of working on, sort of.'

He looked Grimma in the eye. 'Something of mine,' he said. 'The most marvellous thing I've ever seen. Even better than frogs in a flower.'

Then he coughed. 'Anyway, there's plenty of room in there,' he said. 'The floors are just earth, er, but the sheds are big and there are lots of places, er, to hide.'

A snore from the human shook the office.

'Besides, I don't like being so close to that thing,' he added.

There was a general murmur of agreement about this.

'Had you thought about what you're going to do with it?' said Dorcas.

'Some people wanted to kill it but I don't think that's a good idea,' said Grimma. 'I think the other humans would get really upset about it.'

'Besides, it doesn't seem right,' said Dorcas.

'I know what you mean.'

'So . . . what shall we do with it?'

Grimma stared at the huge face. Every pore, every hair, was huge. It was strange to think that if there were creatures smaller than nomes, little people perhaps the size of ants, her own face might look like that. If you looked at it philosophically, the whole thing about big and small was just a matter of size.

'We'll leave it,' she said. 'But . . . is there any paper here?'

'Loads of it on the desk,' said Nooty.

'Go and fetch some, please. Dorcas, you've always got something to write with, haven't you?'

Dorcas fumbled in his pockets until he found a stub of pencil lead.

'Don't waste it,' he said. 'Don't know if I'll ever get some more.'

Eventually Nooty came back towing a yellowing sheet of paper. At the top of it, in heavy black lettering, were the words: Blackbury Sand & Gravel PLC. Below that was the word: Invoice.

Grimma thought for a while, and then licked the stub and, in big letters, started to write.

'What are you doing?' said Dorcas.

'Trying to communicate,' said Grimma. She carefully traced another word, pressing quite hard.

'I've always thought it might be worth trying,' said Dorcas, 'but is this the right time?'

'Yes,' said Grimma. She finished the last word.

'What do you think?' she said, handing Dorcas the pencil lead.

The writing was a bit jagged where she had pressed hard, and her grasp of grammar and writing wasn't as good as her skill at reading, but it was clear enough.

'I would have done it differently,' said Dorcas, reading it.

'Perhaps you would, but this is the way *I've* done it.'

'Yes.' Dorcas put his head on one side. 'Well, it's definitely a communication. You can't get much more communicating than that. Yes.'

Grimma tried to sound cheerful. 'And now,' she said, 'let's see this shed of yours.'

Two minutes later the office shed was empty of nomes. The human snored on the floor, one hand outstretched.

There was a piece of paper in it now.

It said: Blackbury Sand & Gravel PLC.

It said: Invoice.

It said: We Could Of Kiled You. LEAV US ALONE.

Now it was quite light outside, and the snow had stopped.

'They'll see our tracks,' said Sacco. 'Even humans will notice this many tracks.'

'It doesn't matter,' said Dorcas. 'Just get everyone into the old sheds.'

'Are you sure, Dorcas?' said Grimma. 'Are you really *sure* this is a good idea?'

'No.'

They joined the stream of nomes hurrying through a crack in the crumbling corrugated iron and entered the vast, echoing chamber of the shed.

Grimma looked around her. Rust and time had eaten large holes in the walls and ceiling. Old tins and coils of wire were stacked willy-nilly in the corners, along with odd-shaped bits of metal and jam jars with nails in them. Everything stank of oil.

'What's the bit we ought to know about?' she said.

Dorcas pointed to the shadows at the far end of the shed, where she could just make out something big and indistinct.

'It just looks like . . . some sort of big cloth . . .' she said.

'It's, um, underneath it. Is everyone in?' Dorcas cupped his hands around his mouth. '*Is everyone in?*' he shouted. He turned to Nooty.

'I need to know where everyone is,' he said. 'I don't want anyone to be frightened, but I don't want unnecessary people getting in the way.'

'Unnecessary for what?' said Grimma, but he ignored her.

'Sacco, you take some of the lads and get those things we put in the hedge,' said Dorcas. 'We'll definitely need the battery and I'm really not certain how much fuel there is.'

'*Dorcas!* What is it?' said Grimma, tapping her foot.

Dorcas got like this sometimes, she knew. When he was thinking about machines or things he could do with his hands, he started to ignore people. His voice changed, too.

He gave her a long, slow look as if he was seeing her for the first time. Then he looked down at his feet.

'You'd better, er, come and see,' he said. 'I shall need you to explain things to everyone. You're so much better at that sort of thing.'

Grimma followed him across the chilly floor as more nomes filed into the shed and huddled apprehensively along the walls.

He led her under the shadow of the tarpaulin, which formed a sort of big, dusty cave.

A tyre like a truck's loomed up a little way away in the gloom, but it was far more knobbly than any she had seen.

'Oh. It's just a truck,' she said, uncertainly. 'You've got a truck in here, have you?'

Dorcas said nothing. He just pointed upwards.

Grimma looked up. And then looked up some more. Into the mouth of Jekub.

13

IV. *Dorcas said, This is Jekub, Great Beast with teeth.*
V. *Needs Must. If we are driven, let us Drive.*

From The Book of Nome *Jekub, Chap. 2, IV–V*

Sometimes words need music too. Sometimes the descriptions are not enough; books should be written with soundtracks, like films.

Something deep on an organ, perhaps.

Grimma stared.

Dee-dah-DAH.

It can't really be alive, she thought desperately. It's not really about to bite me. Dorcas wouldn't have brought me in here if he knew there was a monster about to bite me. I'm not going to be frightened. I'm not frightened at all. I am a thinking nome and I'm not *frightened!*

'I think the knobbly wheels are just to make it grip the ground better,' said Dorcas, his voice sounding a long way off. 'Now, I've had a good look around it and, you know, there's nothing really wrong with it, it's just very old – '

Grimma's gaze travelled along the huge yellow neck.

Dee-dah-dee-dah-DUM.

'Then I thought, I'm sure he could be started up. These diesel engines are quite easy really, and of course there were pictures in one of the books, although I'm not sure about these pipes, hydraulics I think it's called, but there was this book on one of the benches, *Workshop Manual*, and I've put grease on things and tidied it up,' Dorcas gabbled.

Dah-dah-dah-DUM.

'I suppose the humans or whatever knew they would be coming back, and I've been up and looked at the controls and, you know, it's probably easier than the truck was, only of course there's these extra levers for the hydraulics, but that shouldn't be a problem if there's enough fuel, which . . .'

He stopped, aware of her silence.

'Is there something the matter?' he said.

'What *is* it?' said Grimma.

'I was just telling you,' said Dorcas. 'It's fascinating. You see, these pipes pump some sort of stuff which make those bits up there move, and those pistons are forced out, which makes the arm thing over there – '

'I didn't ask you what it does, I asked you what it *is*,' said Grimma, impatiently.

'Didn't I say?' said Dorcas innocently. 'Well, there's its name painted on it. Just up there, look.'

She looked where he pointed. Grimma's brow wrinkled.

'J . . . C . . . B,' she said. 'Jcb? Jekub? It's got no vowels in it. What sort of name is that?'

'Dunno,' said Dorcas. 'I'm not a good man at names. Anyway, it sounds right. Come over this side.'

She followed him dreamily, and, once more, stared into the darkness under the tarpaulin.

'There,' he said. 'There's no mistaking what *they* are, I hope.'

'Oh, my,' said Grimma, and raised her hand to her mouth.

'Yes,' said Dorcas. 'That's what I thought. When I first found this I thought, Oh, it's a sort of truck, well,

well, and then I walked up here and I found it was a truck with — '

'Teeth,' said Grimma, softly. 'Great big metal teeth.'

'That's right,' said Dorcas proudly. 'Jekub. A sort of truck. A truck with teeth.'

Dah-DUM.

'Does it — does it work?' said Grimma.

'It should do. It should do. I've tested what I can. Basic principle *is* like a truck, but there's a lot of extra levers and things — '

'Why didn't you tell me about this before?' Grimma demanded.

'Dunno. Because I didn't have to, I suppose,' said Dorcas.

'But it's *huge*. You can't keep something like this to yourself!'

'Everyone has to have something they can keep to themselves,' said Dorcas vaguely. 'Anyway, the size isn't important. It's just so, well, so perfect.' Dorcas patted a knobbly tyre. 'You know you said humans think someone made the world in a week? When I saw Jekub for the first time I thought, OK, this is what he used.'

He stared up into the shadows.

'First thing we've got to do is get the tarpaulin off,' he said. 'It'll be very heavy, so we'll need lots of people. You'd better warn them. Jekub can be a bit scary when you see him for the first time.'

'Didn't frighten me a bit,' said Grimma.

'I know,' said Dorcas. 'I was watching your face.'

The nomes looked expectantly at Grimma.

'The thing to remember,' she said, 'is that it's just a machine. Just a sort of truck. But when you first see it, it can be rather frightening, so hold on to small children's hands. And run smartly backwards when the tarpaulin comes down.'

There was a chorus of nods.

'All right. Grab hold.'

Six hundred nomes spat on their hands and grasped the edge of the heavy sheet.

'When I say pull, I want you to pull.'

The nomes took the strain.

'*Pull!*'

The creases in the tarpaulin flattened out and disappeared.

'*Pull!*'

It began to move. Then, as it slid over Jekub's angular shape, its own weight started to tug at it . . .

'*Run!*'

It came down like an oily green avalanche, piling up into a mountain of folds, but no one bothered about it because the sun shone through the dusty, cobwebbed windows and made Jekub glow.

Several nomes screamed. Mothers picked up their children. There was a movement towards the doors.

It *does* look like a head, Grimma thought. On a long neck. And he's got another one at the other end. What am I saying? *It* has got another one at the other end.

'I said it's all right!' she shouted, over the rising din. 'Look! It's not even moving!'

'Hey!' shouted another voice. She looked up. Nooty and Sacco had climbed out along Jekub's neck, and were sitting there waving cheerfully.

That did it. The tide of nomes reached the wall and stopped. You always feel foolish, running away from something that isn't chasing you. They hesitated and then, slowly, inched their way back.

'Well, well,' said Granny Morkie hobbling forward. 'So that's what they looked like. I always wondered.'

Grimma stared at her.

'What what looked like?' she said.

'Oh, the big diggers,' said Granny. 'They'd all gone

when I was born, but our dad saw 'em. Great big yellow things with teeth that et dirt, he said. I always thought he was just having me on.'

Jekub was still not eating people. Some of the more adventurous nomes started to climb on him.

'It was when the motorway was built,' Granny went on, leaning on her stick. 'They were all over the place, Dad said. Big yellow things with teeth and knobbly tyres.'

Grimma stared at her with the kind of expression reserved for people who turn out, against all expectation, to have interesting and secret histories.

'And there was others, too,' the old woman went on. 'Things that shoved dirt in heaps and everything. This would have been, oh, fifteen years ago now. Never thought I'd see one.'

'You mean the roads were *made*?' said Grimma. Jekub was covered with young nomes now. She could see Dorcas in the back of the cab, explaining what various levers did.

'That's what he said,' said Granny. 'You didn't think they was nat'ral, did you?'

'Oh. No. No. Of course not,' said Grimma. 'Don't be silly.'

And she thought: I wonder if Dorcas is right? Perhaps everything was made. Some bits early, some bits later. You start with hills and clouds and things, and then you add roads and Stores. Perhaps the job of humans is to make the world, and they're still doing it. That's why the machines have to suit them.

Gurder would have understood this sort of thing. I wish he was back, she thought.

And then Masklin would be back, too.

She tried to think about something else.

Knobbly tyres. That was a good start. Jekub's back wheels were nearly as high as a human. It doesn't need roads. Of course it doesn't. It *makes* roads. So it has to be able to go where roads aren't.

She pushed her way through the crowds to the back of the cab, where another group of nomes were already nomehandling a plank into position, and scrambled up to where Dorcas was trying to make himself heard in the middle of an excited crowd.

'You're going to drive this out of here?' she demanded.

He looked up.

'Oh, yes,' he said happily. 'I think so. I hope so. I imagine we've got at least an hour before any more humans come, and it's not a lot different to a truck.'

'We know how to do it!' shouted one of the younger nomes. 'My dad told me all about the strings and stuff.'

Grimma looked around the cab. It seemed to be full of levers.

It'd been more than half a year since the Long Drive, and she'd never taken much notice of mechanical things, but she couldn't help thinking the old lorry cab had been a lot less crowded. There had been some pedals and a lever and the steering wheel, and that had been about it.

She turned back to Dorcas.

'Are you sure?' she said doubtfully.

'No,' he said. 'You know I'm never sure. But a lot of the controls are for his mou . . . for the bucket. The thing with the teeth in it. At the end of his neck. I mean, the digging bits. We needn't bother with them. They're amazingly ingenious, though, and all you have to do — '

'Where's everyone going to sit? There isn't much room.'

Dorcas shrugged. 'I suppose the older people can travel in the cab. The youngsters will have to hang on where they can. We can wrap wires and things around the place. For handholds, I mean. Look, don't worry. We'll be driving in the light and we don't have to go fast.'

'And then we'll get to the barn, won't we, Dorcas?'

said Nooty. 'Where it'll be warm and there's lots of food.'

'I hope so,' said Dorcas. 'Now, let's get on with things. We haven't got much time. Where's Sacco with the battery?'

Grimma thought: Will there be lots of food at the barn? Where did we get that idea? Angalo said that turnips or something were stored up there, and there may be some potatoes. That's not exactly a feast.

Her stomach, thinking thoughts of its own, rumbled in disagreement. It had been a very long night to pass on a tiny piece of sandwich.

Anyway, we can't stay here now. Anywhere will be better than here.

'Dorcas,' she said, 'is there anything I can help with?'

He looked up. 'You could read the instruction book,' he said. 'See if it says how to drive it.'

'Don't you know?'

'Er. Not in so many words. Not *exactly*. I mean, I know how to do it, it's just that I don't know what to do.'

The book was under the bench on one side of the shed. Grimma propped it up and tried to concentrate above the noise. I bet he does know, she thought. But this is his moment, and he doesn't want me getting in the way.

The nomes moved like people with a purpose. Things were far too bad to spend time grumbling. Funny thing, she thought as she turned the grubby pages, that people only seem to stop complaining when things get really bad. That's when they start using words like pulling together, shoulders to the wheel, and noses to the grindstone. She'd found 'nose to the grindstone' in a book. Apparently it meant 'to get on with things'. She didn't see why people were supposed to work hard if you ground their noses; it seemed more likely that they'd work hard if you promised to grind their noses if they didn't.

It had been the same with *Road Works Ahead* on the

Long Drive. The road ahead works. How could it mean anything else? But the road had been full of holes. Where was the sense in that? Words ought to mean what they meant.

She turned the page.

There was a big brown ring on this one, where a human had put down a cup.

Across the floor a group of nomes swarmed past around the slowly moving bulk of the battery. They were rolling it on rusty ball bearings.

The can of fuel wobbled past after it.

Grimma stared at the pictures of levers with numbers on. Suddenly people were keen on the barn. Suddenly, when things were not just averagely awful but promising to be really dreadful, they seemed almost happy. Masklin had known about that. It's amazing what people would do, he said, if you found the right place to push.

She stared at the pages, and tried to get interested in levers.

The clouds running before the sun were spreading across the pink of the sky. Red sky in the morning, Grimma had read once. It meant people who kept sheep were happy. Or not happy. Or perhaps it was cows.

In the dark office the human awoke, mooed for a while, and tried to jerk free of the cobweb of wires that held it down. After a lot of effort it wriggled most of one arm free.

What the human did next would have surprised most nomes. It caught hold of a chair and, with a great deal of grunting, managed to tip it over. It pulled it across the floor, manipulated the leg under a couple of strands of wire, and heaved.

A minute later it was sitting upright, pulling more wires free.

Its huge eyes fell on the scrap of paper on the floor.

It stared at it for a moment, rubbing its arms, and then it picked up the telephone.

Dorcas prodded vaguely at a wire.

'Are you sure the battery is connected the right way round, sir?' said Sacco.

'I can tell the difference between red wires and black wires, you know,' said Dorcas mildly, prodding another wire.

'Then perhaps the battery doesn't have enough electricity,' said Grimma helpfully, trying to see over their shoulders. 'Perhaps it's all run to the bottom, or gone dry.'

Dorcas and Sacco exchanged glances.

'Electricity doesn't sink,' said Dorcas patiently. 'Or dry up, as far as I know. It's either there or it isn't. Excuse me.' He peered up into the mass of wires again, and gave one a poke. There was a pop, and a fat blue spark.

'It's there all right,' he added. 'It's just that it isn't where it should be.'

Grimma walked back across the greasy floor of the cab. Groups of nomes were standing around, waiting. Hundreds of them were clutching the strings lashed to the big steering wheel above them. Other teams stood by with bits of wood pressing, like battering rams, on the pedals.

'Just a bit of a delay,' she said. 'All the electricity's got lost.'

There were nomes everywhere. On the Long Drive there had been a whole truck for them. But Jekub's cab was smaller, and people had to pack themselves in where they could.

What a ragged bunch, Grimma thought. And it was true. Even in the sudden rush from the Store the nomes had been able to bring quite a lot of stuff. And they had been plump and well-dressed.

Now they were thinner and leaner and much dirtier and all they were taking with them were the torn and grubby clothes they stood up in. Even the books had been left behind. A dozen books took up the space of three dozen nomes, and while Grimma privately thought that some of the books were more useful than many of the nomes, she'd accepted Dorcas's promise that they would come back, one day, and try to retrieve them from their hiding place under the floor.

Well, thought Grimma. We tried. We really made an effort. We came to the quarry to dig in, look after ourselves, live proper lives. And we failed. We thought all we had to do was bring the right things from the Store, but we brought a lot of wrong things too. This time we'll need to go as far away from humans as possible, and I don't actually think anywhere is far enough.

She climbed up on to the rickety driving platform, which had been made by tying a plank across the cab. There were even nomes on this. They watched her expectantly.

At least driving Jekub should be easier. The leaders of the teams on the controls could see her, so she wouldn't have to mess around with semaphore and bits of thread like they'd done when they left the Store. And a lot of the nomes had done this before, too . . .

She heard Dorcas shout: 'Try it this time!'

There was a click. There was a whirr. Then Jekub roared.

The sound bounced around the cave of the shed. It was so loud and so deep it wasn't really sound at all, just something that turned the air hard and then hit you with it. Nomes flung themselves flat on the trembling deck of the cab.

Grimma, clutching at her ears, saw Dorcas running across the floor waving his hands. The team on the accelerator pedal gave him a 'Who, us?' look and stopped pushing.

The sound died down to a deep rumbling, a *mummummummum* that still had a feel-it-in-the-bone quality. Dorcas hurried back and climbed, with a lot of stopping for breath, up to the plank. When he got there he sat down and rubbed his brow.

'I'm getting too old for this sort of thing,' he said. 'When a nome gets to a certain age, it's time to stop stealing giant vehicles. Well-known fact. Anyway. It's ticking over nicely. You might as well take us out.'

'What, all by myself?' said Grimma.

'Yes. Why not?'

'It's just that, well, I thought Sacco or someone would be up here.' I thought a male nome would be driving, she thought.

'They'd *like* to,' said Dorcas. 'They'd *love* to. And we'd be zipping all over the place, I don't doubt it, with them crying "Yippee!" and whatnot. No. I want a nice peaceful drive across the fields, thank you very much. The gentle touch.'

He leaned down.

'Everyone ready down there?' he yelled.

There was a chorus of nervous 'yesses', and one or two cheerful ones.

'I wonder if putting Sacco in charge of the go-faster pedal is really a good idea?' mused Dorcas. He straightened up. 'Er. You're not *worried*, are you?' he said.

Grimma snorted. 'What? Me? No. Of course not. It does not,' she added, 'present a problem.'

'O–kay,' he said. 'Let's go.'

There was silence, except for the deep thrumming of the engine.

Grimma paused.

If Masklin were here, she thought, he'd do this better than me. No one mentions him any more. Or Angalo.

Or Gurder. They don't like thinking about them. That must be something nomes learnt hundreds of years ago, in this place full of foxes and rushing things and a hundred nasty ways to die. If someone goes missing, you must stop thinking about them, you must put them out of your mind. But I think about him all the time.

I just went on about the frogs in the flowers, and I never thought about his dreams.

Dorcas gently put his arm around her. She was shaking.

'We should have sent some people to the airport,' she muttered. 'It would have showed that we cared, and — '

'We didn't have the time, and we didn't have the people,' said Dorcas softly. 'When he comes back we can explain about that. He's bound to understand.'

'Yes,' she whispered.

'And now,' said Dorcas, standing back, 'let's go!'

Grimma took a deep breath.

'First gear,' she bellowed, 'and go forward verrrry slowly.'

The teams pushed and pulled their way over the deck. There was a slight shudder and the engine noise dropped. Jekub lurched forward and jolted to a stop. The engine coughed and died.

Dorcas looked thoughtfully at his fingernails.

'Handbrake, handbrake, handbrake,' he hummed softly.

Grimma glared at him, and cupped her hands round her mouth. 'Take the handbrake off!' she shouted. 'Right! *Now* get into first gear and go forward very slowly!'

There was a click, and silence.

'Starttheengine, starttheengine, starttheengine,' murmured Dorcas, rocking back and forth on his heels.

Grimma sagged. 'Put everything back where it was and start the engine,' she screamed.

Nooty, in charge of the handbrake team, called up, 'Do you want the handbrake on or off, miss?'

'What?'

'You haven't told us what to do with the handbrake, miss,' said Sacco. The nomes with him started to grin.

Grimma shook a finger at him. 'Listen,' she snapped, 'if I have to come down there and tell you what to do with the handbrake, you'll all be *extremely sorry*, all right? Now stop giggling like that and *get this thing moving! Quickly!*'

There was a click. Jekub roared again and started to move. A cheer went up from the nomes.

'Right,' said Grimma. 'That's more like it.'

'The doors, the doors, the doors, we didn't open the do—ors,' hummed Dorcas.

'Of course we didn't open the doors,' said Grimma, as the digger began to go faster. 'What do we need to open the doors for? This is Jekub!'

14

v. *There is nothing that can* be *in our way, for this is Jekub, that Laughs at Barriers, and says* brrm-brrm.

From The Book of Nome, *Jekub, Chap. 3, v.V*

It was a very old shed. It was a very rusty shed. It was a shed that wobbled in high winds. The only thing even vaguely new about it was the padlock on the door, which Jekub hit at about six miles an hour. The rickety building rang like a gong, leapt off its foundations and was dragged halfway across the quarry before it fell apart in a shower of rust and smoke. Jekub emerged like a very angry chick from a very old egg and then rolled to a stop.

Grimma picked herself up from the plank and nervously started to pick bits of rust off herself.

'We've stopped,' she said vaguely, her ears still ringing. 'Why have we stopped, Dorcas?'

He didn't bother to try to get up. The thump of Jekub hitting the door had knocked all the breath out of him.

'I think,' he said, 'that everyone might have been flung about a bit. Why did you want it to go so fast?'

'Sorry!' Sacco called up. 'Bit of a misunderstanding there, I think!'

Grimma pulled herself together. 'Well,' she said, 'I got us out, anyway. I've got the hang of it now. We'll just . . . we'll just . . . we'll . . .'

Dorcas heard her voice fade into silence. He looked up.

There was a truck parked in front of the quarry. And three humans were running towards Jekub in big, floating bounds.

'Oh dear,' he said.

'Didn't it read my note?' wondered Grimma aloud.

'I'm afraid it did,' said Dorcas. 'Now, we shouldn't panic. We've got a choice. We can either – '

'Go forward,' snapped Grimma. 'Right now!'

'No, no,' said Dorcas weakly, 'I wasn't going to suggest that . . .'

'First gear!' Grimma commanded. 'And lots of fast!'

'No, you don't want to do that,' Dorcas murmured.

'Watch me,' said Grimma. 'I warned them! They can read, we know they can read! If they're really intelligent, they're intelligent enough to know better!'

Jekub gathered speed.

'You mustn't do this,' said Dorcas. 'We've always kept away from humans!'

'They don't keep away from us!' shouted Grimma.

'But – '

'They demolished the Store, they tried to stop us escaping, now they're taking our quarry *and they don't even know what we are!*' said Grimma. 'Remember the Gardening Department in the Store? Those horrible statues of garden ornaments? Well, I'm going to show them *real* nomes . . .'

'You can't beat humans!' shouted Dorcas, above the roar of the engine. 'They're too big! You're too small!'

'They may be big,' said Grimma, 'and I may be small. But *I'm* the one with the giant truck. With *teeth*.' She leaned over the plank. 'Everyone hang on down there,' she shouted. 'This may be rough.'

It had dawned on the great slow creatures outside that something was wrong. They stopped their lumbering charge and, very slowly, tried to dodge out of the way.

Two of them managed to leap into the empty office as Jekub bowled past.

'I see,' said Grimma. 'They must think we're stupid. Take a big left turn. More. More. Now stop. OK.' She rubbed her hands together.

'What are you going to do?' whispered Dorcas, terrified.

Grimma leaned over the plank.

'Sacco,' she said. 'You see those other levers?'

The pale round blobs of the humans' faces appeared at the dusty windows of the shed.

Jekub was twenty feet away, vibrating gently in the early morning mist. Then the engine roared. The big front shovel came up, catching the sunlight . . .

Jekub leapt forward, bouncing across the quarry floor and taking out one wall of the shed like ripping the lid off a can. The other walls and the roof folded up gently, as if it was a house of cards with the Ace of Spades flipped away.

The digger careered around in a big circle, so that when the two humans crawled out of the wreckage it was the first thing they saw. Throbbing, with the big metal mouth poised to bite.

They ran.

They ran almost as fast as nomes.

'I've always wanted to do that,' said Grimma, in a satisfied voice. 'Now, where did the other human go?'

'Back to the truck, I think,' said Dorcas.

'Fine,' said Grimma. 'Lots of right, Sacco. Stop. Now forwards, slowly.'

'Can we sort of stop this and just go, now? Please?' pleaded Dorcas.

'The humans' truck is in the way,' said Grimma, reasonably enough. 'They've stopped right in the entrance.'

'Then we're trapped,' said Dorcas.

Grimma laughed. It wasn't a very amusing sound. Dorcas suddenly felt almost as sorry for the humans as he was feeling for himself.

The humans must have been having similar thoughts, if humans had thoughts. He could see their pale faces watching Jekub lurch towards them.

They're wondering why they can't see a human inside, he thought. They can't work it out. Here's this machine, moving all by itself. A bit of a puzzler, for humans.

They reached some sort of conclusion, though. He saw both truck doors fly open and the humans jumped out just as Jekub —

There was a crunch, and the truck jerked as Jekub hit it. The knobbly wheels spun for a moment, and then the truck rolled backwards. Clouds of steam poured out.

'That's for Nisodemus,' said Grimma.

'I thought you didn't like him,' said Dorcas.

'Yes, but he was a nome.'

Dorcas nodded. They were all, when you got right down to it, nomes. It was just as well to remember whose side you were on.

'May I suggest you change gear?' he said quietly.

'Why? What's wrong with the one we've got?'

'You'll be able to push better if you go down a gear. Trust me.'

Humans were watching. They *were* watching, because a machine rolling around by itself is something that you do watch, even if you've just had to climb a tree or hide behind a hedge.

They saw Jekub roll backwards, change gear with a roar, and attack the truck again. The windows shattered.

Dorcas was really unhappy about this.

'You're killing a truck,' he said.

'Don't be silly,' said Grimma. 'It's a machine. Just bits of metal.'

'Yes, but someone made it,' said Dorcas. 'They must be very hard to make. I hate destroying things that are hard to make.'

'They ran over Nisodemus,' said Grimma. 'And when we used to live in a hole, nomes were always being squashed by cars.'

'Yes, but nomes aren't hard to make,' said Dorcas. 'You just need other nomes.'

'You're weird.'

Jekub struck again. One of the truck's headlights exploded. Dorcas winced.

Then the truck was pushed clear. Smoke was billowing out from it now, where fuel had spilled over the hot engine. Jekub backed off and rumbled around it. The nomes were really getting the hang of him now.

'Right,' said Grimma. 'Straight ahead.' She nudged Dorcas. 'We'll go and find this barn now, shall we?'

'Just go down the lane, and I think there's a gateway into the fields,' Dorcas mumbled. 'It had an actual gate in it,' he added. 'I suppose it would be too much to ask you to let us open it first?'

Behind them the truck burst into flames. Not spectacularly, but in a workmanlike way, as if it was going to go on burning all day. Dorcas saw a human take off its coat and flap uselessly at the fire. He felt quite sorry for it.

Jekub rolled unopposed down the lane. Some of the nomes started to sing as they sweated over the ropes.

'Now, then,' said Grimma, 'where's this gateway? Through the gate and across the fields, you said, and – '

'It's just before you get to the car with the flashing lights on top,' said Dorcas slowly. 'The one that's just coming up the lane.'

They stared at it.

'Cars with lights on the top are bad news,' said Grimma.

'You're right there,' said Dorcas. 'They're often full of humans who very seriously want to know what's going on. There were lots of them down at the railway.'

Grimma looked along the hedge.

'This is the gateway coming up, is it?' she said.

'Yes.'

Grimma leaned down.

'Slow down and turn sharp right,' she said.

The teams swung into action. Sacco even changed gear without being asked. Nomes hung like spiders from the steering wheel, hauling it around.

There *was* a gate in the gateway. But it was old and held to the post with bits of string in proper agricultural fashion. It wouldn't have stopped anything very determined, and it had no chance with Jekub.

Dorcas winced again. He hated to see things broken.

The field on the other side was brown soil. Corrugated earth, the nomes called it, after the corrugated cardboard you sometimes got in the Packing Department in the Store. There was snow between the furrows. The big wheels churned it into mud.

Dorcas was half expecting the car to follow them. It stopped instead, and two humans in dark blue suits got out and started to lumber across the field. There's no stopping humans, he thought glumly. They're like the weather.

The field ran gently uphill, around the quarry. Jekub's engine thudded.

There was a wire fence ahead, with a grassy field beyond it. The wire parted with a twang. Dorcas watched it roll back, and wondered whether Grimma would let him stop and collect a bit of it. You always knew where you were with wire.

The humans were still following. Out of the corner of his eye, because up here there was altogether too much outside to look at, Dorcas saw flashing lights on the main road, far away.

He pointed them out to Grimma.

'I know,' she said. 'I've seen them. But what else could we have done?' she added desperately. 'Gone off and lived in the flowers like good little *pixies*?'

'I don't know,' said Dorcas wearily. 'I'm not sure about anything any more.'

Another wire fence twanged. There was shorter grass up here, and the ground curved –

And then there was nothing but sky, and Jekub speeding up as the wheels bounced over the field at the top of the hill.

Dorcas had never seen so much sky. There was nothing around them, just a bit of scrub in the distance. And it was silent. Well, not silent at all, because of Jekub's roar. But it looked the kind of place that *would* be silent if diggers full of desperate nomes weren't thundering across it.

Frantic sheep ran out of the way.

'There's the barn up ahead, that stone building on the horiz – ' Grimma began. Then she said, 'Are you all right, Dorcas?'

'If I keep my eyes shut,' he whispered.

'You look dreadful.'

'I *feel* worse.'

'But you've been outside before.'

'Grimma, we're the highest thing there is! There's nothing higher than us for miles, or whatever you call those things! If I open my eyes I'll fall into the sky!'

Grimma leaned down to the perspiring drivers.

'Right just a bit!' she shouted. 'That's it! Now all the fast you can!'

'Hold on to Jekub!' she shouted to Dorcas, as the engine noise grew. 'You know *he* can't fly!'

The machine bumped up on a stony track that led in the general direction of the distant barn. Dorcas risked opening one eye. He'd never been to the barn. Was anyone certain there was food there, or was it just a guess? Perhaps at least it'd be warm . . .

But there was a flashing light near it, coming towards them.

'Why won't they leave us *alone*?' shouted Grimma. 'Stop!'

Jekub rolled to a halt. The engine ticked over in the chilly air.

'This must lead down to the road,' said Dorcas.

'We can't go back,' said Grimma.

'No.'

'Or forwards.'

'No.'

Grimma drummed her fingers on Jekub's metal.

'Have you got any other ideas?'

'We could try going across the fields,' said Dorcas.

'Where would that take us?' said Grimma.

'Away from here, for a start.'

'But we wouldn't know where we were going!' said Grimma.

Dorcas shrugged. 'It's either that or paint flowers.'

Grimma tried to smile.

'And those little wings wouldn't suit me,' she said.

'What's going on up there?' Sacco yelled up.

'We ought to tell people,' Grimma whispered. 'Everyone thinks we're going to the barn – '

She looked around. The car was closer, bumping heavily over the rough track. The two humans were still coming the other way. 'Don't humans ever give up?' she said to herself.

She leaned over the edge of the plank.

'Some left, Sacco,' she said. 'And then just go steadily.'

Jekub bounced off the track and rolled over the cold grass. There was another wire fence in the far distance and a few more sheep.

We don't know where we're going, she thought. The only important thing is to *go*. Masklin was right. This isn't our world.

'Perhaps we should have talked to humans,' she said aloud.

'No, you were right,' said Dorcas. 'In this world everything belongs to humans and we would belong to them, too. There wouldn't be any room for us to be *us*.'

The fence came closer. There was a road on the other side. Not a track, but a proper road with black stone on it.

'Right or left?' said Grimma. 'What do you think?'

'It doesn't matter,' said Dorcas, as the digger twanged through the fence.

'We'll try going left, then,' she said. 'Slow down, Sacco! Left a bit. More. More. Steady at that. Oh, no!'

There was another car in the distance. It had a flashing light on the top.

Dorcas risked a look behind them.

There was another flashing light there.

'No,' he said.

'What?' said Grimma.

'Just a little while ago you asked if humans ever gave up,' he said. 'They don't.'

'Stop,' said Grimma.

The teams trotted obediently across Jekub's floor. The digger rolled gently to a halt again, engine ticking over.

'This is it,' said Dorcas.

'Are we at the barn yet?' a nome called up.

'No,' said Grimma. 'Not yet. Nearly.'

Dorcas made a face.

'We might as well accept it now,' he said. 'You'll end up waving a stick with a star on it. I just hope they don't force me to mend their shoes.'

Grimma looked thoughtful. 'If we drove as hard as we could at that car coming towards us – ' she began.

'No,' said Dorcas, firmly. 'It really wouldn't solve anything.'

'It'd make me feel a lot better,' said Grimma.

She looked around at the fields.

'Why's it gone all dark?' she said. 'We can't have been running all day. It was early morning when we started out.'

'Doesn't time fly when you're enjoying yourselves?' said Dorcas gloomily. 'And I don't like milk much. I don't mind doing their housework if I *don't* have to drink milk, but – '

'Just *look*, will you?'

Darkness was spreading across the fields.

'It might be an ellipse,' said Dorcas. 'I read about them, it all goes dark when the sun covers the moon. And possibly vice versa,' he added doubtfully.

The car ahead of them squealed to a halt, crashed backwards across the road into a stone wall, and came to an abrupt stop.

In the field by the road the sheep were running away. It wasn't the ordinary panic of sheep ordinarily disturbed. They had their heads down and were pounding across the ground with one aim in mind. They were sheep who had decided that this was no time to waste energy panicking when it could be used for galloping away as fast as possible.

A loud and unpleasant humming noise filled the air.

'My word,' Dorcas said weakly. 'They're pretty damn terrifying, these ellipses.' Down below, the nomes *were* panicking. They weren't sheep, every nome could think

147

for itself, and when you started to think hard about sudden darkness and mysterious humming noises, panicking seemed a logical idea.

Little lines of crawling blue fire crackled over Jekub's battered paintwork. Dorcas felt his hair standing on end.

Grimma stared upwards.

The sky was totally black.

'It's . . . all . . . right,' she said, slowly. 'Do you know, I think it's all right!'

Dorcas looked at his hands. Sparks crackled off his fingertips.

'It is, is it?' was all he could think of to say.

'That isn't night, it's a shadow. There's something huge floating above us.'

'And that's better than night, is it?' said Dorcas.

'I think so. Come on, let's get off.'

She shinned down the rope to Jekub's deck. She was smiling madly. That was almost as terrifying as everything else put together. They weren't used to Grimma smiling.

'Give me a hand,' she said. 'We've got to get down. So he can be sure it's us.'

They looked at her in astonishment as she wrestled with the gangplank.

'Come on,' she repeated. 'Help me, can't you?'

They helped. Sometimes, when you're totally confused, you'll listen to anyone who seems to have any sort of aim in mind. They grabbed the plank and shoved it out of the back of the cab until it tilted and swung down towards the floor.

At least there wasn't so much sky now. The blue was a thin line around the edge of the solid darkness overhead.

Not entirely solid. When Dorcas's eyes grew used to it, he could make out squares and rectangles and circles.

Nomes scurried down the plank and milled around on the road below, uncertain whether to run or stay.

Above them one of the dark squares in the shadow moved aside. There was a clank, and then a rectangle of darkness whirred down very gently, like a lift without wires, and landed softly on the road. It was quite big.

There was something on it. Something in a pot. Something red and yellow and green.

The nomes craned forward to see what it was.

15

> 1. *Thus ended the journey of Jekub, and the nomes fled, looking not behind.*
>
> *From* The Book of Nome, *Strange Frogs, Chap. 1, v.I.*

Dorcas clambered down awkwardly on to Jekub's oily deck. It was empty now, except for the bits of string and wood that the nomes had used.

They've dropped things just any old how, he thought, listening to the distant chattering of the nomes. It's not right, leaving litter. Poor old Jekub deserves more than this.

There was some sort of excitement going on outside, but he didn't pay it much attention.

He bumbled around for a bit, trying to coil up the string and push the wood into tidy heaps. He pulled down the wires that had let Jekub taste the electricity. He got down on his hands and knees and tried to rub out the muddy footprints.

Jekub made noises, even with the engine stopped. Little pops and sizzles, and the occasional ping.

Dorcas sat down and leaned against the yellow metal. He didn't know what was going on. It was so far outside anything he'd ever seen before that his mind wasn't letting him worry about it.

Perhaps it's just another machine, he thought wearily. A machine for making night come down suddenly.

He reached out and patted Jekub.

'Well done,' he said.

Sacco and Nooty found him sitting with his head against the cab wall, staring vacantly at his feet.

'Everyone's been looking for you!' Sacco said. 'It's like an aeroplane without wings! It's just floating there in the air! So you must come and tell us what makes it go . . . I say, are you all right?'

'Hmm?'

'Are you all right?' said Nooty. 'You look rather odd.'

Dorcas nodded slowly. 'Just a bit worn out,' he said.

'Yes, but, you see, we need you,' said Sacco insistently.

Dorcas groaned and allowed himself to be helped to his feet. He took a last look around the cab.

'It really went, didn't it?' he said. 'It really went very well. All things considered. For his age.'

He tried to give Sacco a cheerful look.

'What are you talking about?' said Sacco.

'All that time in that shed. Since the world was made, perhaps. And I just greased him and fuelled him up and away he went,' said Dorcas.

'The machine? Oh, yes. Well done,' said Sacco.

'But — ' Nooty pointed upwards.

Dorcas shrugged.

'Oh, I'm not bothered about that,' he said. 'It's probably Masklin's doing. Perfectly simple explanation. Grimma is right. It's probably that flying thing he went off to get.'

'But something's come out of it!' said Nooty.

'Not Masklin, you mean?'

'It's some kind of plant!'

Dorcas sighed. Always one thing after another. He patted Jekub again.

'Well, *I* care,' he said.

He straightened up, and turned to the others. 'All right,' he said, 'show me.'

It was in a metal pot in the middle of the floating platform. The nomes craned and tried to climb on one another's shoulders to look at it, and none of them knew what it was except for Grimma, who was staring at it with a strange quiet smile on her face.

It was a branch from a tree. On the branch was a flower the size of a bucket.

If you climbed high enough, you could see that inside it, held with its glistening petals was a pool of water. And from the depths of the pool little yellow frogs stared up at the nomes.

'Have *you* any idea what it is?' said Sacco.

Dorcas smiled. 'Masklin's found out that it's a good idea to send a girl flowers,' he said. 'And I think everything's all right.' He glanced at Grimma.

'Yes, but *what* is it?'

'I seem to remember it's called a bromeliad,' said Dorcas. 'It grows on the top of very tall trees in wet forests a long way away, and little frogs spend their whole lives in it. Your whole life in one flower. Imagine that. Grimma once said she thought it was the most astonishing thing in the world.'

Sacco bit his lip thoughtfully.

'Well, there's electricity,' he said. 'Electricity is quite astonishing.'

'Or hydraulics,' said Nooty, taking his hand. 'You told me hydraulics was fascinating.'

'Masklin must have got it for her,' said Dorcas. 'Very literal-minded lad, that lad. Very active imagination.'

He stared from the flower to Jekub looking small and old under the humming shadow of the ship.

And felt, suddenly, quite cheerful. He was still tired enough to go to sleep standing up, but he felt his mind fizzing with ideas. Of course there were a lot of questions, but right now the answers didn't matter; it was enough just to enjoy the questions, and know that the world was full of astonishing things, and that he wasn't a frog.

Or at least he was the kind of frog who was interested in how flowers grew and whether you could get to other flowers if you jumped hard enough.

And, just when you'd got out of the flower, and were feeling really proud of yourself, you'd look at the new, big, wide endless world around you.

And eventually you'd notice that it had petals around the horizon.

Dorcas grinned.

'I'd very much like to know,' he said, 'what Masklin has been doing these past few weeks . . .'

Wings

The Third Book of the Nomes

TERRY PRATCHETT

WINGS

THE THIRD BOOK OF THE NOMES

CORGI BOOKS

To Lyn and Rhianna
and the sandwich-eating alligator
at the Kennedy Space Center, Florida

Author's Note

No character in this book is intended to resemble any living creature of whatever size on any continent, especially if they've got lawyers.

I've also taken liberties with Concorde itself, despite British Airways' kindness in letting me have a look around one. It really does look like shaped sky. But it doesn't fly non-stop to Miami; it makes a stop in Washington. But who wants to stop in Washington? Nomes couldn't do anything in Washington except cause trouble.

It's also just possible that people on Concorde don't have to eat special airline-food pink wobbly stuff. But everybody else has to.

In the Beginning . . .

. . . was Arnold Bros (est. 1905), the great department store.

It was the home of several thousand nomes – as they called themselves – who'd long ago given up life in the countryside and settled down under the floorboards of mankind.

Not that they had anything to do with humans. Humans were big and slow and stupid.

Nomes live fast. To them, ten years is like a century. Since they'd been living in the Store for more than eighty years, they'd long ago forgotten that there were things like Sun and Rain and Wind. All there was was the Store – created by the legendary Arnold Bros (est. 1905) as a Proper Place for nomes to live.

And then, into the Store from an Outside the nomes didn't believe existed, came Masklin and his little tribe. They knew what Rain and Wind were, all right. That's why they'd tried to get away from them.

With them they brought the Thing. For years they had thought of the Thing as a sort of talisman or lucky charm. Only in the Store, near electricity, did it wake up and tell a few selected nomes things they hardly understood . . .

They learned that they had originally come from the stars, in some sort of Ship, and that somewhere up in the sky that Ship had been waiting for thousands of years to take them HOME . . .

And they learned that the Store was going to be demolished in three weeks.

How Masklin tricked, bullied and persuaded the nomes into leaving the Store by stealing one of its huge trucks is recounted in *Truckers*.

They made it to an old quarry, and for a little while things went well enough.

But when you're four inches high in a world full of giant people, things never go very well for very long.

They found that humans were going to reopen the quarry.

At the same time, they also found a scrap of newspaper which had a picture of Richard Arnold, grandson of one of the Brothers who founded Arnold Bros. The company that owned the Store was now a big international concern, and Richard Arnold — said the newspaper — was going to Florida to watch the launch of its first communications satellite.

The Thing admitted to Masklin that, if it could get into space, it could call the Ship. He decided to take a few nomes and go to the airport and find some way of getting to Florida to get the Thing into the sky. Which of course was ridiculous, as well as impossible. But he didn't know this, so he tried to do it anyway.

Thinking that Florida was five miles away and that there were perhaps several hundred human beings in the world, and not knowing where exactly to go or what to do when they got there, but determined to get there and do it *anyway*, Masklin and his companions set out.

The nomes that stayed behind fought the humans in *Diggers*. They defended their quarry as long as they could and fled on Jekub, the great yellow digging machine.

But this is Masklin's story . . .

1

AIRPORTS: A place where people hurry up and wait.

From *A Scientific Encyclopedia for the Enquiring Young Nome*
by Angalo de Haberdasheri

Let the eye of your imagination be a camera . . .

This is the universe, a glittering ball of galaxies like the ornament on some unimaginable Christmas tree.

Find a galaxy . . .

Focus

This is a galaxy, swirled like the cream in a cup of coffee, every pinpoint of light a star.

Find a star . . .

Focus

This is a solar system, where planets barrel through the darkness around the central fires of the sun. Some planets hug close, hot enough to melt lead. Some drift far out, where the comets are born.

Find a blue planet . . .

Focus

This is a planet. Most of it is covered in water. It's called Earth.

Find a country . . .

Focus

. . . blues and greens and browns under the sun, and here's a pale oblong which is . . .

Focus

. . . an airport, a concrete hive for silver bees, and there's a . . .

Focus

. . . building full of people and noise and . . .

Focus

. . . a hall of lights and bustle and . . .

Focus

. . . a bin full of rubbish and . . .

Focus

. . . a pair of tiny eyes . . .

Focus

Focus

Focus

Click!

Masklin slid cautiously down an old burger carton.

He'd been watching humans. Hundreds and hundreds of humans. It was beginning to dawn on him that getting on a jet plane wasn't like stealing a truck.

Angalo and Gurder had nestled deep into the rubbish and were gloomily eating the remains of a cold, greasy chip.

This has come as a shock to all of us, Masklin thought.

I mean, take Gurder. Back in the Store he was the Abbot. He believed that Arnold Bros made the Store for nomes. And he still thinks there's some sort of Arnold Bros somewhere, watching over us, because we are important. And now we're out here and all we've found is that nomes aren't important at all . . .

And there's Angalo. He doesn't believe in Arnold Bros but he likes to think Arnold Bros exists just so that he can go on not believing in him.

And there's me.

I never thought it would be this hard.

I thought jet planes were just trucks with more wings and less wheels.

There's more humans in this place than I've ever seen before. How can we find Grandson Richard, 39, in a place like this?

I hope they're going to save me some of that chip . . .

Angalo looked up.

'Seen him?' he said, sarcastically.

Masklin shrugged. 'There's lots of humans with beards,' he said. 'They all look the same to me.'

'I *told* you,' said Angalo. 'Blind faith never works.' He glared at Gurder.

'He could have gone already,' said Masklin. 'He could have walked right past me.'

'So let's get back,' said Angalo. 'People will be missing us. We've made the effort, we've seen the airport, we've nearly got trodden on *dozens* of times. Now let's get back to the real world.'

'What do you think, Gurder?' said Masklin.

The Abbot gave him a long, despairing look.

'I don't know,' he said. 'I really don't know. I'd hoped . . .'

His voice trailed off. He looked so downcast that even Angalo patted him on the shoulder.

'Don't take it so hard,' he said. 'You didn't *really* think some sort of Grandson Richard, 39, was going to swoop down out of the sky and carry us off to Florida, did you? Look, we've given it a try. It hasn't worked. Let's go home.'

'Of course I didn't think *that*,' said Gurder irritably. 'I just thought that . . . maybe in some way . . . there'd be a way.'

'The world belongs to humans. They built everything. They run everything. We might as well accept it,' said Angalo.

Masklin looked at the Thing. He knew it was listening. Even though it was just a small black cube, it somehow always looked more alert when it was listening.

The trouble was, it only spoke when it felt like it. It'd always give you just enough help, and no more. It seemed to be testing him the whole time.

Somehow, asking the Thing for help was like admitting that you'd run out of ideas. But . . .

'Thing,' he said, 'I know you can hear me, because there must be loads of electricity in this building. We're at the airport. We can't find Grandson Richard, 39. We don't know how to *start* looking. Please help us.'

The Thing stayed silent.

'If you *don't* help us,' said Masklin quietly, 'we'll go back to the quarry and face the humans, but that won't matter to you because we'll leave you here. We really will. And no nomes will ever find you again. There will never be another chance. We'll die out, there will be no more nomes anywhere, and it will be because of you. And in years and years to come you'll be all alone and useless and you'll think "Perhaps I should have helped Masklin when he asked me," and then you'll think, "If I had my time all over again, I *would* have helped him." Well, Thing, imagine all that has happened and you've magically got your wish. Help us.'

'It's a machine!' snapped Angalo. 'You can't blackmail a machine — !'

One small red light lit up on the Thing's black surface.

'I know you can tell what other machines are thinking,' said Masklin. 'But can you tell what nomes are thinking? Read my mind, Thing, if you don't think I'm serious. You want nomes to act intelligently. Well, I *am* acting intelligently. I'm intelligent enough to know when I need help. I need help now. And you can help. I know you can. If you don't help us, we'll leave right now and forget you ever existed.'

A second light came on, very faintly.

Masklin stood up, and nodded to the others.

'All right,' he said. 'Let's go.'

The Thing made the little electronic noise which was the machine's equivalent of a nome clearing his throat.

'*How can I be of assistance?*' it said.

Angalo grinned at Gurder.

Masklin sat down again.

'Find Grandson Richard Arnold, 39,' he said.

'*This will take a long time,*' said the Thing.

'Oh.'

A few lights moved on the Thing's surface. Then it said, '*I have located a Richard Arnold, aged thirty-nine. He has just gone into the first-class departure lounge for flight 205 to Miami, Florida.*'

'That didn't take a very long time,' said Masklin.

'*It was three hundred microseconds,*' said the Thing. '*That's long.*'

'I don't think I understood all of it, either,' Masklin added.

'*Which parts didn't you understand?*'

'Nearly all of them,' said Masklin. 'All the bits after "gone into".'

'*Someone with the right name is here and waiting in a special room to get on a big silver bird that flies in the sky to go to a place called Florida,*' said the Thing.

'What big silver bird?' said Angalo.

'It means jet plane. It's being sarcastic,' said Masklin.

'Yeah? How does it know all this stuff?' said Angalo, suspiciously.

'*This building is full of computers,*' said the Thing.

'What, like you?'

The Thing managed to looked offended. '*They are very, very primitive,*' it said. '*But I can understand them. If I think slowly enough. Their job is to know where humans are going.*'

'That's more than most humans do,' said Angalo.

'Can you find out how we can get to him?' said Gurder, his face alight.

'Hold on, hold on,' said Angalo, quickly. 'Let's not rush into things here.'

'We came here to find him, didn't we?' said Gurder.

'Yes! But what do we actually *do*?'

'Well, of course, we . . . we . . . that is, we'll . . .'

'We don't even know what a departure lounge is.'

'The Thing said it's a room where humans wait to get on an aeroplane,' said Masklin.

Gurder prodded Angalo with an accusing finger.

'You're frightened, aren't you,' he said. 'You're frightened that if we see Grandson Richard it'll mean there really *is* an Arnold Bros and you'll have been *wrong*! You're just like your father. He could never stand being wrong, either!'

'I'm frightened about *you*,' said Angalo. 'Because you'll see that Grandson Richard is just a human. Arnold Bros was just a human, too. Or two humans. They just built the Store for humans. They didn't even know about nomes! And you can leave my father out of this, too.'

The Thing opened a small hatch on its top. It did that sometimes. When the hatches were shut you couldn't see where they were, but whenever the Thing was really interested in something it opened up and extended a small silver dish on a pole, or a complicated arrangement of pipes.

This time it was a piece of wire mesh on a metal rod. It started to turn, slowly.

Masklin picked up the box.

While the other two argued he said, quietly, 'Do you know where this lounge thing is?'

'*Yes,*' said the Thing.

'Let's go, then.'

Angalo looked round.

'Hey, what are you doing?' he said.

Masklin ignored him. He said to the Thing: 'And do

you know how much time we have before he starts going to Florida?'

'*About half an hour.*'

Nomes live ten times faster than humans. They're harder to see than a high-speed mouse.

That's one reason why most humans hardly ever see them.

The other is that humans are very good at not seeing things they know aren't there. And, since sensible humans know that there are no such things as people four inches high, a nome who doesn't want to be seen probably *won't* be seen.

So no one noticed three tiny blurs darting across the floor of the airport building. They dodged the rumbling wheels of luggage trolleys. They shot between the legs of slow-moving humans. They skidded around chairs. They became nearly invisible as they crossed a huge, echoing corridor.

And they disappeared behind a potted plant.

It has been said that everything everywhere affects everything else. This may be true.

Or perhaps the world is just full of patterns.

For example, in a tree nine thousand miles away from Masklin, high on a cloudy mountainside, was a plant that looked like one large flower. It grew wedged in a fork of the trees, its roots dangling in the air to trap what nourishment they could from the mists. Technically, it was an epiphytic bromeliad, although not knowing this made very little difference to the plant.

Water condensed into a tiny pool in the centre of the bloom.

And there were the frogs.

Very, very small frogs.

They had such a tiny life cycle it still had trainer wheels on it.

They hunted insects among the petals. They laid their eggs in the central pool. Tadpoles grew up and became more frogs. And made more tadpoles. Eventually they died and sank down and joined the compost at the base of the leaves which, in fact, helped nourish the plant.

And this had been the way things were for as far back as the frogs could remember.*

Except that on this day, while it hunted for flies, one frog lost its way and crawled around the side of one of the outermost petals, or possibly leaves, and saw something it had never seen before.

It saw the universe.

More precisely, it saw the branch stretching away into the mists.

And several yards away, glistening with droplets of moisture in a solitary shaft of sunlight, was another flower.

The frog sat and stared.

'Hngh! Hngh! Hngh!'

Gurder leaned against the wall and panted like a hot dog on a sunny day.

Angalo was almost as badly out of breath but was going red in the face trying not to show it.

'Why didn't you *tell* us!' he demanded.

'You were too busy arguing,' said Masklin. 'So I knew the only way to get you running was to start moving.'

'Thank . . . you . . . very much,' Gurder heaved.

'Why aren't you puffed out?' said Angalo.

---

* About three seconds. Frogs don't have good memories.

'I'm used to running fast,' said Masklin, peering around the plant. 'OK, Thing. Now what?'

'*Along this corridor,*' said the Thing.

'It's full of humans!' squeaked Gurder.

'Everywhere's full of humans. That's why we're doing this,' said Masklin. He paused, and then added, 'Look, Thing, isn't there any other way we can go? Gurder nearly got squashed just now.'

Coloured lights moved in complicated patterns across the Thing. Then it said, '*What is it you want to achieve?*'

'We must find Grandson Richard, 39,' panted Gurder.

'No. Going to the Florida place is the important thing,' said Masklin.

'It isn't!' said Gurder. 'I don't want to go to any Florida!'

Masklin hesitated. Then he said, 'This probably isn't the right time to say this, but I haven't been totally honest with you . . .'

He told them about the Thing, and space, and the Ship in the sky. Around them there was the endless thundering noise of a building full of busy humans.

Eventually Gurder said, 'You're not trying to find Grandson Richard at all?'

'I think he's probably very important,' said Masklin hurriedly. 'But you're right. At Florida there's a place where they have sort of jet planes that go straight up to put kind of bleeping radio things in the sky.'

'Oh, come *on*,' said Angalo. 'You can't just put things in the sky! They'd fall down.'

'I don't really understand it myself,' Masklin admitted. 'But if you go up high enough, there is *no* down. I think. Anyway, all we have to do is to go to Florida and put the

Thing on one of these going-up jets and it can do the rest, it says.'

'All?' said Angalo.

'It can't be harder than stealing a truck,' said Masklin.

'You're not suggesting we *steal* a plane?' said Gurder, by this time totally horrified.

'Wow!' said Angalo, his eyes lighting up as if by some internal power source. He loved vehicles of all sorts – especially when they were travelling fast.

'You would, too, wouldn't you,' said Gurder accusingly.

'Wow!' said Angalo again. He seemed to be looking at a picture only he could see.

'You're mad,' said Gurder.

'No one said anything about stealing a plane,' said Masklin quickly. 'We aren't going to steal a plane. We're just going for a ride on one, I hope.'

'Wow!'

'And we're *not* going to try to drive it, Angalo!'

Angalo shrugged.

'All right,' he said. 'But suppose I'm on it, and the driver becomes ill, then I expect I'll have to take over. I mean, I drove the Truck pretty well – '

'You kept running *into* things!' said Gurder.

'I was learning. Anyway, there's nothing to run into in the sky except clouds, and they look pretty soft,' said Angalo.

'There's the *ground*!'

'Oh, the ground wouldn't be a problem. It'd be too far away.'

Masklin tapped the Thing. 'Do you know where the jet plane is that's going to Florida?'

'*Yes.*'

'Lead us there, then. Avoiding too many humans, if you can.'

It was raining softly and, because it was early evening, lights were coming on around the airport.

Absolutely no one heard the faint tinkle as a little ventilation grille dropped off an outside wall.

Three blurred shapes lowered themselves down on to the concrete and sped away.

Towards the planes.

Angalo looked up. And up some more. And there was still more up to come. He ended up with his head craned right back.

He was nearly in tears. 'Oh, wow!' he kept saying.

'It's too big,' muttered Gurder, trying not to look. Like most of the nomes who had been born in the Store he hated looking up and not seeing a ceiling. Angalo was the same, but more than being Outside he hated not going fast.

'I've seen them go up in the sky,' said Masklin. 'They really do fly. Honestly.'

'Wow!'

It loomed over them, so big that you had to keep on stepping back and back to see how big it was. Rain glistened on it. The airport lights made smears of green and white bloom on its flanks. It wasn't a *thing*, it was a bit of shaped sky.

'Of course, they look smaller when they're a long way off,' Masklin muttered.

He stared up at the plane. He'd never felt smaller in his life.

'I *want* one,' moaned Angalo, clenching his fists. '*Look* at it. It looks as though it's going too fast even when it's standing still!'

'How do we get on it, then?' said Gurder.

'Can't you just see their faces back home if we turned up with this?' said Angalo.

'Yes. I can. Horribly clearly,' said Gurder. 'But how do we get on it?'

'We could – ' Angalo began. He hesitated. 'Why did you have to say that?' he snapped.

'There's the holes where the wheels stick through,' said Masklin. 'I think we could climb up there.'

'*No,*' said the Thing, which was tucked under his arm. '*You would not be able to breathe. You must be properly inside. Where the planes go, the air is thin.*'

'I should hope so,' said Gurder, stoutly. 'That's why it's air.'

'*You would not be able to breathe,*' said the Thing patiently.

'Yes I would,' said Gurder. 'I've always been able to breathe.'

'You get more air close to the ground,' said Angalo. 'I read that in a book. You get lots of air low down, and not much when you go up.'

'Why not?' said Gurder.

'Dunno. It's frightened of heights, I guess.'

Masklin waded through the puddles on the concrete so that he could see down the far side of the aircraft. Some way away a couple of humans were using some sort of machines to load boxes into a hole in the side of the plane. He walked back, around the huge tyres, and squinted up at a long, high tube that stretched from the building.

He pointed.

'I think that's how humans are loaded on to it,' he said.

'What, through a pipe? Like water?' said Angalo.

'It's better than standing out here getting wet, anyway,' said Gurder. 'I'm soaked through already.'

'There's stairs and wires and things,' said Masklin.

'It shouldn't be too difficult to climb up there. There's bound to be a gap we can slip in by.' He sniffed. 'There always is,' he added, 'when humans build things.'

'Let's do it!' said Angalo. 'Oh, wow!'

'But you're not to try to steal it,' said Masklin, as they helped the slightly plump Gurder lumber into a run. 'It's going where we want to go anyway — '

'Not where I want to go,' moaned Gurder. 'I want to go home!'

' — and you're not to try to drive it. There's not enough of us. Anyway, I expect it's a lot more complicated than a truck. It's a — do you know what it's called, Thing?'

'*A Concorde.*'

'There,' said Masklin. 'It's a Concorde. Whatever that is. And you've got to promise not to steal it.'

2

CONCORDE: It goes twice as fast as a bullet and you get smoked salmon.

From *A Scientific Encyclopedia for the Enquiring Young Nome*
by Angalo de Haberdasheri

Squeezing through a gap in the human-walking-on-to-planes pipe wasn't as hard as coming to terms with what was on the other side.

The floors of the sheds in the quarry had been bare boards or stamped earth. In the airport building it was squares of a sort of shiny stone. But here —

Gurder flung himself face down and buried his nose in it.

'Carpet!' he said, almost in tears. 'Carpet! I never thought I'd see you again!'

'Oh, get up,' said Angalo, embarrassed at the Abbot acting like that in front of someone who, however much of a friend he was, hadn't been born a Store nome.

Gurder stood up awkwardly. 'Sorry,' he mumbled, brushing himself off. 'Don't know what possessed me there It just took me back, that's all. Real carpet. Haven't seen real carpet for *months*.'

He blew his nose noisily. 'We had some beautiful carpets in the Store, you know. Beautiful. Some of them had patterns on.'

Masklin looked up the pipe. It was like one of the Store's corridors, and quite brightly lit.

'Let's move on,' he said. 'It's too exposed here. Where are all the humans, Thing?'

'They will be arriving shortly.'

'How does it *know*?' Gurder complained.

'It listens to other machines,' said Masklin.

'There are also many computers on this plane,' said the Thing.

'Well, that's nice,' said Masklin vaguely. 'You'll have someone to talk to, then.'

'They are quite stupid,' said the Thing, and managed to express disdain without actually having anything to express it with.

A few feet away the corridor opened into a new space. Masklin could see a curtain, and what looked like the edge of a chair.

'All right, Angalo,' he said. 'Lead the way. I know you want to.'

It was two minutes later.

The three of them were sitting under a seat.

Masklin had never really thought about the insides of aircraft. He'd spent days up on the cliff behind the quarry, watching them take off. Of course, he'd assumed there were humans inside. Humans got everywhere. But he'd never really thought about the insides. If ever there was anything that looked made up of outsides, it was a plane flying.

But it had been too much for Gurder. He was in tears.

'Electric light,' he moaned. 'And more carpets! And big soft seats! They've even got napkins on! And there isn't any mud *anywhere*! There's even *signs*!'

'There, there,' said Angalo helplessly, patting him on the shoulder. 'It was a *good* Store, I know.' He looked up at Masklin.

'You've got to admit it's unsettling,' he said. 'I

was expecting . . . well, wires and pipes and exciting levers and things. Not something like the Arnold Bros Furnishing Department!'

'We shouldn't stay here,' said Masklin. 'There'll be humans all over the place pretty soon. Remember what the Thing said.'

They helped Gurder up and trotted under the rows of seats with him between them. But it wasn't like the Store in one important way, Masklin realized. There weren't many places to hide. In the Store there was always something to get behind or under or wriggle through . . .

He could already hear distant sounds. In the end they found a gap behind a curtain, in a part of the aircraft where there were no seats. Masklin crawled inside, pushing the Thing in front of him.

They weren't distant sounds now. They were very close. He turned his head, and saw a human foot a few inches away.

At the back of the gap there was a hole in the metal wall where some thick wires passed through. It was just big enough for Angalo and Masklin, and big enough for a terrified Gurder with the two of them pulling on his arms. There wasn't too much room, but at least they couldn't be seen.

They couldn't see, either. They lay packed together in the gloom, trying to make themselves comfortable on the wires.

After a while Gurder said, 'I feel a bit better now.'
Masklin nodded.

There were noises all around them. From somewhere far below came a series of metallic 'clonks'. There was the mournful sound of human voices, and then a jolt.

'Thing?' he whispered.
'Yes?'
'What's happening?'

'*The plane is getting ready to become airborne.*'

'Oh.'

'*Do you know what that means?*'

'No. Not really.'

'*It is going to fly in the air. Borne means to be carried, and air means air. To be borne in the air. Air-borne.*'

Masklin could hear Angalo's breathing.

He settled himself as best he could between the metal wall and a heavy bundle of wires, and stared into the darkness.

The nomes didn't speak. After a while there was a faint jerk and a sensation of movement.

Nothing else happened. It went on not happening.

Eventually Gurder, his voice trembling with terror, said, 'Is it too late to get off, if we — ?'

A sudden distant thundering noise finished the sentence for him. A dull rumbling shook everything around them very gently but very firmly.

Then there was a heavy pause, like the moment a ball must feel between the time it's thrown up and the time it starts to come down, and something picked up all three of them and slid them into a struggling heap. The floor tried to become the wall.

The nomes hung on to one another, stared into one another's faces, and screamed.

After a while, they stopped. There didn't seem much point in continuing. Besides, they were out of breath.

The floor, very gradually, became a proper floor again and didn't show any further ambitions to become a wall.

Masklin pushed Angalo's foot off his neck.

'I think we're flying,' he said.

'Is that what it was?' said Angalo weakly. 'It looks kind of more graceful when you see it from the ground.'

'Is anyone hurt?'

Gurder pulled himself upright.

'I'm all bruises,' he said. He brushed himself down. And then, because there is no changing nomish nature, he added, 'Is there any food around?'

They hadn't thought about food.

Masklin stared behind him into the tunnel of wires.

'Maybe we won't need any,' he said, uncertainly. 'How long will it take to get to Florida, Thing?'

'The captain has just said it will be six hours and forty-five minutes,' said the Thing.*

'We'll starve to death!' said Gurder.

'Maybe there's something to hunt?' said Angalo hopefully.

'I shouldn't think so,' Masklin said. 'This doesn't look a mouse kind of place.'

'The humans'll have food,' said Gurder. 'Humans always have food.'

'I *knew* you were going to say that,' said Angalo.

'It's just common sense.'

'I wonder if we can see out of a window?' said Angalo. 'I'd like to see how fast we're going. All the trees and things whizzing past, and so on?'

'Look,' said Masklin, before things got out of hand. 'Let's just wait for a while, eh? Everyone calm down. Have a bit of a rest. *Then* maybe we can look for some food.'

They settled down again. At least it was warm and dry. Back in the days when he'd lived in a hole in a bank, Masklin had spent far too much time cold and wet to turn up his nose at a chance to sleep warm and dry.

He dozed . . .

Airborne.

Air . . . born . . .

Perhaps there were hundreds of nomes who lived in

---

* About as long as two and a half days, to a nome.

27

the aeroplanes in the same way that nomes had lived in the Store. Perhaps they got on with their lives under the carpeted floor somewhere, while they were whisked to all the places Masklin had seen on the only map the nomes had ever found. It had been in a pocket diary, and the names of the faraway places written on it were like magic – Africa, Australia, China, Equator, Printed in Hong Kong, Iceland . . .

Perhaps they'd never looked out of the windows. Perhaps they'd never know that they were moving at all.

He wondered if this was what Grimma had meant by all the stuff about the frogs in the flower. She'd read it in a book. You could live your whole life in some tiny place and think it was the whole world. The trouble was, he'd been angry. He hadn't wanted to listen.

Well, he was out of the flower now and no mistake . . .

The frog had brought some other young frogs to its spot among the leaves at the edge of the world of the flower.

They stared at the branch. There wasn't just one flower out there, there were dozens, although the frogs weren't able to think like this because frogs can't count beyond one.

They saw lots of ones.

They stared at them. Staring is one of the few things frogs are good at.

Thinking isn't. It would be nice to say that the tiny frogs thought long and hard about the new flower, about life in the old flower, about the need to explore, about the possibility that the world was bigger than a pool with petals around the edge.

In fact, what they thought was:.−.−.mipmip.−.−.-mipmip.−.−.mipmip.'

But what they *felt* was too big for one flower to contain.

Carefully, slowly, not at all certain why, they plopped down on to the branch.

There was a polite beeping from the Thing.

'You may be interested to know,' it said, *'that we've broken the sound barrier.'*

Masklin turned wearily to the others.

'All right, own up,' he said. 'Who broke it?'

'Don't look at me,' said Angalo. 'I didn't touch anything.'

Masklin crawled to the edge of the hole and peered out.

There were human feet out there. Female human feet, by the look of it. They usually were the ones with the less practical shoes.

You could learn a lot about humans by looking at their shoes. It was about all a nome had to look at, most of the time. The rest of the human was normally little more than the wrong end of a pair of nostrils, a long way up.

Masklin sniffed.

'There's food somewhere,' he said.

'What kind?' said Angalo.

'Never mind what kind,' said Gurder, pushing him out of the way. 'Whatever it is, I'm going to *eat* it.'

'Get back!' Masklin snapped, pushing the Thing into Angalo's arms. 'I'll go! Angalo, don't let him move!'

He darted out, ran for the curtain, and slid behind it. After a few seconds, he moved just enough to let one eye and a frowning eyebrow show.

The room was some sort of food place. The human females were taking trays of food out of the wall. Nomish sense of smell is sharper than a fox's; it was all Masklin could do not to dribble. He had to admit it – it was all very well hunting and growing things, but what you got wasn't a patch on the food you found around humans.

One of the females put the last tray on a trolley and wheeled it past Masklin. The wheels were almost as tall as he was.

As it squeaked past he darted out of his hiding place and leapt on to it, squeezing himself amongst the bottles. It was a stupid thing to do, he knew. It was just better than being stuck in a hole with a couple of idiots.

Rows and rows of shoes. Some black, some brown. Some with laces, some without. Quite a few of them without feet in them, because the humans had taken them off.

Masklin looked up as the trolley inched forward.

Rows and rows of legs. Some in skirts, but most in trousers.

Masklin looked up further. Nomes rarely saw humans sitting down.

Rows and rows of bodies, topped with rows and rows of heads with faces at the front. Rows and rows of –

Masklin crouched back among the bottles.

Grandson Richard was watching him.

It was the face in the newspaper. It had to be. There was the little beard, and the smiling mouth with lots of teeth in it. And the hair that looked as though it had been dramatically carved out of something shiny rather than been grown in the normal way.

Grandson Richard. 39.

The face stared at him for a moment, and then looked away.

He can't have seen me, Masklin told himself. I'm hidden away here.

What will Gurder say when I tell him?

He'll go mad, that's what.

I think I'll keep it to myself for a while. That might be an amazingly good idea. We've got enough to worry about as it is.

39. Either there've been thirty-eight other Grandson Richards, and I don't think that's what it means, or it's a newspaper human way of saying he's thirty-nine years old. Nearly half as old as the Store. And the Store nomes say the Store is as old as the world. I know that can't be true, but –

I wonder what it feels like to live nearly *for ever*?

He burrowed further into the things on the shelf. Mostly they were bottles, but there were a few bags containing knobbly things a bit smaller than Masklin's fist. He stabbed at the paper with his knife until he'd cut a hole big enough, and pulled one of them out.

It was a salted peanut. Well, it was a start.

He grabbed the packet just as a hand reached past.

It was close enough to touch.

It was close enough to touch *him*.

He could see the red of its fingernails as they slid by him, closed slowly over another packet of nuts, and withdrew.

It dawned on Masklin later that the giving-out-food woman wouldn't have been able to see him. She just reached down and into the tray for what she knew would be there, and this almost certainly didn't include Masklin.

That's what he decided later. At the time, with a human hand almost brushing his head, it all looked a lot different. He took a running dive off the trolley, rolled when he hit the carpet, and scurried under the nearest seat.

He didn't even wait to catch his breath. Experience had taught him that it was when you stopped to catch your breath that things caught you. He charged from seat to seat, dodging giant feet, discarded shoes,

dropped newspapers and bags. By the time he crossed
the bit of aisle to the food-place he was a blur even by
nome standards. He didn't stop even when he reached
the hole. He just leapt, and went through it without
touching the sides.

'A peanut?' said Angalo. 'Between three? That's not a
mouthful each!'

'What do you suggest?' said Masklin, bitterly. 'Do
you want to go to the giving-out-food-woman and say
there's three small hungry people down here?'

Angalo stared at him. Masklin had got his breath
back now, but was still very red in the face.

'You know, that could be worth a try,' he said.

'What?'

'Well, if you were a human, would you expect to see
nomes on a plane?' said Angalo.

'Of course I wouldn't – '

'I bet you'd be amazed if you *did* see one, eh?'

'Are you suggesting we deliberately show ourselves to
a human?' Gurder said suspiciously. 'We've never done
that, you know.'

'I nearly did just now,' said Masklin. 'I won't do it
again in a hurry!'

'We've always preferred to starve to death on one
peanut, you mean?'

Gurder looked longingly at the piece of nut in his
hand. They'd eaten peanuts in the Store, of course.
Around Christmas Fayre, when the Food Hall was
crammed with food you didn't normally see in the other
seasons, they made a nice end to a meal. Probably they
made a nice start to a meal, too. What they didn't make
was a meal.

'What's the plan?' he said, wearily.

One of the giving-out-food humans was pulling trays

off a shelf when a movement made it look up. Its head turned very slowly.

Something small and black was being lowered down right by its ear.

It stuck tiny thumbs in small ears, wagged its fingers, and put out its tongue.

'Thrrrrrrrrp,' said Gurder.

The tray in the human's hands crashed on to the floor in front of it. It made a long-drawn-out noise which sounded like a high-pitched foghorn and backed away, raising its hands to its mouth. Finally it turned, very slowly, like a tree about to fall, and fled between the curtains.

When it came back, with another human being, the little figure had gone.

So had most of the food.

'I don't know when I last had smoked salmon,' said Gurder, happily.

'Mmmph,' said Angalo.

'You're not supposed to eat it like that,' said Gurder severely. 'You're not supposed to shove it all in your mouth and then cut off whatever won't fit. Whatever will people think?'

"S'no people here,' said Angalo, but indistinctly. "S'just you an' Masklin.'

Masklin cut the lid off a container of milk. It was practically nome-sized.

'This is more like it, eh?' said Gurder. 'Proper food the natural way, out of tins and things. None of this having to clean the dirt off it, like in the quarry. And it's nice and warm in here, too. It's the only way to travel. Anyone want some of this − ' he prodded a dish vaguely, not sure of what was in it ' − stuff?'

The others shook their heads. The dish contained something shiny and wobbly and pink with a cherry on it, and in some strange way it managed to look like something you wouldn't eat even if it was pushed on to your plate after a week's starvation diet.

'What does it taste of?' said Masklin, after Gurder had chewed a mouthful.

'Tastes of pink,' said Gurder.*

'Anyone fancy the peanut to finish with?' said Angalo. He grinned. 'No? I'll chuck it away, shall I?'

'No!' said Masklin. They looked at him. 'Sorry,' he said. 'I mean, you shouldn't. It's wrong to waste good food.'

'It's *wicked*,' said Gurder primly.

'Mmm. Don't know about wicked,' said Masklin. 'But it's stupid. Put it in your pack. You never know when you might need it.'

Angalo stretched his arms and yawned.

'A wash would be nice,' he said.

'Didn't see any water,' Masklin said. 'There's probably a sink or a lavatory somewhere, but I wouldn't know where to start looking.'

'Talking of lavatories – ' said Angalo.

'Right down the other end of the pipe, please,' said Gurder.

'*And keep away from any wiring*,' volunteered the Thing. Angalo nodded in a puzzled fashion, and crawled away into the darkness.

Gurder yawned and stretched his arms.

'Won't the giving-out-food humans look for us?' he said.

'I don't think so,' said Masklin. 'Back when we used to live Outside, before we found the Store, I'm sure humans saw us sometimes. I don't think they really

---

* Little dishes of strange wobbly stuff tasting of pink turn up in nearly every meal on all aeroplanes. No one knows why. There's probably some sort of special religious reason.

believe their eyes. They wouldn't make those weird garden ornaments if they'd ever seen a *real* nome.'

Gurder reached into his robe and pulled out the picture of Grandson Richard. Even in the dim light of the pipe, Masklin recognized it as the human in the seat. He hadn't got creases on his face from being folded up, and he wasn't made up of hundreds of tiny dots, but apart from that . . .

'Do you think he's here somewhere?' said Gurder wistfully.

'Could be. Could be,' said Masklin, feeling wretched. 'But, look, Gurder . . . maybe Angalo goes a bit too far, but he could be right. Maybe Grandson Richard is just another human being, you know. Probably humans *did* build the Store just for humans. Your ancestors just moved in because, well, it was warm and dry. And — '

'I'm not listening, you know,' said Gurder. 'I'm not going to be told that we're just things like rats and mice. We're special.'

'The Thing is quite definite about us coming from somewhere else, Gurder,' said Masklin meekly.

The Abbot folded up the picture. 'Maybe we did. Maybe we didn't,' he said. 'That doesn't matter.'

'Angalo thinks it matters if it's true.'

'Don't see why. There's more than one kind of truth.' Gurder shrugged. 'I might say: you're just a lot of dust and juices and bones and hair, and that's true. And I might say: you're something inside your head that goes away when you die. That's true, too. Ask the Thing.'

Coloured lights flickered across the Thing's surface.

Masklin looked shocked. 'I've *never* asked it that sort of question,' he said.

'Why not? It's the first question *I'd* ask.'

'It'll probably say something like "Does not compute" or "Inoperative parameters". That's what it says when it doesn't know and doesn't want to admit it. Thing?'

The Thing didn't reply. Its lights changed their pattern.

'Thing?' Masklin repeated.

'I am monitoring communications.'

'It often does that when it's feeling bored,' said Masklin to Gurder. 'It just sits there listening to invisible messages in the air. Pay attention, Thing. This is important. We want — '

The lights moved. A lot of them went red.

'Thing! We — '

The Thing made the little clicking noise that was its equivalent of clearing its throat.

'A nome has been seen in the pilot's cabin.'

'Listen, Thing, we — what?'

'I repeat: a nome has been seen in the pilot's cabin.'

Masklin looked around wildly.

'Angalo?'

'That is an extreme probability,' said the Thing.

3

The sound of Masklin and Gurder's voices echoed up and
down the pipe as they scrambled over the wires.

'I *thought* he was taking too long!'

'You shouldn't have let him go off by himself! You
know what he's like about driving things!'

'*I* shouldn't have let him?'

'He's just got no sense of — which way now?'

Angalo had said he thought the inside of a plane would
be a mass of wires and pipes. He was nearly right. The
nomes squeezed their way through a narrow, cable-hung
world under the floor.

'I'm too old for this! There comes a time in a nome's
life when he shouldn't crawl around the inside of terrible
flying machines!'

'How many times have you done it?'

'Once too often!'

'*We are getting closer,*' said the Thing.

'This is what comes of showing ourselves! It's a Judgement,' declared Gurder.

'Whose?' said Masklin grimly, helping him up.

'What do you mean?'

'There has to be someone to make a judgement!'

'I meant just a judgement in general!'

Masklin stopped.

'Where now, Thing?'

'The message told the giving-out-food people that a strange little creature was on the flight deck,' said the Thing. *'That is where we are. There are many computers here.'*

'They're talking to you, are they?'

'A little. They are like children. Mostly they listen,' said the Thing smugly. *'They are not very intelligent.'*

'What are we going to *do*?' said Gurder.

'We're going to – ' Masklin hesitated. The word 'rescue' was looming up somewhere in the sentence ahead.

It was a good, dramatic word. He longed to say it. The trouble was that there was another, simpler, nastier word a little further beyond.

It was 'How?'

'I don't think they'd try to hurt him,' he said, hoping it was true. 'Maybe they'll put him somewhere. We ought to find a place where we can see what's happening.' He looked helplessly at the wires and intricate bits of metal in front of them.

'You'd better let me lead, then,' said Gurder, in a matter-of-fact voice.

'Why?'

'You might be very good in wide open spaces,' said the Abbot, pushing past him. 'But in the Store we knew all about getting around inside things.'

He rubbed his hands together.

'Right,' he said, and then grabbed a cable and slid through a gap Masklin hadn't even noticed was there.

'Used to do this sort of thing when I was a

boy,' he said. 'We used to get up to all sorts of tricks.'

'Yes?' said Masklin.

'Down this way, I think. Mind the wires. Oh, yes. Up and down the lift shafts, in and out of the telephone switchboard . . .'

'I thought you always said kids spent far too much time running around and getting into mischief these days?'

'Ah. Yes. Well, *that's* juvenile delinquency,' said Gurder sternly. 'It's quite different from our youthful high spirits. Let's try up here.'

They crawled between two warm metal walls. There was daylight ahead.

Masklin and Gurder lay down and pulled themselves forward.

There was an odd-shaped room, not a lot bigger than the cab of the truck itself. Like the cab, it was really just a space where the human drivers fitted into the machinery.

There was a *lot* of that.

It covered the walls and ceiling. Lights and switches, dials and levers. Masklin thought: if Dorcas were here, we'd never get him to leave. Angalo's here somewhere, and we want *him* to leave.

There were two humans kneeling on the floor. One of the giving-out-food females was standing by them. There was a lot of mooing and growling going on.

'Human talking,' muttered Masklin. 'I wish we could understand it.'

'*Very well,*' said the Thing. '*Stand by.*'

'You can understand human noises?'

'*Certainly. They're only nome noises slowed down.*'

'What? *What*? You never told us that! You never told us that before!'

39

'There are many billions of things I have not told you. Where would you like me to start?'

'You can start by telling me what they're saying now,' said Masklin. 'Please?'

'One of the humans has just said, "It must have been a mouse or something," and the other one said, "You show me a mouse wearing clothes and I'll admit it was a mouse." And the giving-out-food woman said, 'It was no mouse I saw. It blew a raspberry at me (exclamation)." '

'What's a raspberry?'

'The small red fruit of the plant Rubus idaeus.'

Masklin turned to Gurder.

'Did you?'

'Me? What fruit? Listen, if there'd been any fruit around I'd have eaten it. I just went "thrrrrp".'

'One of the humans has just said, "I looked round and there it was, staring out of the window." '

'That's Angalo all right,' said Gurder.

'Now the other kneeling-down human has said, "Well, whatever it is, it's behind this panel and it can't go anywhere." '

'It's taking off a bit of the wall!' said Masklin. 'Oh, no! It's reaching inside!'

The human mooed.

'The human said, "It bit me! The little devil bit me!" ' said the Thing, conversationally.

'Yep. That's Angalo,' said Gurder. 'His father was like that, too. A fighter in a tight corner.'

'But they don't know what they've got!' said Masklin urgently. 'They've seen him but he ran away! They're arguing about it! They don't really believe in nomes! If we can get him out before he's caught, they're bound to think it was a mouse or something!'

'I suppose we could get round there inside the walls,' said Gurder. 'But it'd take too long.'

Masklin looked desperately around the cabin. Besides

the three people trying to catch Angalo there were two humans up at the front. They must be the drivers, he thought.

'I'm right out of ideas,' he said. 'Can you think of anything, Thing?'

'There is practically no limit to what I can think of.'

'I *mean*, is there anything you can do to help us rescue Gurder?'

'Yes.'

'You'd better do it, then.'

'Yes.'

A moment later they heard the low clanging of alarms. Lights began to flash. The drivers shouted and leaned forward and started doing things to switches.

'What's going on?' said Masklin.

'It is possible that the humans are startled that they are no longer flying this machine,' said the Thing.

'They're not? Who is, then?'

The lights rippled smoothly across the Thing.

'I am.'

One of the frogs fell off the branch and disappeared quietly into the leafy canopy far below. Since very small, light animals can fall a long way without being hurt, it's quite likely that it survived in the forest world under the tree and had the second most interesting experience any tree frog has ever had.

The rest of them crawled onward.

Masklin helped Gurder along another metal channel full of wires. Overhead they could hear human feet and the growling of humans in trouble.

'I don't think they're very happy about it,' said Gurder.

'But they haven't got time to look for something that was probably a mouse,' said Masklin.

'It's not a mouse, it's Angalo!'

'But afterwards they'll *think* it was a mouse. I don't think humans want to know things that disturb them.'

'Sound just like nomes to me,' said Gurder.

Masklin looked at the Thing under his arm.

'Are you really driving the Concorde?' he said.

'*Yes.*'

'I thought to drive things you had to turn wheels and change gears and things?' said Masklin.

'*That is all done by machines. The humans press buttons and turn wheels just to tell machines what to do.*'

'So what are *you* doing, then?'

'*I,*' said the Thing, '*am being in charge.*'

Masklin listened to the muted thunder of the engines.

'Is that hard?' he said.

'*Not in itself. However, the humans keep trying to interfere.*'

'I think we'd better find Angalo quickly, then,' said Gurder. 'Come on.'

They inched their way along another cable tunnel.

'They ought to thank us for letting our Thing do their job for them,' said Gurder solemnly.

'I don't think they see it like that, exactly,' said Masklin.

'*We are flying at a height of 55,000 feet at 1,352 miles per hour,*' said the Thing.

When they didn't comment, it added, '*That's very high and very fast.*'

'That's good,' said Masklin, who realized that some sort of remark was expected.

'*Very, very fast.*'

The two nomes squeezed through the gap between a couple of metal plates.

'*Faster than a bullet, in fact.*'

'Amazing,' said Masklin.

'*Twice the speed of sound in this atmosphere,*' the Thing went on.

'Wow.'

'*I wonder if I can put it another way,*' said the Thing, and it managed to sound slightly annoyed. '*It could get from the Store to the quarry in under fifteen seconds.*'

'Good job we didn't meet it coming the other way, then,' said Masklin.

'Oh, stop teasing it,' said Gurder. 'It wants you to tell it it's a good boy . . . Thing,' he corrected himself.

'*I do not,*' said the Thing, rather more quickly than usual. '*I was merely pointing out that this is a very specialized machine and requires skilful control.*'

'Perhaps you shouldn't talk so much, then,' said Masklin.

The Thing rippled its lights at him.

'That was nasty,' said Gurder.

'Well, I've spent a year doing what the Thing's told me and I've never had so much as a "thank you",' said Masklin. 'How high are fifty-five thousand feet, anyway?'

'*Ten miles. Twice as far as the distance from the Store to the quarry.*'

Gurder stopped.

'Up?' he said. 'We're that far *up*?'

He looked down at the floor.

'Oh,' he said.

'Now don't *you* start,' said Masklin quickly. 'We've got enough problems with Angalo. Stop holding on to the wall like that!'

Gurder had gone white.

'We must be as high as all those fluffy white cloud things,' he breathed.

'*No,*' said the Thing.

'That's some comfort, then,' said Gurder.

'*They're all a long way below us.*'

'Oh.'

Masklin grabbed the Abbot's arm.

'Angalo, remember?' he said.

Gurder nodded slowly and inched his way forward, holding on to things with his eyes closed.

'We mustn't lose our heads,' said Masklin. 'Even if we *are* up so high.' He looked down. The metal below him was quite solid. You needed to use imagination to see through it to the ground below.

The trouble was that he had a very good imagination.

'Ugh,' he said. 'Come on, Gurder. Give me your hand.'

'It's right in front of you.'

'Sorry. Didn't see it with my eyes shut.'

They spent ages cautiously moving up and down among the wiring, until eventually Gurder said, 'It's no good. There isn't a hole big enough to get through. He'd have found it, if there was.'

'Then we've got to find a way into the cab and get him out like that,' said Masklin.

'With all those humans in there?'

'They'll be too busy to notice us. Right, Thing?'

'*Right.*'

There is a place so far up there is no down.

A little lower, a white dart seared across the top of the sky, outrunning the night, overtaking the sun, crossing in a few hours an ocean that was once the edge of the world . . .

Masklin lowered himself carefully to the floor and crept forward. The humans weren't even looking in his direction.

I hope the Thing really knows how to drive this plane, he thought.

He sidled along towards the panels where, with any luck, Angalo was hiding.

This wasn't right. He hated being exposed like this. Of course, it had probably been worse in the days when he used to have to hunt alone. If anything had caught him then, he would never have known it. He'd have been a mouthful. Whereas no one knew what humans would do to a nome if they caught one . . .

He darted into the blessed shadows.

'Angalo!' he hissed.

After a while a voice from behind the wiring said, 'Who is it?'

Masklin straightened up. 'How many guesses do you want?' he said in his normal voice.

Angalo dropped down. 'They chased me!' he said. 'And one of them stuck its arm — '

'I know. Come on, while they're busy.'

'What's happening?' said Angalo, as they hurried out into the light.

'The Thing is flying us.'

'How? It's got no arms. It can't change gear or anything — '

'Apparently it's being bossy to the computers which do all that. Come *on*.'

'I looked out of the window,' bubbled Angalo. 'There's sky all over the place!'

'Don't remind me,' said Masklin.

'Let me just have one more look — ' Angalo began.

'Listen, Gurder's waiting for us and we don't want any more trouble— '

'But this is better than any truck — '

There was a strangled kind of noise.

The nomes looked up.

One of the humans was watching them. Its mouth was open and it had an expression on its face of someone who is going to have a lot of difficulty explaining what they have just seen, especially to themselves.

The human was already getting to its feet.

Angalo and Masklin looked at one another.

'Run!' they shouted.

45

Gurder was lurking suspiciously in a patch of shadow by the door when they came past, arms and legs going like pistons. He caught up the skirts of his robe and scurried after them.

'What's happening? What's happening?'

'There's a human after us!'

'Don't leave me behind! Don't leave me behind!'

Masklin was just ahead of the other two as they raced up the aisle between the rows of humans, who paid no attention at all to three tiny blurs running between the seats.

'We shouldn't have . . . stood around . . . looking!' Masklin gasped.

'We might . . . never . . . have a chance . . . like that again!' panted Angalo.

'You're *right*!'

The floor tilted slightly.

'*Thing!* What are you doing!'

'*Creating a distraction.*'

'Don't! Everyone this way!'

Masklin darted between two seats, around a pair of giant shoes, and threw himself flat on the carpet. The others hurled themselves down behind him.

Two huge human feet were a few inches away from them.

Masklin pulled the Thing up close to his face.

'Let them have their aeroplane back!' he hissed.

'*I was hoping to be allowed to land it,*' said the Thing. Even though its voice was always flat and expressionless, Masklin still thought that it sounded wistful.

'Do you know how to land one of these things?' said Masklin.

'*I should like the opportunity to learn —* '

'Let them have it back right *now*!'

There was a faint lurch and a change in the pattern of the lights on the Thing's surface. Masklin breathed out.

46

'Now, will everyone act sensibly for five minutes?' he said.

'Sorry, Masklin,' said Angalo. He tried to look apologetic, but it didn't work. Masklin recognized the wide-eyed, slightly mad smile of someone very nearly in their own personal heaven. 'It was just that . . . do you know it's even blue below us? It's like there's no ground down there at all! And – '

'If the Thing tries any more flying lessons we might all find out if that's true,' said Masklin gloomily. 'So let's just sit down and be quiet, shall we?'

They sat in silence for a while, under the seat.

Then Gurder said, 'That human has got a hole in his sock.'

'What about it?' said Angalo.

'Dunno, really. It's just that you never think of humans as having holes in their socks.'

'Where you get socks, holes aren't far behind,' said Masklin.

'They're good socks, though,' said Angalo.

Masklin stared at them. They just looked like basic socks to him. Nomes in the Store used them as sleeping bags.

'How can you tell?' he said.

'They're Histyle Odourprufe,' said Angalo. 'Guaranteed eighty-five per cent Polyputheketlon. We used to sell them in the Store. They cost a lot more than other socks. Look, you can see the label.'

Gurder sighed.

'It was a good Store,' he muttered.

'And those shoes,' said Angalo, pointing to the great white shapes like beached boats a little way away. 'See them? Crucial Street Drifters with Real Rubber Soul. Very expensive.'

'Never approved of them, myself,' said Gurder. 'Too flashy. I preferred Men's, Brown, Laced. A nome could get a good night's sleep in one of those.'

'Those Drifter things are Store shoes too, are they?' said Masklin, carefully.

'Oh, yes. Special range.'

'Hmm.'

Masklin got up and walked over to a large leather bag half-wedged under the seat. The others watched him scramble up it and then pull himself up until he could, very quickly, glance over the armrest. He slid back down.

'Well, well,' he said, in a mad, cheerful voice. 'That's a Store bag, isn't it?'

Gurder and Angalo gave it a critical look.

'Never spent much time in Travel Accessories,' said Angalo. 'But now that you mention it, it could be the Special Calf-Skin Carry-On Bag.'

'For the Discerning Executive?' Gurder added. 'Yes. Could be.'

'Have you wondered how we're going to get off?' said Masklin.

'Same way as we got on?' said Angalo, who hadn't.

'I think that could be difficult. I think the humans might have other ideas,' Masklin said. 'I think, in fact, they might start looking for us. Even if they think we're mice. I wouldn't put up with mice on something like this if I was them. You know what mice are like for widdling on wires. Could be dangerous when you're ten miles high, a mouse going to the lavatory inside your computer. I think the humans will take it very seriously. So we ought to get off when the humans do.'

'We'd get stamped on!' said Angalo.

'I was thinking maybe we could sort of . . . get in this bag, sort of thing,' said Masklin.

'Ridiculous!' said Gurder.

Masklin took a deep breath.

'It belongs to Grandson Richard, you see,' he said.

'I checked,' he added, watching the expressions on their faces. 'I saw him before, and he's in the seat up there. Grandson Richard,' he went on, '39. He's up there right now. Reading a paper. Up there. Him.'

Gurder had gone red. He prodded Masklin with a finger. 'Do you expect me to believe,' he said, 'that Richard Arnold, the grandson of Arnold Bros (est. 1905) has *holes* in his *socks?*'

'That'd make them holy socks,' said Angalo. 'Sorry. Sorry. Just trying to lighten the mood a bit. You didn't have to glare at me like that.'

'Climb up and see for yourself,' said Masklin. 'I'll help you. Only be careful.'

They hoisted Gurder up.

He came down quietly.

'Well?' said Angalo.

'It's got "R.A." in gold letters on the bag, too,' said Masklin.

He made frantic signs to Angalo. Gurder was looking as though he had seen a ghost.

'Yes, you can get that,' said Angalo, hurriedly. ' "Gold Monogram at Only Five Ninety-Nine Extra," it used to say on the sign.'

'*Speak* to us, Gurder,' said Masklin. 'Don't just sit there looking like that.'

'This is a very solemn moment for me,' said Gurder.

'I thought I could cut through some of the stitching and we could get in at the bottom,' said Masklin.

'I am not worthy,' said Gurder.

'Probably not,' said Angalo cheerfully. 'But we won't tell anyone.'

'And Grandson Richard will be helping us, you see,' said Masklin, hoping that Gurder was in a state to take all this in. 'He won't know it, but he'll be helping us. So it'll be all right. Probably it's *meant.*'

Not meant *by* anyone, he told himself conscientiously. Just meant in general.

Gurder considered this.

'Well, all right,' he said. 'But no cutting the bag. We can get in through the zippers.'

They did. It stuck a bit halfway, since zippers always do, but it didn't take long to get an opening big enough for the nomes to climb down inside.

'What shall we do if he looks in?' said Angalo.

'Nothing,' said Masklin. 'Just smile, I suppose.'

The tree frogs were far out on the branch now. What had looked like a smooth expanse of grey-green wood was, close to, a maze of rough bark, roots and clumps of moss. It was unbearably frightening for frogs who had spent their life in a world with petals round the edge.

But they crawled onward. They didn't know the meaning of the word 'retreat'. Or any other word.

4

> HOTELS: A place where TRAVELLING HUMANS are parked at night. Other humans bring them food, including the famous BACON, LETTUCE AND TOMATO SANDWICH. There are beds and towels and special things that rain on people to get them clean.
>
> From *A Scientific Encyclopedia for the Enquiring Young Nome*
> by Angalo de Haberdasheri

Blackness.

'It's very dark in here, Masklin.'

'Yes, and I can't get comfortable.'

'Well, you'll have to make the best of it.'

'A hairbrush! I've just sat down on a hairbrush!'

'We will be landing shortly.'

'Good.'

'And there's a tube of something — '

'I'm hungry. Isn't there anything to eat?'

'I've still got that peanut.'

'Where? Where?'

'Now you've made me drop it.'

'Gurder?'

'Yes?'

'What are you *doing?* Are you cutting something?'

'He's cutting a hole in his sock.'

Silence.

'Well? What of it? I can if I want to. It's my sock.'

More silence.

'I shall just feel better for doing it.'

Still more silence.

'It's just a human, Gurder. There's nothing special about it.'

'We're in its bag, aren't we?'

'Yes, but you said yourself that Arnold Bros is something in our heads. Didn't you?'

'Yes.'

'Well, then?'

'This just makes me feel better, that's all. Subject closed.'

'We're about to land.'

'How will we know when — '

'I am sure I could have done it better. Eventually.'

'Is this the Florida place? Angalo, get your foot out of my face.'

'Yes. This country traditionally welcomes immigrants.'

'Is that what we are?'

'Technically you are en route to another destination.'

'Which?'

'The stars.'

'Oh. Thing?'

'Yes?'

'Is there any record of nomes being here before?'

'What do you mean? *We're* the nomes!'

'Yes, but there may have been others.'

'We're all that there is! Aren't we?'

Tiny coloured lights flickered in the darkness of the bag.

'Thing?' Masklin repeated.

'I am searching available data. Conclusion: no reliable sighting of nomes. All recorded immigrants have been in excess of four inches high.'

'Oh. I just wondered. I wondered if we were all that there was.'

'You heard the Thing. No reliable sightings, it said.'

'No one saw *us* until today.'

'Thing, do you know what happens next?'

'*We will pass through Immigration and Customs. Are you now, or have you ever been, a member of a subversive organization?*'

Silence.

'What, us? Why are you asking us that?'

'*It is the sort of question that gets asked. I am monitoring communications.*'

'Oh. Well, I don't think we have. Have we?'

'No.'

'No.'

'No. I didn't think we had been. What does subversive mean?'

'*The question seeks to establish whether you've come here to overthrow the Government of the United States.*'

'I don't think we want to do that. Do we?'

'No.'

'No.'

'No, we don't. They don't have to worry about us.'

'Very clever idea, though.

'What is?'

'Asking the questions when people arrive. If anyone was coming here to do some subversive overthrowing, everyone'd be down on him like a pound of bricks as soon as he answered "Yes".'

'It's a sneaky trick, isn't it,' said Angalo, in an admiring tone of voice.

'No, we don't want to do any overthrowing,' said Masklin to the Thing. 'We just want to steal one of their going-straight-up jets. What are they called again?'

'*Space Shuttles.*'

'Right. And then we'll be off. We don't want to cause any trouble.'

The bag bumped around and was put down.

There was a tiny sawing noise, totally unheard amongst the noise of the airport. A very small hole appeared in the leather.

'What's he doing?' said Gurder.

'Stop pushing,' said Masklin. 'I can't concentrate. Now . . . it looks like we're in a line of humans.'

'We've been waiting for *ages*,' said Angalo.

'I expect everyone's being asked if they're going to do any overthrowing,' said Gurder wisely.

'I hardly like to bring this up,' said Angalo, 'but how are we going to find this Shuttle?'

'We'll sort that out when the time comes,' said Masklin, uncertainly.

'The time's come,' said Angalo. 'Hasn't it?'

Masklin shrugged helplessly.

'You didn't think we'd arrive in this Florida place and there'd be signs up saying "This way to space", did you?' said Angalo sarcastically.

Masklin hoped his thoughts didn't show up on his face. 'Of course not,' he said.

'Well, what do we do next?' Angalo insisted.

'We . . . we . . . we ask the Thing,' said Masklin. He looked relieved. 'That's what we'll do. Thing?'

'*Yes?*'

Masklin shrugged. 'What do we do next?'

'Now that,' said Angalo, 'is what I call planning.'

The bag shifted. Grandson Richard, 39, was moving up the queue.

'Thing? I said, what do we do — '

'*Nothing.*'

'How can we do nothing?'

'*By performing an absence of activity.*'

'What good is that?'

'*The paper said Richard Arnold was going to Florida for the launch of the communications satellite. Therefore, he is now going to the place where the satellite is. Ergo, we will go with him.*'

'Who's Ergo?' said Gurder, looking around.

The Thing flickered its lights at him.

'It means "Therefore",' it said.

Masklin looked doubtful. 'Do you think he'll take this bag with him?'

'Uncertain.'

There wasn't a lot in the bag, Masklin had to admit. It contained mainly socks, papers, a few odds and ends like hairbrushes, and a book called *The Spy With No Trousers*. This last item had caused them some concern when the bag had been unzipped just after the plane landed, but Grandson Richard had thrust the book among the papers without glancing inside. Now that there was a little light to see by, Angalo was trying to read it. Occasionally he'd mutter under his breath.

'It seems to me,' Masklin said eventually, 'that Grandson Richard isn't going to go straight off to watch the satellite fly away. I'm sure he'll go somewhere and sleep first. Do you know when this Shuttle jet flies, Thing?'

'Uncertain. I can only talk to other computers when they are within my range. The computers here know only about airport matters.'

'He's going to have to go to sleep soon, anyway,' said Masklin. 'Humans sleep through most of the night. I think that's when we'd better leave the bag.'

'And then we can talk to him,' said Gurder.

The others stared at him.

'Well, that's why we came, isn't it?' said the Abbot.

'Originally? To ask him to save the quarry?'

'He's a *human*!' snapped Angalo. 'Even you must realize that by now! He's not going to help us! Why should he help us? He's just a human whose ancestors built a store! Why do you go on believing he's some sort of great big nome in the sky?'

'Because I haven't got anything else to believe in!'

55

shouted Gurder. 'And if you don't believe in Grandson Richard, why are you in his bag?'

'That's just a coincidence – '

'You *always* say that! You always say it's just a coincidence!'

The bag moved, so that they lost their balance again and fell over.

'We're moving,' said Masklin, still peering out of the hole and almost glad of anything that would stop the argument. 'We're walking across the floor. There's a lot of humans out there. A *lot* of humans.'

'There always are,' sighed Gurder.

'Some of them are holding up signs with names on them.'

'That's just like humans,' Gurder added.

The nomes were used to humans with signs. Some of the humans in the Store used to wear their names all the time. Humans had strange long names, like Mrs J. E. Williams Supervisor and Hello My Name is Tracey. No one knew why humans had to wear their names. Perhaps they'd forget them otherwise.

'Hang on,' said Masklin, 'this can't be right. One of them is holding up a sign saying "Richard Arnold". We're walking towards it! We're talking to it!'

The deep muffled rumble of the human voice rolled above the nomes like thunder.

Hoom-voom-boom?

Foom-hoom-zoom-boom.

Hoom-zoom-*boom*-foom?

Boom!

'Can you understand it, Thing?' said Masklin.

'*Yes. The man with the sign is here to take our human to a hotel. It's a place where humans sleep and are fed. All the rest of it was just the things humans say to each other to make sure that they're still alive.*'

'What do you mean?' said Masklin.

56

'They say things like "How are you?" and "Have a nice day" and "What do you think of this weather, then?" What these sounds mean is: I am alive and so are you.'

'Yes, but nomes say the same sort of things, Thing. It's called "getting along with people". You might find it worth a try.'

The bag swung sideways and hit something. The nomes clung desperately to the insides. Angalo clung with one hand. He was trying to keep his place in the book.

'I'm getting hungry again,' said Gurder. 'Isn't there anything to eat in this bag?'

'There's some toothpaste in this tube.'

'I'll give the toothpaste a miss, thanks.'

Now there was a rumbling noise. Angalo looked up. 'I know *that* sound,' he said. 'Infernal combustion engine. We're in a vehicle.'

'*Again?*' said Gurder.

'We'll get out as soon as we can,' said Masklin.

'What kind of truck is it, Thing?' said Gurder.

'*It is a helicopter.*'

'It's certainly noisy,' said Gurder, who had never come across the word.

'It is a "plane without wings",' said Angalo, who had.

Gurder gave this a few moments' careful and terrified thought.

'Thing?' he said, slowly.

'*Yes?*'

'What keeps it up in the — ' Gurder began.

'*Science.*'

'Oh. Well. Science? Good. That's all right, then.'

The noise went on for a long time. After a while it became part of the nomes' world, so that when it stopped the silence came as a shock.

They lay in the bottom of the bag, too discouraged even to talk. They felt the bag being carried, put down, picked up, carried again, put down, picked up one more time, and then thrown on to something soft.

And then there was blessed stillness.

Eventually Gurder's voice said: 'All right. What *flavour* toothpaste?'

Masklin found the Thing among the heap of paper-clips, dust, and screwed-up bits of paper at the bottom of the bag.

'Any idea where we are, Thing?' he said.

'*Room 103, Cocoa Beach New Horizons Hotel,*' said the Thing. '*I am monitoring communications.*'

Gurder pushed past Masklin. 'I've got to get out,' he said. 'I can't stand it in here any more. Give me a leg up, Angalo. I reckon I can just reach the top of the bag – '

There was the long-drawn-out rumble of the zipper. Light flooded in as the bag was opened. The nomes dived for whatever cover was available.

Masklin watched a hand taller than he was reach down, close around a smaller bag with the toothpaste and flannel in it, and pull it out.

The nomes didn't move.

After a while there came the distant sound of rushing water.

The nomes still didn't move.

Boom-boom foom zoom-hoom-hoom, choom zoom hoooom . . .

The human noise rose above the gushing. It echoed even more than normal.

'It . . . sounds like it's . . . singing?' whispered Angalo.

. . . Hoom . . . hoom-boom-boom hoom . . . zoom-hoom-boom *H000oooo000*mmm Boom.

'What's happening, Thing?' Masklin hissed.

'*It has gone into a room to have water showering on it,*' said the Thing.

'What does it want to do that for?'

'I assume it wants to keep clean.'

'So is it safe to get out of the bag now?'

' "Safe" is a relative word.'

'What? What? Like "uncle", you mean?'

'I mean that nothing is totally safe. But I suggest that the human will be wetting itself for some time.'

'Yeah. There's a lot of human to clean,' said Angalo. 'Come on. Let's do it.'

The bag was lying on a bed. It was easy enough to climb down the covers on to the floor.

. . . Hoom-hoom booOOOOM boom . . .

'What do we do now?' said Angalo.

'After we've eaten, that is,' said Gurder firmly.

Masklin trotted across the thick carpet. There was a tall glass door in the nearest wall. It was slightly open, letting in a warm breeze and the sounds of the night.

A human would have heard the click and buzz of crickets and other small mysterious creatures whose role in life is to sit in bushes all night and make noises that are a lot bigger than they are. But nomes hear sounds slowed down and stretched out and deeper, like a record player in a power cut. The dark was full of the thud and growl of the wilderness.

Gurder joined Masklin and squinted anxiously into the blackness.

'Could you go out and see if there is something to eat?' he said.

'I've a horrible feeling,' said Masklin, 'that if I go out there now, there *will* be something to eat, and it'll be me.'

Behind them the human voice sang on.

. . . Boom-hoom-hoom — BOOOooooMMM womp womp . . .

'What's the human singing about, Thing?' said Masklin.

'It is a little difficult to follow. However, it appears that the singer wishes it to be known that he did something his way.'

'Did what?'

'*Insufficient data at this point. But whatever it was, he did it at a) each step along life's highway and b) not in a shy way . . .*'

There was a knock at the door. The singing stopped. So did the gushing of the water. The nomes ran for the shadows.

'Sounds a bit dangerous,' Angalo whispered. 'Walking along highways, I mean. Each step along life's pavement would be better — '

Grandson Richard came out of the shower-room with a towel around its waist. It opened the door. Another human, with all its clothes on, came in with a tray. There was a brief exchange of hoots, and the clothed human put down the tray and went out again. Grandson Richard disappeared into the shower-room again.

. . . Buh-buh buh-buh hoom hoOOOmm . . .

'Food!' Gurder whispered. 'I can smell it! There's food on that tray!'

'*A bacon, lettuce and tomayto sandwich with coleslaw,*' said the Thing. '*And coffee.*'

'How did you know?' said all three nomes in unison.

'*He ordered it when he checked in.*'

'Coleslaw!' moaned Gurder ecstatically. 'Bacon! *Coffee!*'

Masklin stared upwards. The tray had been left on the edge of a table.

There was a lamp near it. Masklin had lived in the Store long enough to know that where there was a lamp, there was a wire.

He'd never found a wire he couldn't climb.

Regular meals, that was the problem. He'd never been used to them. When he'd lived Outside, before the Store, he'd got accustomed to going for days without food and then, when food *did* turn up, eating until he was greasy to the eyebrows. But the Store nomes expected something to eat several times an hour. The Store nomes ate all the time. They only had to miss half a dozen meals and they started to complain.

'I think I could get up there,' he said.

'Yes. Yes,' said Gurder.

'But is it all right to eat Grandson Richard's sandwich?' Masklin added.

Gurder opened his eyes. He blinked.

'That's an important theological point,' he muttered. 'But I'm too hungry to think about it, so let's eat it first, and then if it turns out to be wrong to eat it, I promise to be very sorry.'

. . . Boom-hoom whop whop, foom hoom . . .

'The human says that the end is now near and he is facing a curtain,' the Thing translated. *'This may be a shower curtain.'*

Masklin pulled himself up the wire and on to the table, feeling very exposed.

It was obvious that the Floridians had a different idea about sandwiches. Sandwiches had been sold back in the Store's Food Hall. The word meant something thin between two slices of damp bread. Floridian sandwiches, on the other hand, filled up an entire tray and if there *was* any bread it lurked deep in a jungle of cress and lettuce.

He looked down.

'Hurry up!' hissed Angalo. 'The water's stopped again!'

. . . Boom-hoom hoom whop hoom whop . . .

Masklin pushed aside a drift of greenstuff, grabbed the sandwich, hauled it to the edge of the tray and pushed it down on to the floor.

. . . foom hoom hoom HOOOOooooOOOOmmmmmm-WHOP.

The shower-room door opened.

'Come on! Come *on!*' Angalo yelled.

Grandson Richard came out. He took a few steps, and stopped.

He looked at Masklin.

Masklin looked at him.

There are times when Time itself pauses.

Masklin realized that he was standing at one of those points where History takes a deep breath and decides what to do next.

I can stay here, he thought. I can use the Thing to translate, and I can try to explain everything to him. I can tell him how important it is for us to have a home of our own. I can ask him if he can do something to help the nomes in the quarry. I can tell him how the Store nomes thought that his grandfather created the world. He'll probably enjoy knowing that. He looks friendly, for a human.

He *might* help us.

Or he'll trap us somehow, and call other humans, and they'll all start milling around and mooing, and we'll be put in a cage or something, and prodded. It'll be just like the Concorde drivers. They probably didn't want to hurt us, they just didn't understand what we were. And we haven't got time to let them find out.

It's their world, not ours.

It's too risky. No. I never realized it before, but we've got to do it *our* way . . .

Grandson Richard slowly reached out a hand and said: 'Whoomp?'

Masklin took a running jump.

Nomes can fall quite a long way without being hurt, and in any case a bacon, lettuce and tomato sandwich broke his fall.

There was a blur of activity and the sandwich rose on three pairs of legs. It raced across the floor, leaking mayonnaise.

Grandson Richard threw a towel at it. It missed.

The sandwich leapt over the doorframe and vanished into the chirping, velvety, dangerous night.

There were other dangers besides falling off the branch. One of the frogs was eaten by a lizard. Several others turned back as soon as they were out of the shade of their flower because, as they pointed out, '.–.–.mipmip.–.–.mipmip.–.–.'

The frog in the lead looked back at his dwindling group. There was one . . . and one . . . and one . . . and one . . . and one, which added up to – it wrinkled its forehead in the effort of calculation – yes, one.

Some of the one were getting frightened. The leading frog realized that if they were ever going to get to the new flower and survive there, there'd need to be a lot more than one frog. They'd need at least one, or possibly even one. He gave them a croak of encouragement.

'Mipmip,' he said.

5

FLORIDA (or FLORIDIA): A place where may be found ALLIGATORS, LONG-NECKED TURTLES and SPACE SHUTTLES. An interesting place which is warm and wet and there are geese. BACON, LETTUCE AND TOMATO SANDWICHES may be found here also. A lot more interesting than many other places. The shape when seen from the air is like a bit stuck on a bigger bit.

From *A Scientific Encyclopedia for the Enquiring Young Nome*
by Angalo de Haberdasheri

Let the eye of your imagination be a camera . . .

This is the globe of the world, a glittering blue and white ball like the ornament on some unimaginable Christmas tree.

Find a continent . . .

Focus

This is a continent, a jigsaw of yellows, green and browns.

Find a place . . .

Focus

This is a bit of the continent, sticking out into the warmer sea to the south-east. Most of its inhabitants call it Florida.

Actually, they don't. Most of its inhabitants don't call it anything. They don't even know it exists. Most of them have six legs, and buzz. A lot of them have eight legs and spend a lot of time in webs waiting for six-legged inhabitants to arrive for lunch. Many of the rest have four legs, and bark or moo or even lie in swamps pretending to be logs. In fact, only a tiny proportion of the inhabitants of Florida have two legs, and even most of *them* don't call it Florida. They just go tweet, and fly around a lot.

Mathematically, an almost insignificant amount of living things in Florida call it Florida. But they're the ones who matter. At least, in their opinion. And their opinion is the one that matters. In their opinion.

Focus

Find a highway . . .

Focus

. . . traffic swishing quietly through the soft warm rain . . .

Focus

. . . high weeds on the bank . . .

Focus

. . . grass moving in a way that isn't quite like grass moving in the wind . . .

Focus

. . . a pair of tiny eyes . . .

Focus

Focus

Focus

Click!

Masklin crept back through the grass to the nomes' camp, if that's what you could call a tiny dry space under a scrap of thrown-away plastic.

It has been hours since they'd *run away* from Grandson Richard, as Gurder kept on putting it. The sun was rising behind the rainclouds.

They'd crossed a highway while there was no traffic, they'd blundered around in damp undergrowth, scurrying away from every chirp and mysterious croak, and finally they'd found the plastic. And they'd slept. Masklin had stayed on guard for a while, but he wasn't certain what he was guarding against.

There was a positive side. The Thing had been listening to radio and television and had found the place the going-straight-up Shuttles went from. It was only eighteen miles away. And they'd definitely made progress. They'd gone – oh, call it half a mile. And at last it was warm. Even the rain was warm. And the bacon, lettuce and tomato sandwich was holding up.

But there were still almost eighteen miles to go.

'When did you say the launch is?' said Masklin.

'*Four hours time,*' said the Thing.

'That means we'll have to travel at more than four miles an hour,' said Angalo gloomily.

Masklin nodded. A nome, trying hard, could probably cover a mile and a half in an hour over open ground.

He hadn't given much thought to how they could get the Thing into space. If he'd thought about it at all, he'd imagined that they could find the Shuttle plane and wedge the Thing on it somewhere. If possible maybe they could go too, although he wasn't too sure about that. The Thing said it was cold in space, and there was no air.

'You could have asked Grandson Richard to help us!' said Gurder. 'Why did you run away?'

'I don't know, said Masklin. 'I suppose I thought we ought to be able to help ourselves.'

'*But you used the Truck. Nomes lived in the Store. You used the Concorde. You're eating human food.*'

Masklin was surprised. The Thing didn't often argue like that.

'That's different,' he said.

'*How?*'

'They didn't know about us. We took what we wanted. We weren't given it. They think it's their world, Thing! They think everything in it belongs to them! They name everything and own everything! I looked up at him and I thought, here's a human in a human's room, doing human things. How can he ever understand about nomes? How can he ever think tiny people are real people with real thoughts? I can't just let a human take over. Not just like that!'

The Thing blinked a few lights at him.

'We've come too far not to finish it ourselves,' Masklin mumbled. He looked up at Gurder.

'Anyway, when it came to it, I didn't exactly see you rushing up ready to shake him by the finger,' he said.

'I was embarrassed. It's always embarrassing, meeting deities,' said Gurder.

They hadn't been able to light a fire. Everything was too wet. Not that they needed a fire, it was just that a fire was more civilized. Someone had managed to light a fire there at some time, though, because there were still a few damp ashes.

'I wonder how things are back home?' said Angalo, after a while.

'All right, I expect,' said Masklin.

'Do you really?'

'Well, more *hope* than expect, to tell the truth.'

'I expect your Grimma's got everyone organized,' said Angalo, trying to grin.

'She's not *my* Grimma,' snapped Masklin.

'Isn't she? Whose is she, then?'

'She's — ' Masklin hesitated. 'Hers, I suppose,' he said lamely.

'Oh. I thought the two of you were set to — ' Angalo began.

'We're not. I told her we were going to get married, and all she could talk about was frogs,' said Masklin.

'That's females for you,' said Gurder. 'Didn't I say that letting them learn to read was a bad idea? It overheats their brains.'

'She said the most important thing in the world was little frogs living in a flower,' Masklin went on, trying to listen to the voice of his own memory. He hadn't been listening very hard at the time. He'd been too angry.

'Sounds like you could boil a *kettle* on her head,' said Angalo.

'It was something she'd read in a book, she said.'

'My point exactly,' said Gurder. 'You know I never really agreed with letting everyone learn to read. It unsettles people.'

Masklin looked gloomily at the rain.

'Come to think of it,' he said. 'it wasn't frogs exactly. It was the *idea* of frogs. She said there's these hills where it's hot and rains all the time, and in the rain forests there are these very tall trees and right in the top branches of the trees there are these like great big flowers called . . . bromeliads, I think, and water gets into the flowers and makes little pools and there's a type of frog that lays eggs in the pools and tadpoles hatch and grow into new frogs and these little frogs live their whole lives in the flowers right at the top of the trees and don't even know about the ground and once you know the world is full of things like that your life is never the same.'

He took a deep breath.

'Something like that, anyway,' he said.

Gurder looked at Angalo.

'Didn't understand *any* of it,' he said.

'*It's a metaphor,*' said the Thing. No one paid it any attention.

Masklin scratched his ear. 'It seemed to mean a lot to her,' he said.

'*It's a metaphor,*' said the Thing.

'Women always want something,' said Angalo. 'My wife is always on about dresses.'

'I'm sure he would have helped,' said Gurder. 'If we'd

talked to him. He'd probably have given us a proper meal and, and – '

' – given us a home in a shoebox,' said Masklin.

' – and given us a home in a shoebox,' said Gurder automatically. 'No! I mean, maybe. I mean, why not? A decent hour's sleep for a change. And then we – '

' – we'd be carried around in his pocket,' said Masklin.

'Not necessarily. Not necessarily.'

'We would. Because he's big and we're small.'

'Launch in three hours and fifty-seven minutes,' said the Thing.

Their temporary camp overlooked a ditch. There didn't seem to be any winter in Florida, and the banks were thick with greenery.

Something like a flat plate with a spoon on the front sculled slowly past. The spoon stuck out of the water for a moment, looked at the nomes vaguely, and then dropped down again.

'What was that thing, Thing?' said Masklin.

The Thing extended one of its sensors.

'A long-necked turtle.'

'Oh.'

The turtle swam peacefully away.

'Lucky, really,' said Gurder.

'What?' said Angalo.

'It having a long neck like that *and* being called a long-necked turtle. It'd be really awkward having a name like that if it had a short neck.'

'Launch in three hours and fifty-six minutes.'

Masklin stood up.

'You know,' said Angalo, 'I really wish I could have read more of *The Spy With No Trousers*. It was getting exciting.'

'Come on,' Masklin said. 'Let's see if we can find a way.'

Angalo, who had been sitting with his chin in his hands, gave him an odd look.

'What, now?'

'We've come too far to just stop, haven't we?'

They pushed their way through the weeds. After a while a fallen log helped them across the ditch.

'Much greener here than at home, isn't it,' said Angalo.

Masklin pushed through a thick stand of leaves.

'Warmer, too,' said Gurder. 'They've got the heating fixed here.'*

'No one fixes heating Outside, it just happens,' said Angalo.

'If I get old, this is the kind of place I'd like to live, if I had to live Outside,' Gurder went on, ignoring him.

'*It's a wild-life preserve,*' said the Thing.

Gurder looked shocked. 'What? Like jam? Made of *animals?*'

'*No. It is a place where animals can live unmolested.*'

'You're not allowed to hunt them, you mean?'

'*Yes.*'

'You're not allowed to hunt anything, Masklin,' said Gurder.

Masklin grunted.

There was something nagging at him. He couldn't quite put his finger on it. Probably it was to do with the animals after all.

'Apart from turtles with long necks,' he said, 'what other animals are there here, Thing?'

The Thing didn't answer for a moment. Then it said, '*I find mention of sea cows and alligators.*'

Masklin tried to imagine what a sea cow looked like.

---

* For generations the Store nomes had known that temperature was caused by air conditioning and the heating system; like many of them, Gurder never quite gave up certain habits of thinking.

But they didn't sound too bad. He'd met cows before. They were big and slow and didn't eat nomes, except by accident.

'What's an alligator?' he said.

The Thing told him.

'What?' said Masklin.

'What?' said Angalo.

'*What?*' said Gurder. He pulled his robe tightly around his legs.

'You idiot!' shouted Angalo.

'Me?' said Masklin hotly. 'How should I know? Is it my fault? Did I miss a sign at the airport saying "Welcome to Floridia, home of large meat-eating amphibians up to twelve feet long"?'

They watched the grasses. A damp warm world inhabited by insects and turtles was suddenly a disguise for horrible terrors with huge teeth.

Something's watching us, Masklin thought. I can feel it.

The three nomes stood back to back. Masklin crouched down, slowly, and picked up a large stone.

The grass moved

'The Thing did say they don't all grow to twelve feet,' said Angalo, in the silence.

'We were blundering around in the darkness!' said Gurder. 'With things like that around!'

The grass moved again. It wasn't the wind that was moving it.

'Pull yourself together,' muttered Angalo.

'If it *is* alligators,' said Gurder, trying to look noble, 'I shall show them how a nome can die with dignity.'

'Please yourself,' said Angalo, his eyes scanning the undergrowth. 'I'm planning to show them how a nome can run away with speed.'

The grasses parted.

A nome stepped out.

There was a crackle behind Masklin. His head spun round. Another nome stepped out.

And another.

And another.

Fifteen of them.

The three travellers swivelled like an animal with six legs and three heads.

It was the fire that I saw, Masklin told himself. We sat right down by the ashes of a fire, and I looked at them, and I didn't wonder who could have made them.

The strangers wore grey. They seemed to be all sizes. And every single one of them had a spear.

I wish I had mine, Masklin thought, trying to keep as many of the strangers as possible in his line of sight.

They weren't pointing their spears at him. The trouble was, they weren't exactly *not* pointing them, either.

Masklin told himself that it was very rare for a nome to kill another nome. In the Store it was considered bad manners, while Outside . . . well, there were so many other things that killed nomes in any case. Besides, it was wrong. There didn't have to be any other reasons.

He just had to hope that these nomes felt the same way.

'Do you know these people?' said Angalo.

'Me?' said Masklin. 'Of course not. How could I?'

'They're Outsiders. I dunno, I suppose I thought all Outsiders would know each other.'

'Never seen them before in my life,' said Masklin.

'I *think*,' said Angalo, slowly and deliberately, 'that the leader is that old guy with the big nose and the topknot with a feather in it. What do you think?'

Masklin looked at the tall, thin, old nome who was scowling at the three of them.

'He doesn't look as if he likes us very much.'

'I don't like the look of him at *all*,' said Angalo.

'Have you got any suggestions, Thing?' said Masklin.

'They are probably as frightened of you as you are of them.'

'I doubt it,' said Angalo.

'Tell them you will not harm them.'

'I'd much rather they told me they're not going to harm *us*.'

Masklin stepped forward, and raised his hands.

'We are peaceful,' he said. 'We don't want anyone to be hurt.'

'Including us,' said Angalo. 'We really mean it.'

Several of the strangers backed away and raised their spears.

'I've got my hands raised,' said Masklin over his shoulder. 'Why should they be so upset?'

'Because you're holding a large rock,' said Angalo flatly. 'I don't know about them, but if you walked towards me holding something like that *I'd* be pretty scared.'

'I'm not sure I want to let go of it,' said Masklin.

'Perhaps they don't understand us — '

Gurder moved.

The Abbot hadn't said a word since the arrival of the new nomes. He'd just gone very pale.

Now some sort of internal timer had gone off. He gave a snort, leapt forward, and bore down on Topknot like an enraged balloon.

'How *dare* you accost us, you — you *Outsider!*' he screamed.

Angalo put his hands over his eyes. Masklin got a firm hold on his rock.

'Er, Gurder — ' he began.

Topknot backed away. The other nomes seemed puzzled by the small explosive figure that was suddenly among them. Gurder was in the grip of the kind of anger that is almost as good as armour.

Topknot screeched something back at Gurder.

'Don't you harangue me, you grubby heathen,' said Gurder. 'Do you think all these spears really frighten us?'

'Yes,' whispered Angalo. He sidled closer to Masklin. 'What's got into him?' he said.

Topknot shouted something at his nomes. A couple of them raised their spears, uncertainly. Several of the others appeared to argue.

'This is getting worse,' said Angalo.

'Yes,' said Masklin. 'I think we should – '

A voice behind them snapped out a command. All the Floridians turned. So did Masklin.

Two nomes had come out of the grass. One was a boy. The other was a small, dumpy woman, the sort you'd cheerfully accept an apple pie from. Her hair was tied in a bun and, like Topknot, it had a long grey feather stuck through it.

The Floridians looked sheepish. Topknot spoke at length. The woman said a couple of words. Topknot spread his arms above him and muttered something at the sky.

The woman walked around Masklin and Angalo as if they were items on display. When she looked Masklin up and down he caught her eye and thought: she looks like a little old lady, but she's in charge. If she doesn't like us, we're in a lot of trouble.

She reached up and took the stone out of his hand. He didn't resist.

Then she touched the Thing.

It spoke. What it said sounded very much like the words the woman had just used. She pulled her hand away sharply, and looked at the Thing with her head on one side. Then she stood back.

At another command the Floridians formed, not a line, but a sort of V-shape with the woman at the tip of it and the travellers inside it.

'Are we prisoners?' said Gurder, who had cooled off a bit.

'I don't think so,' said Masklin. 'Not exactly prisoners, yet.'

The meal was some sort of a lizard. Masklin quite enjoyed it; it reminded him of his days as an Outsider, before they found the Store. The other two ate it only because not eating it would be impolite, and it probably wasn't a good idea to be impolite to people who had spears when you didn't.

The Floridians watched them solemnly.

There were at least thirty of them, all wearing identical grey clothes. They looked quite like the Store nomes, except for being slightly darker and much skinnier. Many of them had large, impressive noses, which the Thing said was perfectly OK and all because of genetics.

The Thing was talking to them. Occasionally it would extend one of its sensors and use it to draw shapes in the dirt.

'Thing's probably telling 'em we-come-from-place-bilong-far-on-big-bird-that-doesn't-go-flap,' said Angalo.

A lot of the time the Thing was simply repeating the woman's own words back at her.

Eventually Angalo couldn't stand it any more.

'What's *happening*, Thing?' he said. 'Why's the woman doing all the talking?'

'*She is the leader of this group,*' said the Thing.

'A woman? Are you serious?'

'*I am always serious. It's built-in.*'

'Oh.'

Angalo nudged Masklin. 'If Grimma ever finds out, we're in *real* trouble,' he said.

'*Her name is Very-small-tree, or Shrub,*' the Thing went on.

'And you can understand her?' said Masklin.

'Gradually. Their language is very close to original nomish.'

'What do you mean, original nomish?'

'The language your ancestors spoke.'

Masklin shrugged. There was no point in trying to understand that now.

'Have you told her about us?' he said.

'Yes. She says — '

Topknot, who had been muttering to himself, stood up suddenly and spoke very sharply at great length, with a lot of pointing to the ground and to the sky.

The Thing flashed a few lights.

'He says you are trespassing on the land belonging to the Maker of Clouds. He says that is very bad. He says the Maker of Clouds will be very angry.'

There was a general murmur of agreement from many of the nomes. Shrub spoke to them sharply. Masklin stuck out a hand to stop Gurder from getting up.

'What does, er, Shrub think?' he said.

'I don't think she is very sympathetic to the topknot person. His name is Person-who-knows-what-the-Maker-of-Clouds-is-thinking.'

'And what is the Maker of Clouds?'

'It's bad luck to say its true name. It made the ground and it is still making the sky. It — '

Topknot spoke again. He sounded angry.

We need to be friends with these people, Masklin thought. There has to be a way.

'The Maker of Clouds is . . .' Masklin thought hard, '. . . a sort of Arnold Bros (est. 1905)?'

'Yes,' said the Thing.

'A real thing?'

'I think so. Are you prepared to take a risk?'

'What?'

'I think I know the identity of the Maker of Clouds. I think I know when it will make some more sky.'

'What? When?' said Masklin.

'*In three hours and ten minutes.*'

Masklin hesitated.

'Hold on a moment,' he said, slowly. 'That sounds like the same sort of time that — '

'*Yes. All three of you, please get ready to run. I will now write the name of the Maker of Clouds.*'

'Why will we have to run?'

'*They might get very angry. But we haven't time to waste.*'

The Thing waved the sensor. It wasn't intended as a writing implement, and the shapes it drew were angular and hard to read.

It scrawled four shapes in the dust.

The effect was instantaneous.

Topknot started to shout again. Some of the Floridians leapt to their feet. Masklin grabbed the other two travellers.

'I'm really going to thump that old nome in a minute,' said Gurder. 'How can anyone be so narrow-minded?'

Shrub sat silently while the row went on around her. Then she spoke, very loudly but very calmly.

'*She is telling them,*' said the Thing, '*that it is not wrong to write the name of the Maker of Clouds. It is often written by the Maker of Clouds itself. How famous the Maker of Clouds must be, that even these strangers know its name, she says.*'

That seemed to satisfy most of the nomes. Topknot started to grumble to himself.

Masklin relaxed a bit, and looked down at the figures in the sand.

'N . . . A . . . 8 . . . A?' he said.

'*It's an "S",*' said the Thing, '*not an "8".*'

'But you've only been talking to them for a little while!' said Angalo. 'How can you know something like this?'

'*Because I know how nomes think,*' said the Thing. '*You always believe what you read, and you've all got very literal minds. Very literal minds indeed.*'

6

GEESE: A type of bird which is slower than, e.g.
CONCORDE, and you don't get anything to eat.
According to nomes who know them well, a goose is
the most stupid bird there is, except for a duck. Geese
spend a lot of time flying to other places. As a form of
transport, the goose leaves a lot to be desired.

From *A Scientific Encyclopedia for the Enquiring Young Nome*
by Angalo de Haberdasheri

In the beginning, said Shrub, there was nothing but
ground. NASA saw the emptiness above the ground and
decided to fill it with sky. It built a place in the middle
of the world and sent up towers full of clouds. Sometimes
they also carried stars because, at night, after one of the
cloud towers had gone up, the nomes could sometimes
see new stars moving across the sky.

The land around the cloud towers was NASA's
special country. There were more animals there, and
fewer humans. It was a pretty good place for nomes.
Some of them believed that NASA had arranged it all
for precisely that reason.

Shrub sat back.

'And does *she* believe that?' said Masklin. He looked
across the clearing to where Gurder and Topknot were
arguing. They couldn't understand what one another was
saying, but they were still arguing.

78

The Thing translated.

Shrub laughed.

'She says, days comes, days go, who needs to believe anything? She sees things happen with her own eyes, and these are things she knows happen. Belief is a wonderful thing for those who need it, she says. But she knows this place belongs to NASA, because its name is on signs.'

Angalo grinned. He was so excited he was nearly in tears.

'They live right by the place the going-up jets go from and they think it's some sort of magic place!' he said.

'Isn't it?' said Masklin, almost to himself. 'Anyway, it's no more strange than thinking the Store was the whole world. Thing, how do they watch the going-up jets? They're a long way away.'

'Not far at all. Eighteen miles is not far at all, she says. She says they can be there in little more than an hour.'

Shrub nodded at their astonishment, and then, without another word, stood up and walked away through the bushes. She signalled the nomes to follow her. Half a dozen Floridians trailed after their leader, making the shape of a V with her at the point.

After a few yards the greenery opened out again beside a small lake.

The nomes were used to large bodies of water. There were reservoirs near the airport. They were even used to ducks. But the things paddling enthusiastically towards them were a lot bigger than ducks. Besides, ducks were like a lot of other animals and recognized in nomes the shape, if not the size, of humans and kept a safe distance away from them. They didn't come haring towards them as if the mere sight of them was the best thing that had happened all day.

Some of these creatures were almost flying in their desire to get to the nomes.

Masklin looked around automatically for a weapon.

Shrub grabbed his arm, shook her head, and said a couple of words.

'*They're friendly,*' the Thing translated.

'They don't look it!'

'*They're geese,*' said the Thing. '*Quite harmless, except to grass and minor organisms. They fly here for the winter.*'

The geese arrived with a bow wave that surged over the nomes' feet, and arched their necks down towards Shrub. She patted a couple of fearsome-looking beaks.

Masklin tried hard not to look like a minor organism.

'*They migrate here from colder climates,*' the Thing went on. '*They rely on the Floridians to pick the right course for them.*'

'Oh, good. That's . . .' Masklin stopped while his brain caught up with his mouth. 'You're going to tell me these nomes fly on them, right?'

'*Certainly. They travel with the geese. Incidentally, you have two hours and forty-one minutes to launch.*'

'I want to make it absolutely clear,' said Angalo slowly, as a great feathery head nabbled in the water a few inches away, 'that if you're suggesting that we ride on a geese — '

'*A goose. One geese is a goose.*'

' — you can think again. Or compute, or whatever it is you do.'

'*You have a better suggestion, of course,*' said the Thing. If it had a face, it would have been sneering.

'Suggesting we don't ride on them strikes me as a whole lot better, yes,' said Angalo.

'I dunno,' said Masklin, who had been watching the geese speculatively. 'I might be prepared to give it a try.'

'*The Floridians have developed a very interesting relationship with the geese,*' said the Thing. '*The geese provide the nomes with wings, and the nomes provide the geese with brains. They fly north to Canada in the summer, and back here for the winter. It's almost a symbiotic relationship, although of course they're not familiar with the term.'*

'Aren't they? Silly old them,' Angalo muttered.

'I don't understand you, Angalo,' said Masklin. 'You're mad for riding in machines with whirring bits of metal pushing them along, yet you're worried about sitting on a perfectly natural bird.'

'That's because I don't understand how birds work,' said Angalo. 'I've never seen an exploded working diagram of a goose.'

'The geese are the reason the Floridians have never had much to do with humans,' the Thing continued. *'As I said, their language is almost original nomish.'*

Shrub was watching them carefully. There was something about the way she was treating them that still seemed odd to Masklin. It wasn't that she was afraid of them, or aggressive, or unpleasant.

'She's not surprised,' he said aloud. 'She's interested, but she's not surprised. They were upset because we were *here*, not because we existed. *How many other nomes has she met?'*

The Thing had to translate.

It was a word that Masklin had only known for a year. Thousands.

The leading tree frog was trying to wrestle with a new idea. It was very dimly aware that it needed a new type of thought.

There had been the world, with the pool in the middle and the petals round the edge. One.

But further along the branch was another world. From here it looked tantalizingly like the flower they had left. One.

The leading frog sat in a clump of moss and swivelled each eye so that it could see both worlds at the same time. One there. And one *there*.

One. And one.

The frog's forehead bulged as it tried to get its mind around a new idea. One and one were one. But if you had one *here* and one *there* . . .

The other frogs watched in bewilderment as their leader's eyes whizzed round and round.

One here and one there couldn't be one. They were too far apart. You needed a word that meant both ones. You needed to say . . . you needed to say . . .

The frog's mouth widened. It grinned so broadly that both ends almost met behind its head.

It had worked it out.

'.—.—.mipmip.—.—!' it said.

It meant: one. And one *more* one.

Gurder was still arguing with Topknot when they got back.

'How do they manage to keep it up? They don't understand what each other's saying!' said Angalo.

'Best way,' said Masklin. 'Gurder? We're ready to go. Come on.'

Gurder looked up. He was very red in the face. The two of them were crouched either side of a mass of scrawled diagrams in the dirt.

'I need the Thing!' he said. 'This idiot refuses to understand anything!'

'You won't win any arguments with him,' said Masklin. 'Shrub says he argues with all other nomes they meet. He likes to.'

'What other nomes?' said Gurder.

'There's nomes everywhere, Gurder. That's what Shrub says. There's other groups even in Floridia. And — and — and in Canadia, where the Floridians go in the summer. There were probably even other nomes back home! We just never found them!'

He pulled the Abbot to his feet.

82

'And we haven't got a lot of time left,' he added.

'I'm not going up on one of those things!'

The geese gave Gurder a puzzled look, as if he was an unexpected frog in their waterweed.

'I'm not very happy about it either,' said Masklin, 'but Shrub's people do it all the time. You just snuggle down in the feathers and hang on.'

'*Snuggle?*' shouted Gurder. 'I've never snuggled in my life!'

'You rode on the Concorde,' Angalo pointed out. 'And that was built and driven by humans.'

Gurder glared like someone who wasn't going to give in easily.

'Well, who built the geese?' he demanded.

Angalo grinned at Masklin, who said: 'What? Dunno. Other geese, I expect.'

'Geese? *Geese?* And what do *they* know about designing for air safety?'

'Listen,' said Masklin. 'They can take us all the way across this place. The Floridians fly thousands of miles on them. Thousands of miles, without even any smoked salmon or pink wobbly stuff. It's worth trying it for eighteen miles, isn't it?'

Gurder hesitated. Topknot muttered something.

Gurder cleared his throat.

'Very well,' he said haughtily. 'I'm sure if this misguided individual is in the habit of flying on these things, I should have no difficulty whatsoever.' He stared up at the grey shapes bobbing out in the lagoon. 'Do the Floridians talk to the creatures?'

The Thing tried this on Shrub. She shook her head. No, she said, geese were quite stupid. Friendly but stupid. Why talk to something that couldn't talk back?

'Have you told her what we're doing?' said Masklin.

'*No. She hasn't asked.*'

'How do we get on?'

Shrub stuck her fingers in her mouth and whistled.

Half a dozen geese waddled up the bank. Close to, they didn't look any smaller.

'I remember reading something about geese once,' said Gurder, in a sort of dreamy terror. 'It said they could break a human's arm with a blow of their nose.'

'Wing,' said Angalo, looking up at the feathery grey bodies looming over him. 'It was their wing.'

'And it was swans that do that,' said Masklin, weakly. 'Geese are the ones you mustn't say boo to.'

Gurder watched a long neck weave back and forth above him.

'Wouldn't dream of it,' he said.

A long time after, when Masklin came to write the story of his life, he described the flight of the geese as the fastest, highest and most terrifying of all.

People said, hold on, that's not right. You said, Masklin, that the plane went so fast it left its sound behind, and so high up there was blue all around it.

And he said, that's the point. It went so fast you didn't know how fast it was going; it went so high you couldn't see how high it was. It was just something that happened. And the Concorde looked as though it was *meant* to fly. When it was on the ground it looked kind of lost.

The geese, on the other hand, looked as aerodynamic as a pillow. They didn't roll into the sky and sneer at the clouds like the plane did. No, they ran across the top of the water and hammered desperately at the air with their wings and then, just when it was obvious they weren't going to achieve anything, they suddenly did; the water dropped away and there was just the slow creak of wings pulling the goose up into the sky.

Masklin would be the first to admit that he didn't understand about jets and engines and machines, so maybe that was why he didn't worry about travelling in them. But he thought he knew a thing or two about muscles, and the knowledge that it was only a couple of big muscles that were keeping him alive was not comforting.

Each traveller shared a goose with one of the Floridians. They didn't do any steering, as far as Masklin could see. That was all done by Shrub, who sat far out on the neck of the leading goose.

The ones behind it followed their leader in a perfect V-shape.

Masklin buried himself in the feather. It was comfortable, if a bit cold. Floridians, he learned later, had no difficulty sleeping on a flying goose. The mere thought gave Masklin nightmares.

He peered out just long enough to see distant trees sweeping by much too fast, and stuck his head down again.

'How long have we got, Thing?' he said.

'I estimate arrival in the vicinity of the launch pad one hour from launch.'

'I suppose there's absolutely no possibility that launches have anything to do with lunches?' said Masklin wistfully.

'No.'

'Pity. Well — have you any suggestions about how we get on the machine?'

'That is almost impossible.'

'I thought you'd say that.'

'But you could put ME on,' the Thing added.

'Yes, but how? Tie you to the outside?'

'No. Get me close enough and I will do the rest.'

'What rest?'

'Call the Ship.'

'Yes, where *is* the Ship? I'm amazed satellites and things haven't bumped into it.'

'*It is waiting.*'

'You're a great help, sometimes.'

'*Thank you.*'

'That was meant to be sarcastic.'

'*I know.*'

There was a rustling beside Masklin and his Floridian co-rider pushed aside a feather. It was the boy he had seen with Shrub. He'd said nothing, but had just stared at Masklin and the Thing. Now he grinned, and said a few words.

'*He wants to know if you feel sick.*'

'I feel fine,' Masklin lied. 'What's his name?'

'*His name is Pion. He is Shrub's oldest son.*'

Pion gave Masklin another encouraging grin.

'*He wants to know what it is like in a jet,*' said the Thing. '*He says it sounds exciting. They see them sometimes, but they keep away from them.*'

The goose canted sideways. Masklin tried to hang on with his toes as well as his feet.

'*It must be much more exciting than geese, he says,*' said the Thing.

'Oh, I don't know,' said Masklin weakly.

Landing was much worse than flying. It would have been better on water, Masklin was told later, but Shrub had brought them down on land. The geese didn't like that much. It meant that they had almost to stand on the air, flapping furiously, and then drop the last few inches.

Pion helped Masklin down on to the ground, which seemed to him to be moving from side to side. The other travellers tottered towards him through the throng of birds.

'The ground!' panted Angalo. 'It was so close! No one seemed to mind!'

He sagged to his knees.

'And they make honking noises!' he said. 'And keep

swinging from side to side! And they're all knobbly under the feathers!'

Masklin flexed his arms to let the tension out.

The land around them didn't seem a lot different to the place they'd left, except that the vegetation was lower and Masklin couldn't see any water.

'*Shrub says that this is as close as the geese can go,*' Thing said. '*It is too dangerous to go any further.*'

Shrub nodded, and pointed to the horizon.

There was a white shape on it.

'That?' said Masklin.

'That's it?' said Angalo.

'*Yes.*'

'Doesn't look very big,' said Gurder quietly.

'It's still quite a long way off,' said Masklin.

'I can see helicopters,' said Angalo. 'No wonder Shrub didn't want to take the geese any closer.'

'We must be going,' said Masklin. 'We've got an hour, and I reckon that's barely enough. Er. We'd better say goodbye to Shrub. Can you explain, Thing? Tell her that — that we'll try and find her again. Afterwards. If everything's all right. I suppose.'

'If there *is* any afterwards,' Gurder added. He looked like a badly washed dishcloth.

Shrub nodded when the Thing had finished translating, and then pushed Pion forward.

The Thing told Masklin what she wanted.

'What? We can't take him with us!' said Masklin.

'*Young nomes in Shrub's people are encouraged to travel,*' said the Thing. '*Pion is only fourteen months old and already he has been to Alaska.*'

'Try and explain that we're not going to a Laska,' said Masklin. 'Try and make her understand that all sorts of things could happen to him!'

The Thing translated.

'She says that is good. A growing boy should always seek out new experiences.'

'What? Are you translating me properly?' said Masklin suspiciously.

'Yes.'

'Well, have you told her it's dangerous?'

'Yes. She says that danger is what being alive is all about.'

'But he could be killed!' Masklin shrieked.

'Then he will go up into the sky and become a star.'

'Is that what they believe?'

'Yes. They believe that the operating system of a nome starts off as a goose. If it is a good goose, it becomes a nome. When a good nome dies, NASA takes it up into the sky and it becomes a star.'

'What's an operating system?' said Masklin. This was religion. He always felt out of his depth with religion.

'The thing inside you that tells you what you are,' said the Thing.

'It means a soul,' said Gurder wearily.

'Never heard such a lot of nonsense,' said Angalo cheerfully. 'At least, not since we were in the Store and believed we came back as garden ornaments, eh?' He nudged Gurder in the ribs.

Instead of getting angry about this, Gurder just looked even more despondent.

'Let the lad come if he likes,' Angalo went on. 'He shows the right spirit. He reminds me of me when I was like him.'

'His mother says that if he gets homesick he can always find a goose to bring him back,' said the Thing.

Masklin opened his mouth to speak.

But there were times when you couldn't say anything because there was nothing to say. If you had to explain anything to someone else, then there had to be something you were both sure of, some place to start, and Masklin wasn't sure that there was any place like that around

Shrub. He wondered how big the world was to her. Probably bigger than he could imagine. But it stopped at the sky.

'Oh, all right,' he said. 'But we have to go right away. No time for long tearful – '

Pion nodded to his mother and came and stood by Masklin, who couldn't think of anything to say. Even later on, when he understood the geese nomes better, he never quite got used to the way they cheerfully parted from one another. Distances didn't seem to mean much to them.

'Come on then,' he managed.

Gurder glowered at Topknot, who had insisted on coming this far. 'I really wish I could talk to that nome,' he said.

'Shrub told me he's quite a decent nome, really,' said Masklin. 'He's just a bit set in his ways.'

'Just like you, Gurder,' said Angalo.

'Me? I'm not – ' Gurder began.

'Of course you're not,' said Masklin, soothingly. 'Now, let's go.'

They jogged through scrub two or three times as high as they were.

'We'll never have time,' Gurder panted.

'Save your breath for running,' said Angalo.

'Do they have smoked salmon on Shuttles?' said Gurder.

'Dunno,' said Masklin, pushing his way through a particularly tough clump of grass.

'No, they don't,' said Angalo authoritatively. 'I remember reading about it in a book. They eat out of tubes.'

The nomes ran in silence while they thought about this.

'What, toothpaste?' said Gurder, after a while.

'No, not toothpaste. Of course not toothpaste. I'm *sure* not toothpaste.'

'Well, what else do you know that comes in tubes?'

Angalo thought about this.

'Glue?' he said, uncertainly.

'Doesn't sound a good meal to me. Toothpaste and glue?'

'The people who drive the space jets must like it. They were all smiling in the picture I saw,' said Angalo.

'That wasn't smiling, that was probably just them trying to get their teeth apart,' said Gurder.

'No, you've got it all wrong,' Angalo decided, thinking fast. 'They have to have their food in tubes because of gravity.'

'What about gravity?'

'There isn't any.'

'Any what?'

'Gravity. So everything floats around.'

'What, in water?' said Gurder.

'No, in air. Because there's nothing to hold it on the plate, you see.'

'Oh.' Gurder nodded. 'Is that where the glue comes in?'

Masklin knew that they could go on like this for hours. What these sounds mean, he thought, is: I am alive and so are you. And we're all very worried that we might not be alive for much longer, so we'll just keep talking, because that's better than thinking.

It all looked better when it was days or weeks away, but now when it was —

'How long, Thing?'

'Forty minutes.'

'We've got to have another rest! Gurder isn't running, he's just falling upright.'

They collapsed in the shade of a bush. The Shuttle didn't look much closer, but they could see plenty of other activity. There were more helicopters. According to frantic signs from Pion, who climbed up the bush, there were humans, much further off.

'I need to sleep,' said Angalo.

'Didn't you sleep on the goose?' said Masklin.

'Did *you*?'

Angalo stretched out in the shade.

'How are we going to get on the Shuttle?' he said.

Masklin shrugged. 'Well, the Thing says we don't have to get on it, we just have to put the Thing on it.'

Angalo pushed himself up on his elbows. 'You mean we don't get to ride on it? I was looking forward to that!'

'I don't think it's like the Truck, Angalo. I don't think they leave a window open for anyone to sneak in,' said Masklin. 'I think it'd take more than a lot of nomes and some string to fly it, anyway.'

'You know, that was the best time of my life, when I drove the Truck,' said Angalo dreamily. 'When I think of all those months I lived in the Store, not even knowing about the Outside . . .'

Masklin waited politely. His head felt heavy.

'Well?' he said.

'Well what?'

'What happens when you think of all those months in the Store not knowing about the Outside?'

'It just seems like a waste. Do you know what I'm going to do if – I mean, when we get home? I'm going to write down everything we've learned. We should be doing that, you know. Making lots of our own books. Not just reading human books, which are full of made-up things. And not just making books like Gurder's *Book of Nome*. Books of *proper* stuff, like Science . . .'

Masklin glanced at Gurder. The Abbot wasn't making any comment. He was asleep already.

Pion curled up and started to snore. Angalo's voice trailed off. He yawned.

They hadn't slept for hours. Nomes slept mainly at night, but needed catnaps to get through the long day. Even Masklin was nodding.

'Thing?' he remembered to say, 'wake me up in ten minutes, will you?'

7

> SATELLITES: They are in SPACE and stay there by going so fast that they never stay in one place long enough to fall down. TELEVISIONS are bounced off them. They are part of SCIENCE.
>
> From *A Scientific Encyclopedia for the Enquiring Young Nome*
> by Angalo de Haberdasheri

It wasn't the Thing that woke Masklin up. It was Gurder.

Masklin lay with his eyes half-closed, listening. Gurder was talking to the Thing in a low voice.

'I believed in the Store,' he said, 'and then it was just a, a sort of thing built by humans. And I thought Grandson Richard was some special person and he turned out to be a human who sings when he wets himself — '

' — *takes a shower* — '

' — and now there's thousands of nomes in the world! Thousands! Believing all sorts of things! That stupid Topknot person believes that the going-up Shuttles make the sky. Do you know what I thought when I heard that? I thought, if he'd been the one arriving in my world instead of the other way around, he'd have thought I was just as stupid! I *am* just as stupid! Thing?'

'*I was maintaining a tactful silence.*'

'Angalo believes in silly machinery and Masklin believes in, oh, I don't know. Space. Or not believing in things. And it all works for them. I try and believe in *important* things and they don't last for five minutes. Where's the fairness in that?'

'*Only another tactful and understanding silence suffices at this point.*'

'I just wanted to make some *sense* out of life.'

'*This is a commendable aim.*'

'I mean, what is the *truth* of everything?'

There was a pause. Then the Thing said: '*I recall your conversation with Masklin about the origin of nomes. You wanted to ask me. I can answer now. I was made. I know this is true. I know that I am a thing made of metal and plastic, but also that I am something which lives inside that metal and plastic. It is impossible for me not to be absolutely certain of it. This is a great comfort. As to nomes, I have data that says nomes originated on another world and came here thousands of years ago. This may be true. It may not be true. I am not in a position to judge.*'

'I knew where I was, back in the Store,' said Gurder, half to himself. 'And even in the quarry it wasn't too bad. I had a proper job. I was important to people. How can I go back now, knowing that everything I believed about the Store and Arnold Bros and Grandson Richard is just . . . is just an *opinion*?'

'*I cannot advise. I am sorry.*'

Masklin decided it was a diplomatic time to wake up. He made a grunting noise just to be sure that Gurder heard him.

The Abbot was very red in the face.

'I couldn't sleep,' he said shortly.

Masklin stood up.

'How long, Thing?'

'*Twenty-seven minutes.*'

'Why didn't you wake me up!'

'*I wished you to be refreshed.*'

'But it's still a long way off. We'll never get you on to it in time. Wake up, you.' Masklin prodded Angalo with

94

his foot. 'Come on, we'll have to run. Where's Pion? Oh, there you are. Come *on*, Gurder.'

They jogged on through the scrub. In the distance, there was the low mournful howl of sirens.

'You're cutting it really fine, Masklin,' said Angalo.

'Faster! Run faster!'

Now that they were closer, Masklin could see the Shuttle. It was quite high up. There didn't seem to be anything useful at ground level.

'I hope you've got a good plan, Thing,' he panted, as the four of them doged between the bushes, 'because I'll never be able to get you all the way up there.'

'Do not worry. We are nearly close enough.'

'What do you mean? It's still a long way off!'

'It is close enough for me to get on.'

'What is it going to do? Take a flying leap?' said Angalo.

'Put me down.'

Masklin obediently put the black box on the ground. It extended a few of its probes, which swung around slowly for a while and then pointed towards the going-up jet.

'What are you playing at?' said Masklin. 'This is wasting *time*!'

Gurder laughed, although not in a very happy way.

'I know what it's doing,' he said. 'It's sending itself on to the Shuttle. Right, Thing?'

'I am transmitting an instruction subset to the computer on the communications satellite,' said the Thing.

The nomes said nothing.

'Or, to put it another way . . . yes, I am turning the satellite computer into a part of me. Although not a very intelligent one.'

'Can you really do that?' said Angalo.

'Certainly.'

'Wow. And you won't miss the bit you're sending?'

'No. Because it will not leave me.'

'You're sending it and keeping it at the same time?'

'*Yes.*'

Angalo looked at Masklin.

'Did you understand any of that?' he demanded.

'I did,' said Gurder. 'The Thing's saying it's not just a machine, it's a sort of . . . a sort of collection of electric thoughts that live in a machine. I think.'

Lights flickered around on top of the Thing.

'Does it take a long time to do?' said Masklin.

'*Yes. Please do not take up vital communication power at this point.*'

'I think he means he doesn't want us to talk to him,' said Gurder. 'He's concentrating.'

'It,' said Angalo. 'It's an it. And it made us run all the way here just so's we can hurry up and wait.'

'It probably has to be close up to do . . . whatever it is it's doing,' said Masklin.

'How long's it going to take?' said Angalo. 'It seems ages since it was twenty-seven minutes to go.'

'Twenty-seven minutes at least,' said Gurder.

'Yeah. Maybe more.'

Pion pulled at Masklin's arm, pointed to the looming white shape with his other hand, and rattled off a long sentence in Floridian or, if the Thing was right, nearly original nomish.

'I can't understand you without the Thing,' said Masklin. 'Sorry.'

'No speaka da goose-oh,' said Angalo.

A look of panic spread across the boy's face. He shouted this time, and tugged harder.

'I think he doesn't want to be near the going-up jets when they start up,' said Angalo. 'He's probably afraid of the noise. Don't — like — the — noise, right?' he said.

Pion nodded furiously.

'They didn't sound too bad at the airport,' said

Angalo. 'More of a rumble. I expect they might frighten unsophisticated people.'

'I don't think Shrub's people are particularly unsophisticated,' said Masklin thoughtfully. He looked up at the white tower. It had seemed a long way away, but in some ways it might be quite close.

Really very close.

'How safe do you think it is here?' he said. 'When it goes up, I mean.'

'Oh, come *on*,' said Angalo. 'The Thing wouldn't have let us come right here if it wasn't safe for nomes.'

'Sure, sure,' said Masklin. 'Right. You're right. Silly to dwell on it, really.'

Pion turned and ran.

The other three looked back at the Shuttle. Lights moved in complicated patterns on the top of the Thing.

Somewhere another siren sounded. There was a sensation of power, as though the biggest spring in the world was being wound up.

When Masklin spoke, the other two seemed to hear him speak their own thoughts.

'Exactly how good,' he said, very slowly, 'do you think the Thing is at judging how close nomes can stand to a going-up jet when it goes up? I mean, how much experience has it got, do you think?'

They looked at one another.

'Maybe we should back off a little bit . . .?' Gurder began.

They turned and walked away.

Then each one of them couldn't help noticing that the others seemed to be walking faster and faster.

Faster and faster.

Then, as one nome, they gave up and ran for it, fighting their way through the scrub and grass, skidding on stones, elbows going up and down like pistons. Gurder, who was normally out of breath at anything above walking pace, bounded along like a balloon.

'Have . . . *you* . . . any . . . any . . . idea . . . how . . . how . . . close . . .?' Angalo panted.

The sound behind them started like a hiss, like the whole world taking a deep breath. Then it turned into . . .

. . . not noise, but something more like an invisible hammer which smacked into both ears at once.

8

After some time, when the ground had stopped shaking, the nomes picked themselves up and stared blearily at one another.

'   !' said Gurder.

'What?' said Masklin. His own voice sounded a long way away, and muffled.

'   ?'' said Gurder.

'   ?' said Angalo.

'   ?'

'What? I can't hear you! Can you hear *me*?'

'   ?'

Masklin saw Gurder's lips move. He pointed to his own ears and shook his head.

'We've gone deaf!'

'   ?'

'   ?'

99

'Deaf, I said.' Masklin looked up.

Smoke billowed overhead and out of it, rising fast even to a nome's high-speed senses, was a long, growing cloud tipped with fire. The noise dropped to something merely very loud and then, very quickly, disappeared.

Masklin stuck a finger in his ear and wiggled it around.

The absence of sound was replaced by the terrible hiss of silence.

'Anyone listening?' he ventured. 'Anyone hearing me?'

'That,' said Angalo, his voice sounding blurred and unnaturally calm, 'was pretty loud. I don't reckon many things come much louder.'

Masklin nodded. He felt as though he'd been pounded hard by something.

'You know about these things, Angalo,' he said, weakly. 'Humans ride on them, do they?'

'Oh, yes. Right at the top.'

'No one makes them do it?'

'Er. I don't think so,' said Angalo. 'I think the book said a lot of them want to do it.'

'They *want* to do it?'

Angalo shrugged. 'That's what it said.'

There was only a distant dot now, at the end of a widening white cloud of smoke.

Masklin watched it.

We must be *mad*, he thought. We're tiny and it's a big world and we never stop to learn enough about where we are before we go somewhere else. At least back when I lived in a hole I knew everything there was to know about living in a hole, and now it's a year later and I'm at a place so far away I don't even know how far away it is, watching something I don't understand go to a place so far up there is no down. And I can't go back. I've got to go right on to the end of whatever all this is, because I can't go back. I can't even stop.

So *that's* what Grimma meant about the frogs. Once

you know things, you're a different person. You can't
help it.

He looked back down. Something was missing.

The Thing . . .

He ran back the way they'd come.

The little black box was where he'd left it. The rods
had withdrawn into it, and there weren't any lights.

'Thing?' he said uncertainly.

One red light came on faintly. Masklin suddenly felt
cold, despite the heat around him.

'Are you all right?' he said.

The light flickered.

'Too quick. Used too much pow . . . ' it said.

'Pow?' said Masklin. He tried hard not to wonder why
the word hadn't been much more than a growl.

The light dimmed.

'Thing? Thing?' He tapped gently on the box. 'Did it
work? Is the Ship coming? What do we do now? Wake
up! *Thing?'*

The light went out.

Masklin picked the Thing up and turned it over and
over in his hands.

'Thing?'

Masklin and Gurder hurried up, with Pion behind
them.

'Did it work?' said Angalo. 'Can't see any Ship
yet.'

Masklin turned his face towards them.

'The Thing's stopped,' he said.

'Stopped?'

'All the lights have gone out!'

'Well, what does that mean?' Angalo started to look
panicky.

'I don't know!'

'Is it dead?' said Gurder.

'It *can't* die! It's existed for thousands of years!'

Gurder shook his head. 'Sounds like a good reason for dying,' he said.

'But it's a, a *thing*.'

Angalo sat down with his arms around his knees.

'Did it say if it got everything sorted out? When's the Ship coming?'

'Listen, don't you care? It's run out of pow!'

'Pow?'

'It must mean electricity. It kind of sucks it out of wires and stuff. I think it can store it for a while, too. And now it must have run out.'

They looked at the black box. It had spent thousands of years being handed down from nome to nome without ever saying a word or lighting a light. It had only woken up again when it had been brought into the Store, near electricity.

'It looks creepy, sitting there doing nothing,' said Angalo.

'Can't we find it some electricity?' said Gurder.

'Around here? There isn't any!' Angalo snapped. 'We're in the middle of nowhere!'

Masklin stood up and gazed around. It was just possible to see some buildings in the distance. There was a movement of vehicles around them.

'What about the *Ship*?' said Angalo. 'Is it on its way?'

'I don't know!'

'How will it find us?'

'I don't know!'

'Who's driving it?'

'I don't — ' Masklin stopped in horror. 'No one! I mean, who *could* be driving it? There hasn't been anyone on it for thousands of years!'

'Who was going to bring it here, then?'

'I don't know! The Thing, maybe?'

'You mean it's on its way and no one's driving it?'

'Yes! No! I don't know!'

Angalo squinted up at the blue sky.

'Oh, wow,' he said, glumly.

'We need to find some electricity for the Thing,' said Masklin. 'Even if it's managed to summon the Ship, the ship will still need to be told where we are.'

'*If* it summoned the Ship,' said Gurder. 'It might have run out of pow before it had time.'

'We can't be sure,' said Masklin. 'Anyway, we must help the Thing. I hate to see it like that.'

Pion, who had disappeared into the scrub, came back dragging a lizard.

'Ah,' said Gurder, without any enthusiasm. 'Here comes lunch.'

'If the Thing was talking we could tell Pion you can get awfully tired of lizard, in time,' said Angalo.

'In about two seconds,' said Gurder.

'Come on,' said Masklin, wearily. 'Let's go and find some shade and think up another plan.'

'Oh, a plan,' Gurder said, as if that was worse than lizard. 'I like plans.'

They ate – not very well – and lay back watching the sky. The brief sleep on the way hadn't been enough. It was easy to doze.

'I must say, these Floridians have got it all worked out,' said Gurder lazily. 'It's cold back home and here they've got the heating turned up just right.'

'I keep telling you, it's not the heating,' said Angalo, straining his eyes for any sign of a descending Ship. 'And the wind isn't the air conditioning, either. It's the sun that makes you warm.'

'I thought that was just for lighting,' said Gurder.

'And it's where all the heat comes from,' said Angalo. 'I read it in a book. It's a great ball of fire bigger than the world.'

Gurder eyed the sun suspiciously.

'Oh, yes?' he said. 'What keeps it up?'

'Nothing. It's just kind of *there*.'

Gurder squinted at the sun again.

'Is this generally known?' he said.

'I suppose so. It was in the book.'

'For anyone to read? I call that irresponsible. That's the sort of thing that can really upset people.'

'There's thousands of suns up there, Masklin says.'

Gurder sniffed. 'Yes, he's told me. It's called the glaxie, or something. Personally, I'm against it.'

Angalo chuckled.

'I don't see what's so funny,' said Gurder coldly.

'Tell him, Masklin,' said Angalo.

'It's all very well for you,' Gurder muttered. 'You just want to drive things fast. *I* want to make sense of them. Maybe there *are* thousands of suns, but *why*?'

'Can't see that it matters,' said Angalo lazily.

'It's the only thing that *does* matter. Tell him, Masklin.'

They both looked at Masklin.

At least, where Masklin had been sitting.

He'd gone.

Beyond the top of the sky was the place the Thing had called the universe. It contained — according to the Thing — everything and nothing. And there was very little everything and more nothing than anyone could imagine.

For example, it was often said that the sky was full of stars. It was untrue. The sky was full of sky. There were unlimited amounts of sky and really, by comparison, very few stars.

It was amazing, therefore, that they made such an impression . . .

Thousands of them looked down now as something round and shiny drifted around the Earth.

It had Arnsat-1 painted on its side, which was a bit of a waste of paint since stars can't read.

It unfolded a silver dish.

It should then have turned to face the planet below it, ready to beam down old movies and new news.

It didn't. It had new orders.

Little puffs of gas jetted out as it turned around and searched the sky for a new target.

By the time it had found it, a lot of people in the old movies and new news business were shouting very angrily at one another down telephones, and some of them were feverishly trying to give it new instructions.

But that didn't matter, because it wasn't listening any more.

Masklin galloped through the scrub. They'd argue and bicker, he thought. I've got to do this quickly. I don't think we've got a lot of time.

It was the first time he'd been really alone since the days when he'd lived in a hole and had to go out hunting by himself because there was no one else.

Had it been better then? At least it had been simpler. You just had to try to eat without being eaten. Just getting through the day was a triumph. Everything had been bad, but at least it had been a kind of understandable, nome-sized badness.

In those days the world had ended at the motorway on one side and the woods beyond the field on the other side. Now it had no kind of boundaries at all, and more problems than he knew what to do with.

But at least he knew where to find electricity. You found it near buildings with humans in them.

The scrub ahead of Masklin opened out on to a track. He turned on to it, and ran faster. Go along any track and you'd find humans on it somewhere . . .

There were footsteps behind him. He turned around, and saw Pion. The young Floridian gave him a worried smile.

'Go away!' Masklin said. 'Go on! Go! Go back! Why are you following me? Go away!'

Pion looked hurt. He pointed up the track and said something.

'I don't understand!' shouted Masklin.

Pion stuck a hand high above his head, palm downward.

'Humans?' Masklin guessed. 'Yes. I know. I know what I'm doing. Go back!'

Pion said something else.

Masklin lifted up the Thing. 'Talking box no go,' he said helplessly. 'Good grief, why should I have to speak like this? You must be at least as intelligent as me. Go on, go away. Go back to the others.'

He turned and ran. He looked back briefly and saw Pion watching him.

How *much* time have I got? he wondered. Thing once told me the Ship flies very fast. Maybe it could be here any minute. Maybe it's not coming at all . . .

He saw figures loomed over the scrub. Yes, follow any track and sooner or later you find humans. They get everywhere.

Yes, maybe the Ship isn't coming at all.

If it isn't, he thought, then what I'm going to do now is probably the most stupid thing any nome has ever done anywhere in the total history of nomekind.

He stepped out into a circle of gravel. A small truck was parked in it, with the name of the Floridian god NASA painted on the side. Close by, a couple of humans were bent over a piece of machinery on a tripod.

They didn't notice Masklin. He walked closer, his heart thumping.

He put down the Thing.

He cupped his hands around his mouth.

He tried to shout as clearly and as slowly as possible.

'Hey, there! You! Hum-mans!'

'He did *what*?' shouted Angalo.

Pion ran through his pantomime of gestures again.

'*Talked* to *humans*?' said Angalo. 'Went in a thing with *wheels*?'

'I thought I heard a truck engine,' said Gurder.

Angalo pounded a fist into his palm.

'He was worried about the Thing,' he said. 'He wanted to find it some electricity!'

'But we must be miles from any buildings!' said Gurder.

'Not the way Masklin's going!' Angalo snarled.

'I *knew* it would come to this!' Gurder moaned. 'Showing ourselves to humans! We never used to do that sort of thing in the Store! What are we going to *do*?'

Masklin thought: up to now, it's not too bad.

The humans hadn't really known what to do about him. They'd even backed away! And then one of them had rushed to the truck and talked into a machine on a string. Probably some sort of telephone, Masklin thought knowledgeably.

When he hadn't moved, one of the humans had fetched a box out of the back of the truck and crept towards him as if expecting Masklin to explode. In fact, when he waved, the human jumped back clumsily.

The other humans said something, and the box was cautiously put down on the gravel a few feet from Masklin.

Then both humans watched him expectantly.

He kept smiling, to put them at their ease, and climbed into the box. The he gave them another wave.

One of the humans reached down gingerly and picked up the box, lifting it up in the air as though Masklin was something very rare and delicate. He was carried to the truck. The human got in and, still holding the box with exaggerated care, placed it on its knees. A radio crackled with deep human voices.

Well, no going back now. Knowing that, Masklin very nearly relaxed. Perhaps it was best to look at it as just another step along life's pavement.

They kept staring at him, as if they didn't believe what they were seeing.

The truck lurched off. After a while it turned on to a concrete road, where another truck was waiting. A human got out, spoke to the driver of Masklin's truck, laughed in a slow human way, looked down at Masklin and stopped laughing very suddenly.

It almost ran back to its own truck and started speaking into another telephone.

I knew this would happen, Masklin thought. They don't know what to do with a real nome. Amazing.

But just so long as they take me somewhere where there's the right kind of electricity . . .

Dorcas, the engineer, had once tried to explain electricity to Masklin, but without much success because Dorcas wasn't too certain about it either. There seemed to be two kinds, straight and wiggly. The straight kind was very boring and stayed in batteries. The wiggly kind was found in wires in the walls and things, and somehow the Thing could steal some of it if it was close enough. Dorcas used to talk about wiggly electricity in the same tone of voice Gurder used for talking about Arnold Bros (est. 1905). He'd tried to study it back in the Store. If it was put into freezers it made things cold, but if the same electricity went into an oven it made things hot, so how did it *know*?

Dorcas used to talk, Masklin thought. I said 'used to'. I hope he *still* does.

He felt light-headed and oddly optimistic. Part of him was saying: that's because if you for one second think seriously about the position you've put yourself in, you'll panic.

Keep smiling.

The truck purred along the road, with the other truck following it. Masklin saw a third truck rattle down a side road and pull in behind them. There were a lot of humans on it, and most of them were watching the skies.

They didn't stop at the nearest building, but drove on to a bigger one with many more vehicles outside. More humans were waiting for them.

One of them opened the truck door, doing it very slowly even for a human.

The human carrying Masklin got out of the truck.

Masklin looked up at dozens of staring faces. He could see every eyeball, every nostril. Every one of them looked worried. At least, every eyeball did. The nostrils just looked like nostrils.

They were worried about *him*.

Keep smiling.

He stared back up at them and, still almost giggling with repressed panic, said, 'Can I help you, gentlemen?'

9

SCIENCE: A way of finding things out and then making them work. Science explains what is happening around us the whole time. So does RELIGION, but science is better because it comes up with more understandable excuses when it's wrong. There is a lot more Science than you think.

From *A Scientific Encyclopedia for the Enquiring Young Nome*
by Angalo de Haberdasheri

Gurder, Angalo and Pion sat under a bush. It gave them a bit of shade. The cloud of gloom over them was almost as big.

'We'll never even get home without the Thing,' said Gurder.

'Then we'll get Masklin out,' said Angalo.

'That'll take for ever!'

'Yeah? Well, that's nearly as long as we've got here, if we can't get home.' Angalo had found a pebble that was almost the right shape to attach to a twig with strips torn off his coat; he'd never seen a stone axe in his life, but he had a definite feeling that there were useful things that could be done with a stone tied to the end of a stick.

'I wish you'd stop fiddling with that thing,' Gurder said. 'What's the big plan, then? Us against the whole of Floridia?'

'Not necessarily. You needn't come.'

'Calm down, Mr To-the-Rescue. One idiot's enough.'

'I don't hear you coming up with any better ideas.' Angalo swished the axe through the air once or twice.

'I haven't got any.'

A small red light started to flash on the Thing.

After a while, a small square hole opened up and there was a tiny whirring sound as the Thing extended a little lens on a stick. This turned around slowly.

Then the Thing spoke.

'*Where,*' it asked, '*is this place?*'

It tilted the lens up and there was a pause while it surveyed the face of the human looking down at it.

'*And why?*' it added.

'I'm not sure,' said Masklin. 'We're in a room in a big building. The humans haven't hurt me. I think one of them has been trying to talk to me.'

'*We appear to be in some sort of glass box,*' said the Thing.

'They even gave me a little bed,' said Masklin. 'And I think the thing over there is some kind of lavatory but, *look*, what about the Ship?'

'*I expect it is on its way,*' said the Thing calmly.

'Expect? *Expect?* You mean you don't know?'

'*Many things can go wrong. If they have gone right, the Ship will be here soon.*'

'If they don't, I'm stuck here for life!' said Masklin bitterly. 'I came here because of you, you know.'

'*Yes. I know. Thank you.*'

Masklin relaxed a bit.

'They're being quite kind,' he said. He thought about this. 'At least, I think so,' he added. 'It's hard to tell.'

He looked through the transparent wall. A lot of humans had been in to look at him in the last few minutes. He wasn't quite certain whether he was an honoured visitor or a prisoner or maybe something in between.

'It seemed the only hope at the time,' he said lamely.

'*I am monitoring communications.*'

'You're always doing that.'

'*A lot of them are about you. All kinds of experts are rushing here to have a look at you.*'

'What kind of experts? Experts in nomes?'

'*Experts in talking to creatures from other worlds. Humans haven't met anyone from another world but they've still got experts in talking to them.*'

'All this had better work,' said Masklin soberly. 'Humans really know about nomes now.'

'*But not what nomes are. They think you have just arrived.*'

'Well, that's true.'

'*Not arrived here. Arrived on the planet. Arrived from the stars.*'

'But we've been here for thousands of years! We *live* here!'

'*Humans find it a lot easier to really believe in little people from the sky than little people from the Earth. They would prefer to think of little green men than leprechauns.*'

Masklin's brow wrinkled. 'I didn't understand any of that,' he said.

'*Don't worry about it. It doesn't matter.*' The Thing let its lens swivel around to see more of the room.

'*Very nice. Very scientific,*' it said.

Then it focused on a wide plastic tray by Masklin.

'*What is that?*'

'Oh, fruit and nuts and meat and stuff,' said Masklin. 'I think they've been watching me to see what I eat. I think these are quite bright humans, Thing. I pointed to my mouth and they understood I was hungry.'

'*Ah,*' said the Thing. '*Take me to your larder.*'

'Pardon?'

'*I will explain. I have told you that I monitor communications?*'

'All the time.'

'*There is a joke. That is, a humorous anecdote or story, known to humans. It concerns a Ship from another world landing on this planet, and strange creatures get out and say to a petrol pump, dustbin, slot-machine or similar mechanical device, "Take me to your leader." I surmise this is because they are unaware of the shape of humans. I have substituted the similar word larder, referring to a place where food is stored. This is a humorous pun, or play on words for hilarious effect.*'

It paused.

'Oh,' said Masklin. He thought about it. 'These would be the little green men you mentioned?'

'*Very . . . wait a moment. Wait a moment.*'

'What? What?' said Masklin urgently.

'*I can hear the Ship.*'

Masklin listened as hard as he could.

'I can't hear a thing,' he said.

'*Not sound. Radio.*'

'Where is it? Where is it, Thing? You've always said the Ship's up there, but *where?*'

The remaining tree frogs crouched among the moss to escape the heat of the afternoon sun.

Low in the eastern sky was a sliver of white.

It would be nice to think that the tree frogs had legends about it. It would be nice to think that they thought the sun and moon were distant flowers — a yellow one by day, a white one by night. It would be nice to think they had legends about them, and said that when a good frog died its soul would go to be big flowers in the sky . . .

The trouble is that it's *frogs* we're talking about here. Their name for the sun was '.−.−mipmip.−.−.' Their name for the moon was '.−.−mipmip.−.−.' Their name for *everything* was '.–.–mipmip.–.–.', and when you're stuck with a vocabulary of one word, it's pretty hard to have legends about anything at all.

The leading frog, however, was dimly aware that there was something wrong with the moon.

It was growing brighter.

'We left the Ship on the *moon?*' said Masklin. 'Why?'

'*That's what your ancestors decided to do,*' said the Thing. '*So they could keep an eye on it, I assume.*'

Masklin's face lit up slowly, like clouds at sunrise.

'You know,' he said, excitedly, 'right back before all this, right back when we used to live in the old hole, I used to sit out at nights and watch the moon. Perhaps in my blood I really knew that up there – '

'*No, what you were experiencing was probably primitive superstition,*' said the Thing.

Masklin deflated. 'Oh. Sorry.'

'*And now, please be quiet. The Ship is feeling lost and wants to be told what to do. It has just woken up after fifteen thousand years.*'

'I'm not very good at mornings myself,' Masklin said.

There is no sound on the moon, but this doesn't matter because there is no one to hear anything. Sound would just be a waste.

But there is light.

Fine moondust billowed high across the ancient plains of the moon's dark crescent, expanding in boiling clouds that went high enough to catch the rays of the sun. They glittered.

Down below, something was digging itself out.

'We left it in a *hole?*' said Masklin.

Lights rippled back and forth across all the surfaces of the Thing.

'*Don't say that's why you always lived in holes,*' it said. '*Other nomes don't live in holes.*'

'No, that's true,' said Masklin. 'I ought to stop thinking only about the — '

He suddenly went quiet. He stared out of the glass tank, where a human was trying to interest him in marks on a blackboard.

'You've got to stop it,' he said. 'Right now. Stop the Ship. We've got it all wrong. Thing, we can't go! It doesn't belong to just us! We can't take the Ship!'

The three nomes lurking near the Shuttle launching place watched the sky. As the sun neared the horizon the moon sparkled like a Christmas decoration.

'It must be caused by the Ship!' said Angalo. 'It must be!' He beamed at the others. 'That's it, then. It's on its way!'

'I never thought it would work . . .' Gurder began.

Angalo slapped Pion on the back, and pointed.

'See that, my lad?' he said. 'That's the Ship, that is! Ours!'

Gurder rubbed his chin, and nodded thoughtfully at Pion.

'Yes,' he said, 'That's right. Ours.'

'Masklin says there's all kinds of stuff up there,' said Angalo dreamily. 'And masses of space. That's what space is well-known for, lots of space. Masklin said the Ship goes faster than light goes, which is probably wrong, otherwise how'd you see anything? You'd turn the lights on and all the light would drop backwards out of the room. But it's pretty fast — '

Gurder looked back at the sky again. Something at the back of his mind was pushing its way to the front and giving him a curious grey feeling.

'Our Ship,' he said. 'The one that brought nomes here.'

'Yeah, that's right,' said Angalo, hardly hearing him.

'And it'll take us all back,' Gurder went on.

'That's what Masklin said, and – '

'All nomes,' said Gurder. His voice was as flat and heavy as a sheet of lead.

'Sure. Why not? I expect I'll soon work out how to drive it back to the quarry, and we can pick them all up. And Pion here, of course.'

'What about Pion's people?' said Gurder.

'Oh, they can come too,' said Angalo expansively. 'There's probably even room for their geese!'

'And the others?'

Angalo looked surprised. 'What others?'

'Shrub said there were lots of other groups of nomes. Everywhere.'

Angalo looked blank. 'Oh, them. Well, I don't know about them. But we *need* the Ship. You know what it's been like ever since we left the Store.'

'But if we take the Ship away, what will *they* have if they need it?'

Masklin had just asked the same question.

The Thing said, '*0100110101010111010101010010 110101110010.*'

'What did you say?'

The Thing sounded tetchy. '*If I lose concentration, there might not be a Ship for anyone,*' it said. '*I am sending fifteen thousand instructions per second.*'

Masklin said nothing.

'*That's a lot of instructions,*' the Thing added.

'By rights the Ship must belong to all the nomes in the world,' said Masklin.

'*010011001010010010 . . .*'

'Oh, shut up and tell me when the Ship is going to get here.'

'*0101011001 . . . Which do you want me to do? . . . 01001100 . . .*'

'What?'

'*I can shut up OR I can tell you when the Ship is going to arrive. I can't do both.*'

'Please tell me when the Ship is going to arrive,' said Masklin patiently, 'and then shut up.'

'*Four minutes.*'

'Four minutes!'

'*I could be three seconds out,*' said the Thing. '*But I calculate it as four minutes. Only now it's three minutes thirty-eight seconds. It'll be three minutes and thirty-seven seconds any second now . . .*'

'I can't hang around in here if it's coming that soon!' said Masklin, all thoughts of his duty to the nomes of the world temporarily forgotten. 'How can I get out? This thing's got a lid on.'

'*Do you want me to shut up first, or get you out and then shut up?*' said the Thing.

'Please!'

'*Have the humans seen you move?*' said the Thing.

'What do you mean?'

'*Do they know how fast you can run?*'

'I don't know,' said Masklin. 'I suppose not.'

'*Get ready to run, then. But first, put your hands over your ears.*'

Masklin thought it would be best to obey. The Thing could be deliberately infuriating at times, but it didn't pay to ignore its advice.

Lights on the Thing made a brief star-shaped pattern.

It started to wail. The sound went up and then went beyond Masklin's hearing. He could feel it even with his hands over his ears; it seemed to be making unpleasant bubbles in his head.

He opened his mouth to shout at the Thing, and the walls exploded. One moment there was glass, and the next there were bits of glass, drifting out like a jigsaw puzzle where every piece had suddenly decided it wanted some personal space. The lid slid down, almost hitting him.

'*Now pick me up and run,*' ordered the Thing, before the shards had spilled across the table.

Humans around the room were turning to look in that slow, clumsy way humans had.

Masklin grabbed the Thing and took off across the polished surface.

'Down!' he said. 'We're high up, how do we get down?' He looked around desperately. There was some sort of machine at the other end of the table, covered with little dials and lights. He'd watched one of the humans using it.

'Wires,' he said. 'There's always wires!'

He skidded around, dodged easily around a giant hand as it tried to grab him, and hared along the table.

'I'll have to throw you over,' he panted. 'I can't carry you down!'

'*I'll be all right.*'

Masklin slid to a stop by the table edge and threw the Thing down. There *were* wires running down towards the floor. He leapt for one, swung around madly, and then half fell and half slid down it.

Humans were lurching towards him from everywhere. He picked up the Thing again, hugging it to his chest, and darted forwards. There was a foot — brown shoe, dark blue sock. He zigged. There were two more feet — black shoes, black socks. And they were about to trip over the first foot . . .

He zagged.

There were more feet, and hands reaching vainly down. Masklin was a blur, dodging and weaving between feet that could flatten him.

And then there was nothing but open floor.

Somewhere an alarm sounded, its shrill note sounding deep and awesome to Masklin.

'*Head for the door,*' suggested the Thing.

'But more humans'll be coming in,' hissed Masklin.

'*That's good, because we're going out.*'

Masklin reached the door just as it opened. A gap of a few inches appeared, with more feet behind it.

There wasn't any time to think. Masklin ran over the shoe, jumped down on the other side, and ran on.

'Where now? Where now?'

'*Outside.*'

'Which way is that?'

'*Every way.*'

'Thank you very much!'

Doors were opening all along the corridor. Humans were coming out. The problem was not evading capture — it would take a very alert human even to *see* a nome running at full speed, let alone catch one — but simply avoiding being trodden on by accident.

'Why don't they have mouseholes? Every building should have mouseholes!' Masklin moaned.

A boot stamped down an inch away. He jumped.

The corridor was filling with humans. Another alarm started to sound.

'Why's all this happening? I can't be causing all this? There can't be all this trouble over just one nome!'

'*It's the Ship. They have seen the Ship.*'

A shoe almost awarded Masklin the prize for the most perfectly flattened nome in Florida. As it was, he almost ran into it.

Unlike most shoes, it had a name on it. It was a Crucial Street Drifter with Real Rubber Soul, Pat'd. The sock above it looked as though it could be a Histyle Odourprufe, made of Guaranteed eighty-five per cent Polyputheketlon, the most expensive sock in the world.

Masklin looked further up. Beyond the great sweep of blue trouser and the distant clouds of sweater was a beard.

It was Grandson Richard, 39.

Just when you thought there was no one watching over nomes, the universe went and tried to prove you wrong . . .

Masklin took a standing jump and landed on the trouser leg, just as the foot moved. It was the safest place. Humans didn't often tread on other humans.

The foot took a step and came down again. Masklin swung backwards and forwards, trying to pull himself up the rough cloth. There was a seam an inch away. He managed to grab it; the stitches gave a better handhold.

Grandson Richard, 39, was in a crush of people all heading the same way. Several other humans banged into him, almost jarring Masklin loose. He kicked his boots off and tried to grip with his toes.

There was a slow thumping as Grandson Richard's feet hit the ground.

Masklin reached a pocket, got a decent foothold, and climbed on. A bulky label helped him up to the belt. Masklin was used to labels in the Store, but this was pretty big even by big label standards. It was covered in lettering and had been riveted to the trousers, as if Grandson Richard was some sort of machine.

' "Grossbergers Hagglers, the First Name in Jeans," ' he read. 'And there's lots of stuff about how good they are, and pictures of cows and things. Why d'you think he wants labels all over him?'

'Perhaps if he hasn't got labels, he doesn't know what his clothes are,' said the Thing.

'Good point. He'd probably put his shoes on his head.'

Masklin glanced back at the label as he grabbed the sweater.

'It says here that these jeans won a gold medal in the Chicago Exhibition in 1910,' he said. 'They've certainly lasted well.'

Humans were streaming out of the building.

The sweater was much easier to climb. Masklin hauled himself up quickly. Grandson Richard had quite long hair, which also helped when it was time to climb up on to the shoulder.

A doorframe passed briefly overhead, and then the deep blue of the sky.

'How long, Thing?' Masklin hissed. Grandson Richard's ear was only a few inches away.

'*Forty-three seconds.*'

The humans spilled out on to the wide concrete space in front of the building. Some more hurried out of the building, carrying machinery. They kept running into one another because they were all staring at the sky.

Another group was clustered around one human, who was looking very worried.

'What's going on, Thing?' Masklin whispered.

'*The human in the middle of the group is the most important one here. It came to watch the Shuttle launch. Now all the others are telling it that it's got to be the one to welcome the Ship.*'

'That's a bit of a cheek. It's not *their* Ship.'

'*Yes, but they think it's coming to talk to them.*'

'Why should they think that?'

'*Because they think they're the most important creatures on the planet.*'

'Hah!'

'*Amazing, isn't it?*' said the Thing.

'Everyone knows nomes are more important,' said Masklin. 'At least . . . every nome does.' He thought about this for a moment, and shook his head. 'So that's the head human, is it? Is it some sort of extra-wise one, or something.'

'*I don't think so. The other humans around it are trying to explain to it what a planet is.*'

'Doesn't it know?'

'*Many humans don't. Mistervicepresident is one of them. 001010011000.*'

'You're talking to the Ship again?'

'*Yes. Six seconds.*'

'It's really coming . . .'

'*Yes.*'

10

GRAVITY: This is not properly understood, but it is what makes small things, like nomes, stick to big things, like planets. Because of SCIENCE, this happens whether you know about gravity or not. Which goes to show that Science is happening all the time.

From *A Scientific Encyclopedia for the Enquiring Young Nome*
by Angalo de Haberdasheri

Angalo looked around.

'Gurder, come *on*.'

Gurder leaned against a tuft of grass and fought to get his breath back.

'It's no good,' he wheezed. 'What are you thinking of? We can't fight humans alone!'

'We've got Pion. And this is a pretty good axe.'

'Oh, that's really going to scare them. A stone axe. If you had two axes I expect they'd give in right away.'

Angalo swung it backwards and forwards. It had a comforting feel.

'You've got to try,' he said simply. 'Come on, Pion. What are you watching? Geese?'

Pion was staring at the sky.

'There's a dot up there,' said Gurder, squinting.

'It's probably a bird,' said Angalo.

'Doesn't look like a bird.'

'Then it's a plane.'

'Doesn't look like a plane.'

Now all three of them were staring upwards, their upturned faces forming a triangle.

There was a black dot up there.

'You don't think he actually *managed* it, do you?' said Angalo, uncertainly.

What had been a dot was now a small dark circle.

'It's not moving, though,' said Gurder.

'It's not moving sideways, anyway,' said Angalo, still speaking very slowly. 'It's moving more sort of down.'

What had been a small dark circle was a larger dark circle, with just a suspicion of smoke or steam around its edges.

'It might be some sort of weather,' said Angalo. 'You know. Special Floridian weather?'

'Oh, yeah? One great big hailstone, right? It's the Ship! Coming for us!'

It was a lot bigger now and yet, and yet . . . still a very long way off.

'If it could come for us just a little way away I wouldn't mind,' Gurder quavered. 'I wouldn't mind walking a little way.'

'Yeah,' said Angalo, beginning to look desperate. 'It's not so much *coming* as, as . . .'

'. . . *dropping*,' said Gurder.

He looked at Angalo.

'Shall we run?' he said.

'It's got to be worth a try,' said Angalo.

'Where shall we run to?'

'Let's just follow Pion, shall we? He started running a while ago.'

Masklin would be the first to admit that he wasn't too familiar with forms of transport, but what they all seemed to have in common was a front, which was in front, and a back, which wasn't. The whole point was that the front was where they went forward from.

The thing dropping out of the sky was a disc — just a top connected to a bottom, with edges round the sides. It didn't make any noise, but it seemed to be impressing the humans no end.

'That's it?' he said.

'*Yes.*'

'Oh.'

And then things seemed to come into focus.

The Ship wasn't big. It needed a new word. It wasn't *dropping* through the thin wisps of cloud up there, it was simply pushing them aside. Just when you thought you'd got some idea of the size, a cloud would stream past and the perspective would wind back. There had to be a special word for something as big as that.

'Is it going to crash?' he whispered.

'*I shall land it on the scrub,*' said the Thing. '*I don't want to frighten the humans.*'

'Run!'

'What do you think I'm doing?'

'It's still right above us!'

'I'm running! I'm running! I can't run any faster!'

A shadow fell across the three running nomes.

'All the way to Floridia to be squashed under our own Ship,' moaned Angalo. 'You never really believed in it, did you? Well, now you're going to believe in it really hard!'

The shadow deepened. They could see it racing across the ground ahead of them — grey around the edges, spreading into the darkness of night. Their own, private night.

'The others are still out there somewhere,' said Masklin.

'*Ah,*' said the Thing. '*I forgot.*'

'You're not supposed to forget things like that!'

'*I've been very busy lately. I can't think of everything. Just nearly everything.*'

'Well don't squash anyone!'

'*I shall stop it before it lands. Don't worry.*'

The humans were all talking at once. Some of them had started to run towards the falling Ship. Some were running away from it.

Masklin risked a glance at Grandson Richard's face. It was watching the Ship with a strange, rapt expression.

As Masklin stared, the big eyes swivelled slowly sideways. The head turned around. Grandson Richard stared down at the nome on his shoulder.

For the second time, the human saw him. And this time, there was nowhere to run.

Masklin rapped the Thing on its lid.

'Can you slow my voice down?' he said quickly. An amazed expression was forming on the human's face.

'*What do you mean?*'

'I mean you just repeat what I say, but slowed down. And louder. So it – so he can understand it?'

'*You want to communicate? With a human?*'

'Yes! Can you do it?'

'*I strongly advise against it! It could be very dangerous!*'

Masklin clenched his fists. 'Compared to what, Thing? Compared to what? How much more dangerous than *not* communicating, Thing? Do it! Right now! Tell him . . . tell him we're not trying to hurt any humans! Right now! I can see his hand moving already! Do it!' He held the box right up to Grandson Richard's ear.

The Thing started to speak in the low, slow tones of human speech.

It seemed to go on for a long time.

The human's expression froze.

'What did you say? What did you say?' said Masklin.

'I said, if he harms you in any way I shall explode and blow his head off,' said the Thing.

'You didn't!'

'I did.'

'You call that communicating?'

'Yes. I call it very effective communicating.'

'But it's a dreadful thing to say! Anyway . . . you never told me you could explode!'

'I can't. But it doesn't know that. It's only human,' said the Thing.

The Ship slowed its fall and drifted down across the scrublands until it met its own shadow. Beside it, the tower where the Shuttle had been launched looked like a pin alongside a very large black plate.

'You landed it on the ground! You said you wouldn't!' said Masklin.

'It's not on the ground. It is floating just above the ground.'

'It looks as though it's on the ground to me!'

'It is floating just above it,' repeated the Thing patiently.

Grandson Richard was looking at Masklin down the length of his nose. He looked puzzled.

'What makes it float?' Masklin demanded.

The Thing told him.

'Auntie who? Who's she? There's relatives on board?'

'Not Auntie. Anti. Anti-gravity.'

'But there's no flames or smoke!'

'Flames and smoke are not essential.'

Vehicles were screaming towards the bulk of the Ship.

'Um. Exactly *how* far off the ground did you stop it?' Masklin enquired.

'Four inches seemed adequate – '

Angalo lay with his face pressed into the sandy soil.

To his amazement, he was still alive. Or at least, if he was dead, then he was still able to think. Perhaps he *was* dead, and this was wherever you went afterwards.

It seemed pretty much like where he'd been before.

Let's see, now. He'd looked up at the great thing dropping out of the sky right towards his head, and had flung himself down, expecting at any second to become just a little greasy mark in a great big hole.

No, he probably hadn't died. He'd have remembered something important like that.

'Gurder?' he ventured.

'Is that you?' said Gurder's voice.

'I hope so. Pion?'

'Pion!' said Pion, somewhere in the darkness.

Angalo pushed himself up on to his hands and knees.

'Any idea where we are?' he said.

'In the Ship?' suggested Gurder.

'Don't think so,' said Angalo. 'There's soil here, and grass and stuff.'

'Then where did the Ship go? Why's it all dark?'

Angalo brushed the dirt off his coat. 'Dunno. Maybe . . . maybe it missed us. Maybe we were knocked out, and now it's night-time?'

'I can see a bit of light around the horizon,' said Gurder. 'That's not right, is it? That's not how nights are supposed to be.'

Angalo looked around. There *was* a line of light in the distance. And there was also a strange sound, so quiet that you could miss it but which, once you had noticed it, also seemed to fill up the world.

He stood up to get a better view.

There was a faint thump.

'Ouch!'

Angalo reached up to rub his head. His hand touched metal. Crouching a little, he risked turning his head to see what it was he'd hit.

He went very thoughtful for a while.

Then he said, 'Gurder, you're going to find this amazingly hard to believe . . .'

* * *

'*This* time,' said Masklin to the Thing, 'I want you to translate *exactly*, do you understand? Don't try to frighten him!'

Humans had surrounded the Ship. At least, they were trying to surround it, but you'd need an awful lot of humans to surround something the size of the Ship. So they were just surrounding it in places.

More trucks were arriving, many of them with sirens blaring. Grandson Richard had been left standing by himself, watching his own shoulder nervously.

'Besides, we owe him something,' said Masklin. 'We used his satellite. And we stole things.'

'*You said you wanted to do it your way. No help from humans, you said,*' said the Thing.

'It's different now. There is the Ship,' said Masklin. 'We've made it. We're not begging any more.'

'*May I point out that you're sitting on his shoulder, not him on yours,*' said the Thing.

'Never mind that,' said Masklin. 'Tell it – I mean, ask him to walk towards the Ship. And say please. And say that we don't want anyone to get hurt. Including me,' he added.

Grandson Richard's reply seemed to take a long time. But he did start to walk towards the crowds around the Ship.

'What did he say?' said Masklin, hanging on tightly to the sweater.

'*I don't believe it,*' said the Thing.

'He doesn't believe me?'

'*He said: his grandfather always talked about the little people, but he never believed it until now. He said: are you like the ones in the old Store?*'

Masklin's mouth dropped open. Grandson Richard was watching him intently.

'Tell him yes,' Masklin croaked.

'*Very well. But I do not think it'll be a good idea.*'

The Thing boomed. Grandson Richard rumbled a reply.

'He says his grandfather made jokes about little people in the Store,' said the Thing. 'He used to say they brought him luck.'

Masklin felt the horrible sensation in his stomach that meant the world was changing again, just when he thought he understood it.

'Did his grandfather ever see a nome?' he said.

'He says no. But he says that when his grandfather and his grandfather's brother were starting the Store and stayed late every night to do the office work, they used to hear sounds in the walls and they used to tell each other there were little Store people. It was a sort of joke. He says that when he was small, his grandfather used to tell him about little people who came out at night to play with the toys.'

'But the Store nomes never did things like that!' said Masklin.

'I didn't say the stories were true.'

The Ship was a lot closer now. There didn't seem to be any doors or windows anywhere. It was as featureless as an egg.

Masklin's mind was in turmoil. He'd always believed that humans were quite intelligent. After all, nomes were very intelligent. Rats were quite intelligent. And foxes were intelligent, more or less. There ought to be enough intelligence sloshing around in the world for humans to have some too. But this was something more than intelligence.

He remembered the book called *Gulliver's Travels*. It had been a big surprise to the nomes. There had never been an island of small people. He was certain of that. It was a, a, a made-up thing. There had been lots of books in the Store that were like that. They'd caused no end of problems for the nomes. For some reason, humans needed things that weren't true.

They never really thought nomes existed, he thought, but they wanted to believe that we did.

'Tell him,' he said, 'tell him I must get into the Ship.'

Grandson Richard whispered. It was like listening to a gale.

'He says there are too many people.'

'Why are all the humans around it?' said Masklin, bewildered. 'Why aren't they frightened?'

Grandson Richard's reply was another gale.

'He says, they think some creatures from another world will come out and talk to them.'

'Why?'

'I don't know,' said the Thing. *'Perhaps they don't want to be alone.'*

'But there's no one in it! It's *our* Ship — ' Masklin began.

There was a wail. The crowd put their hands over their ears.

Lights appeared on the darkness of the Ship. They twinkled all over the hull in patterns which raced backwards and forwards and disappeared. There was another wail.

'There *isn't* anyone in it, is there?' said Masklin. 'No nomes were left on it in hibernation or anything?'

High up on the ship a square hole opened. There was a whiffling noise and a beam of red light shot out and set fire to a patch of scrub several hundred yards away.

People started to run.

The Ship rose a few feet, wobbling alarmingly. It drifted sideways a little. Then it went straight up so fast that it was just a blur and jerked to a halt high over the crowd. And then it turned over. And then it went on its edge for a while.

It floated back down again and landed, more or less. That is, one side touched the ground and the other rested on the air, on nothing.

The Ship spoke, loudly.

To the humans it must have sounded like a high-pitched chattering.

What it actually said was: 'Sorry! Sorry! Is this a microphone? Can't find the button that opens the door . . . let's try this one . . .'

Another square hole opened. Brilliant blue light flooded out.

The voice boomed out across the country again.

'Got it!' There was the distorted thud-thud of someone who isn't certain if their microphone is working and who is tapping it experimentally. 'Masklin, are you out there?'

'That's Angalo!' said Masklin. 'No one else drives like that! Thing, tell Grandson Richard I must get on the Ship! Please!'

The human nodded.

Humans were milling around the base of the Ship. The doorway was too high up for them to reach.

With Masklin hanging on grimly, Grandson Richard pushed his way through the throng.

The Ship wailed again.

'Er,' came Angalo's hugely amplified voice, apparently talking to someone else. 'I'm not sure about this switch, but maybe it's . . . Certainly I'm going to press it, why shouldn't I press it? It's next to the door one, it must be safe. Look, shut up . . .'

A silver ramp wound out of the doorway. It looked big enough for humans.

'See? See?' said Angalo's voice.

'Thing, can you speak to Angalo?' said Masklin. 'Tell him I'm out here, trying to get to the Ship?'

'No. *He appears to be randomly pressing buttons. It is to be hoped that he does not press the wrong ones.*'

'I thought you could tell the Ship what to do!' said Masklin.

The Thing managed to sound shocked. '*Not when a nome is in it,*' it said. '*I can't tell it not to do what a nome tells it to do. That's what being a machine is all about.*'

Grandson Richard was shoving his way through the pushing, shouting mass of humans, but it was hard going.

Masklin sighed.

'Ask Grandson Richard to put me down,' he said. Then he added, 'And say thank you. Say it . . . it would have been nice to talk more.'

The Thing did the translation.

Grandson Richard looked surprised. The Thing spoke again. Then he reached up a hand towards Masklin.

If he had to make that list of horrible moments, Masklin would have put this one at the top. He'd faced foxes, he'd helped to drive the Truck, he'd flown on a goose — but none of them was half so bad as letting a human being actually touch him. The huge whorled fingers uncurled and passed on either side of his waist. He shut his eyes.

Angalo's booming voice said, 'Masklin? Masklin? If anything bad's happened to you, there's going to be *trouble*.'

Grandson Richard's fingers gripped Masklin lightly, as though the human was holding something very fragile. Masklin felt himself being slowly lowered towards the ground. He opened his eyes. There was a forest of human legs around him.

He looked up into Grandson's Richard's huge face and, trying to make his voice as deep and slow as possible, said the only word any nome had said directly to a human in five thousand years.

'Goodbye.'

Then he ran through the maze of feet.

Several humans with official-looking trousers and big boots were standing at the bottom of the ramp. Masklin scurried between them and ran on upwards.

Ahead of him blue light shone out of the open hatchway. As he ran he saw two dots appear on the lip of the entrance.

The ramp was long. Masklin hadn't slept for hours. He wished he'd got some sleep on the bed when the humans were studying him; it had looked quite comfortable.

Suddenly, all his legs wanted to do was go somewhere close and lie down.

He staggered to the top of the ramp and the dots became the heads of Gurder and Pion. They reached out and pulled him into the Ship.

He turned around and looked down into a sea of human faces, below him. He'd never looked down on a human before.

They probably couldn't even see him. They're waiting for the little green men, he thought.

'Are you all right?' said Gurder urgently. 'Did they do anything to you?'

'I'm fine, I'm fine,' murmured Masklin. 'No one hurt me.'

'You look dreadful.'

'We should have talked to them, Gurder,' said Masklin. 'They *need* us.'

'Are you *sure* you're all right?' said Gurder, peering anxiously at him.

Masklin's head felt full of cotton wool. 'You know you believed in Arnold Bros (est. 1905)?' he managed to say.

'Yes,' said Gurder.

Masklin gave him a mad, triumphant grin.

'Well, he believed in you, too! How about that?'

And Masklin folded up, very gently.

11

> THE SHIP: The machine used by nomes to leave Earth.
> We don't yet know everything about it but, since it was
> built by nomes using SCIENCE, we will.
>
> From *A Scientific Encyclopedia for the Enquiring Young Nome*
> by Angalo de Haberdasheri

The ramp wound in. The doorway shut. The Ship rose
in the air until it was high above the buildings.

And it stayed there, while the sun set.

The humans below tried shining coloured lights at it,
and playing tunes at it, and eventually just speaking to
it in every language known to humans.

It didn't seem to take any notice.

Masklin woke up.

He was on a very uncomfortable bed. It was all soft.
He hated lying on anything softer than the ground. The
Store nomes liked sleeping on fancy bits of carpet, but
Masklin's bed had been a bit of wood. He'd used a piece
of rag for a cover and thought that was luxury.

He sat up and looked around the room. It was fairly
empty. There was just the bed, a table, and a chair.

A table and a chair.

In the Store, the nomes had made their furniture out
of matchboxes and cotton reels; the nomes living Outside
didn't even know what furniture *was*.

This looked rather like human furniture, but it was nome-sized.

Masklin got up and padded across the metal floor to the door. Nome-sized, again. A doorway made by nomes for nomes to walk through.

It led into a corridor, lined with doors. There was an old feel about it. It wasn't dirty or dusty. It just felt like somewhere that had been absolutely clean for a very, very long time.

Something purred towards him. It was a small black box, rather like the Thing, mounted on little treads. A small revolving brush on the front was sweeping dust into a slot. At least, if there had been any dust it would have been sweeping it. Masklin wondered how many times it had industriously cleaned this corridor, while it waited for nomes to come back . . .

It bumped into his foot, beeped at him, and then bustled off in the opposite direction. Masklin followed it.

After a while he passed another one. It was moving along the ceiling with a faint clicking noise, cleaning it.

He turned the corner, and almost walked into Gurder. 'You're up!'

'Yes,' said Masklin. 'Er. We're on the Ship, right?'

'It's amazing —!' Gurder began. He looked wild-eyed, and his hair was sticking up at all angles.

'I'm sure it is,' said Masklin reassuringly.

'But there's all these . . . and there's great big . . . and there's these *huge* . . . and you'd never believe how wide . . . and there's so much . . .' Gurder's voice trailed off. He looked like a nome who would have to learn new words before he could describe things.

'It's too big!' he blurted out. He grabbed Masklin's arm. 'Come on,' he said, and half ran along the corridor.

'How did you get on?' said Masklin, trying to keep up.

'It was amazing! Angalo touched this panel thing and it just moved aside and then we were inside and there was an elevator thing and then we were in this great big room with a seat and Angalo sat down and all these lights came on and he started pressing buttons and moving things!'

'Didn't you try to stop him?'

Gurder rolled his eyes. 'You know Angalo and machines,' he said. 'But the Thing is trying to get him to be sensible. Otherwise we'd be crashing into stars by now,' he added gloomily.

He led the way through another arch into –

Well, it had to be a room. It was inside the Ship. It was just as well he knew that, Masklin thought, because otherwise he'd think it was Outside. It stretched away, as big as one of the departments in the Store.

Vast screens and complicated-looking panels covered the walls. Most of them were dark. Shadowy gloom stretched away in every direction, except for a little puddle of light in the very centre of the room.

It illuminated Angalo, almost lost in a big padded chair. He had the Thing in front of him, on a sloping metal board studded with switches. He had obviously been arguing with it – when Masklin walked up he glared at him and said, 'It won't do what I tell it!'

The Thing looked as small and black and square as it could.

'He wants to drive the Ship,' it said.

'You're a machine! You *have* to do what you're told!' snapped Angalo.

'I'm an intelligent *machine, and I don't want to end up very flat at the bottom of a deep hole,'* said the Thing. *'You can't pilot the Ship yet.'*

'How do you know? You won't let me try! I drove the Truck, didn't I? It wasn't my fault all those trees and street lights and things got in the way,' he added, after catching Masklin's eye.

'I expect the Ship is more difficult,' said Masklin diplomatically.

'But I'm learning about it all the time,' said Angalo. 'It's easy. All the buttons have got little pictures on them. Look . . .'

He pressed a button.

One of the big screens lit up, showing the crowds outside the ship.

'They've been waiting there for ages,' said Gurder.

'What do they want?' said Angalo.

'Search me,' said Gurder. 'Who knows what humans want?'

Masklin stared at the throng below the Ship.

'They've been trying all sorts of stuff,' said Angalo. 'Flashing lights and music and stuff like that. And radio too, the Thing says.'

'Haven't you tried talking back to them?' said Masklin.

'No. Haven't got anything to say,' said Angalo. He rapped on the Thing with his knuckles. 'Right, Mr Clever — if I'm not going to do the driving, who is?'

'*Me.*'

'How?'

'*There is a slot by the seat.*'

'I see it. It's the same size as you.'

'*Put me in it.*'

Angalo shrugged, and picked up the Thing. It slid smoothly into the floor until only the top of it was showing.

'Look, er,' said Angalo, 'can't I do something? Operate the windscreen wipers or something? I'd feel a twerp sitting here doing nothing.'

The Thing didn't seem to hear him. Its light flickered on and off for a moment, as if it was making itself comfortable in a mechanical kind of way. Then it said, in a much deeper voice than it had ever used before: *'RIGHT.'*

Lights came on all over the Ship. They spread out from the Thing like a tide; panels lit up like little skies full of stars, big lights in the ceiling flickered on, there was a distant banging and fizzing as electricity was woken up, and the air began to smell of thunderstorms.

'It's like the Store at Christmas Fayre,' said Gurder.

'ALL SYSTEMS IN WORKING ORDER,' boomed the Thing. *'NAME OUR DESTINATION.'*

'What?' said Masklin. 'And don't shout.'

'Where are we going?' said the Thing. *'You have to name our destination.'*

'It's got a name already. It's called the quarry, isn't it?' said Masklin.

'Where is it?' said the Thing.

'It's — ' Masklin waved an arm vaguely. 'Well, it's over that way somewhere.'

'Which way?'

'How should I know? How many ways are there?'

'Thing, are you telling us you don't know the way back to the quarry?' said Gurder.

'That is correct.'

'We're lost?'

'No. I know exactly what planet we're on,' said the Thing.

'We can't be lost,' said Gurder. 'We're here. We know where we are. We just don't know where we aren't.'

'Can't you find the quarry if you go up high enough?' said Angalo. 'You ought to be able to see it, if you go up high enough.'

'Very well.'

'Can I do it?' said Angalo. 'Please?'

'Press down with your left foot and pull back on the green lever, then,' said the Thing.

There wasn't so much a noise as a change in the type

of silence. Masklin thought he felt heavy for a moment, but then the sensation passed.

The picture in the screen got smaller.

'Now, this is what I call proper flying,' said Angalo, happily. 'No noise and none of that stupid flapping.'

'Yes, where's Pion?' said Masklin.

'He wandered off,' said Gurder. 'I think he was going to get something to eat.'

'On a machine that no nome has been on for fifteen thousand years?' said Masklin.

Gurder shrugged. 'Well, maybe there's something at the back of a cupboard somewhere,' he said. 'I want a word with you, Masklin?'

'Yes?'

Gurder moved closer and glanced over his shoulder at Angalo, who was lying back in the control seat with a look of dreamy contentment on his face.

He lowered his voice.

'We shouldn't be doing this,' he said. 'I know it's a dreadful thing to say, after all we've been through. But this isn't just *our* Ship. It belongs to all nomes, everywhere.'

He looked relieved when Masklin nodded.

'A year ago you didn't even believe there *were* any other nomes anywhere,' Masklin said.

Gurder looked sheepish. 'Yes. Well. That was then. This is now. I don't know what I believe in any more, except that there must be thousands of nomes out there we don't know about. There might even be other nomes living in Stores! We're just the lucky ones who had the Thing. So if we take the Ship away, there won't be any hope for them.'

'I know, I know,' said Masklin wretchedly. 'But what can we do? *We* need the Ship right now. Anyway, how could we find these other nomes?'

'We've got the Ship!' said Gurder.

Masklin waved a hand at the screen, where the land-scape was spreading out and becoming misty.

'It'd take for ever to find nomes down there. You couldn't do it even with the Ship. You'd have to be on the ground. Nomes keep hidden! You nomes in the Store didn't know about my people, and we lived a few miles away. We'd never have found Pion's people except by accident. Besides – ' he couldn't resist prodding Gurder gently, ' – there's a bigger problem, too. You know what we nomes are like. Those other nomes probably wouldn't even *believe* in the Ship.'

He was immediately sorry he'd said that. Gurder looked more unhappy than he'd ever seen him.

'That's true,' the Abbot said. 'I wouldn't have believed it. I'm not sure I believe it now, and I'm *on* it.'

'Maybe, when we've found somewhere to live, we can send the Ship back and collect any other nomes we can find,' Masklin hazarded. 'I'm sure Angalo would enjoy that.'

Gurder's shoulders began to shake. For a moment Masklin thought the nome was laughing, and then he saw the tears rolling down the Abbot's face.

'Um,' he said, not knowing what else to say.

Gurder turned away. 'I'm sorry,' he muttered. 'It's just that there's so much . . . changing. Why can't things stay the same for five minutes? Every time I get the hang of an idea it suddenly turns into something different and *I* turn into a fool! All I want is something real to believe in! Where's the harm in that?'

'I think you just have to have a flexible mind,' said Masklin, knowing even as he said the words that this probably wasn't going to be a lot of help.

'Flexible? Flexible? My mind's got so flexible I could pull it out of my ears and tie it under my chin!' snapped Gurder. 'And it hasn't done me a whole lot of good, let me tell you! I'd have done better just believing everything I was taught when I was young! At least I'd only have been wrong once! This way I'm wrong all the time!'

He stamped away down one of the corridors.

Masklin watched him go. Not for the first time he wished he believed in something as much as Gurder did so he could complain to it about his life. He wished he was back — yes, even back in the hole. It hadn't been too bad, apart from people being cold and wet and getting eaten all the time. But at least he had been with Grimma. They would have been cold and wet and hungry together. He wouldn't have been so lonely . . .

There was a movement by him. It turned out to be Pion, holding a tray of what had to be . . . fruit, Masklin decided. He put aside being lonely for a moment, and realized that hunger had been waiting for an opportunity to make itself felt. He'd never seen fruit that shape and colour.

He took a slice from the proffered tray. It tasted like a nutty lemon.

'It's kept well, considering,' he said, weakly. 'Where did you get it?'

It turned out to have come from a machine in a nearby corridor. It looked fairly simple. There were hundreds of pictures of different sorts of food. If you touched a picture, there was a brief humming noise and then the food dropped on to a tray in a slot. Masklin tried pictures at random and got several different sorts of fruit, a squeaky green vegetable thing, and a piece of meat that tasted rather like smoked salmon.

'I wonder how it does it?' he said aloud.

A voice from the wall beside him said: *'Would you understand if I told you about molecular breakdown and reassembly from a wide range of raw materials?'*

'No,' said Masklin, truthfully.

'Then it's all done by Science.'

'Oh. Well, that's all right, then. That *is* you, Thing, isn't it?'

'*Yes.*'

Chewing on the fish-meat, Masklin wandered back to the control-room and offered some of the food to Angalo. The big screen was showing nothing but clouds.

'Won't see any quarry in all this,' he said.

Angalo pulled one of the levers back a bit. There was that brief feeling of extra weight again.

They stared at the screen.

'Wow,' said Angalo.

'That looks familiar,' said Masklin. He patted his clothes until he found the folded, crumpled map they'd brought all the way from the Store.

He spread it out, and glanced from it to the screen.

The screen showed a disc, made up mainly of different shades of blue and wispy bits of cloud.

'Any idea what it is?' said Angalo.

'No, but I know what some of the bits are called,' said Masklin. 'That one that's thick at the top and thin at the bottom is called South America. Look, it's just like it is on the map. Only it should have the words "South America" written on it.'

'Still can't see the quarry, though,' said Angalo.

Masklin looked at the image in front of them. South America. Grimma had talked about South America, hadn't she? That's where the frogs lived in flowers. She'd said that once you knew about things like frogs living in flowers, you weren't the same person.

He was beginning to see what she meant.

'Never mind about the quarry for now,' he said. 'The quarry can wait.'

'*We should get there as soon as possible, for everybody's sake,*' said the Thing.

Masklin thought about this for a while. It was true, he had to admit. All kinds of things might be happening back home. He had to get the Ship back quickly, for everybody's sake.

And then he thought: I've spent a long time doing things for everybody's sake. Just for once, I'm going to do something for me. I don't think we can find other nomes with this Ship, but at least I know where to look for frogs.

'Thing,' he said, 'take us to South America. And don't argue.'

12

FROGS: Some people think that knowing about frogs is important. They are small and green, or yellow, and have four legs. They croak. Young frogs are tadpoles. In my opinion, this is all there is to know about frogs.

From *A Scientific Encyclopedia for the Enquiring Young Nome*
by Angalo de Haberdasheri

Find a blue planet . . .
Focus
This is a planet. Most of it is covered in water but it's still called Earth.
Find a country . . .
Focus
. . . blues and greens and browns under the sun, and long wisps of raincloud being torn by the mountains . . .
Focus
. . . on a mountain, green and dripping, and there's a . . .
Focus
. . . tree, hung with moss and covered with flowers and . . .
Focus
. . . on a flower with a little pool in it. It's an epiphytic bromeliad.
Its leaves, although they might be petals, hardly

quiver at all as three very small and very golden frogs pull themselves up and gaze in astonishment at the fresh clear water. Two of them look at their leader, waiting for it to say something suitable for this historic occasion.

It's going to be '.—.—.mipmip.—.—.'

And then they slide down the leaf and into the water.

Although the frogs can spot the difference between day and night, they're a bit hazy on the whole idea of Time. They know that some things happen after other things. Really intelligent frogs might wonder if there is something which prevents everything happening all at once, but that's about as close as they can get to it.

So how long it was before a strange night came in the middle of the day is hard to tell, from a frog's point of view . . .

A wide black shadow drifted over the treetops, and came to a halt. After a while there were voices. The frogs could hear them although they didn't know what they meant or even what they were. They didn't sound like the kind of voices frogs were used to.

What they heard went like this: 'How many mountains are there, anyway? I mean, it's ridiculous! Who needs this many mountains? I call it inefficient. One would have done. I'll go mad if I see another mountain. How many more have we got to search?'

'I like them.'

'And some of the trees are the wrong height.'

'I like them too, Gurder.'

'And I don't trust Angalo doing the driving.'

'I think he's getting better, Gurder.'

'Well, I just hope no more aeroplanes come flying around, that's all.'

Gurder and Masklin swung in a crude basket made out of bits of metal and wire. It hung from a square hatchway under the Ship.

There were still huge rooms in the Ship that they

hadn't explored yet. Odd machines were everywhere. The Thing had said the Ship had been used for exploring.

Masklin hadn't quite trusted any of it. There were probably machines that could have lowered and pulled up the basket easily, but he'd preferred to loop the wire around a pillar inside the Ship and, with Pion helping inside, to pull themselves up and down by sheer nomish effort.

The basket bumped gently on the tree branch.

The trouble was that humans wouldn't leave them alone. No sooner had they found a likely-looking mountain than aeroplanes or helicopters would buzz around, like insects around an eagle. It was distracting.

Masklin looked along the branch. Gurder was right. This would have to be the last mountain.

But there were certainly flowers here.

He crawled along the branch until he reached the nearest flower. It was three times as high as he was. He found a foothold and pulled himself up.

There was a pool in there. Six little yellow eyes peered up at him.

Masklin stared back.

So it was true, after all . . .

He wondered if there was anything he should say to them, if there was anything they could possibly understand.

It was quite a long branch, and quite thick. But there were tools and things in the Ship. They could let down extra wires to hold the branch and winch it up when it was cut free. It would take some time, but that didn't matter. It was important.

The Thing had said there were ways of growing plants under lights the same colour as the sun, in pots full of a sort of weak soup that helped plants grow. It should be the easiest thing to keep a branch alive. The easiest thing in . . . the world.

If they did everything carefully and gently, the frogs would never know.

If the world was a bathtub, the progress of the Ship through it would be like the soap, shooting backwards and forwards and never being where anyone was expecting it to be. You could spot where it had just been by aeroplanes and helicopters taking off in a hurry.

Or maybe it was like the ball in a roulette wheel, bouncing around and looking for the right number . . .

Or maybe it was just lost.

They searched all night. If there *was* a night. It was hard to tell. The Thing tried to explain that the Ship went faster than the sun, although the sun actually stood still. Some parts of the world had night while other parts had day. This, Gurder said, was bad organization.

'In the Store,' he said, 'it was always dark when it should be. Even if it *was* just somewhere built by humans,' It was the first time they'd heard him admit the Store was built by humans.

There didn't seem to be anywhere familiar.

Masklin scratched his chin.

'The Store was in a place called Blackbury,' he said. 'I know that much. So the quarry couldn't have been far away.'

Angalo waved his hand irritably at the screens.

'Yes, but it's not like the map,' he said. 'They don't stick names on places! It's ridiculous! How's anyone supposed to know where anywhere is?'

'All right,' said Masklin. 'But you're *not* to fly down low again to try to read the signposts. Every time you do that, humans rush into the streets and we get lots of shouting on the radio.'

'*That's right,*' said the Thing. '*People are bound to get excited when they see a ten-million-ton starship trying to fly down the street.'*

'I was very careful last time,' said Angalo stoutly. 'I even stopped when the traffic lights went red. I don't see why there was such a fuss. All the trucks and cars started crashing into one another, too. And you call *me* a bad driver.'

Gurder turned to Pion, who was learning the language fast. The geese nomes had a knack for that. They were used to meeting nomes who spoke other languages.

'Your geese never got lost,' he said. 'How did they manage it?'

'They just did not get lost,' said Pion. 'They knew always where they going.'

'It can be like that with animals,' said Masklin. 'They've got instincts. It's like knowing things without knowing you know them.'

'Why doesn't the Thing know where to go?' said Gurder. 'It could find Floridia, so somewhere important like Blackbury ought to be *no* trouble.'

'I can find no radio messages about Blackbury. There are plenty about Florida,' said the Thing.

'At least land *somewhere*,' said Gurder. Angalo pressed a couple of buttons.

'There's just sea under us right now,' he said. 'And — what's that?'

Below the Ship and a long way off, something tiny and white skimmed over the clouds.

'Could be goose,' said Pion.

'I . . . don't . . . think . . . so,' said Angalo carefully. He twiddled a knob. 'I'm really learning about this stuff,' he said.

The picture on the screen flickered a bit, and then expanded.

There was a white dart sliding across the sky.

'Is it the Concorde?' said Gurder.

'Yes,' said Angalo.

'It's going a bit slow, isn't it?'

'Only compared to us,' said Angalo.

'Follow it,' said Masklin.

'We don't know where it's going,' said Angalo, in a reasonable tone of voice.

'I do,' said Masklin. 'You looked out of the window when we were on the Concorde. We were going towards the sun.'

'Yes. It was setting,' said Angalo. 'Well?'

'It's morning now. It's going towards the sun again,' Masklin pointed out.

'Well? What about it?'

'It means it's going home.'

Angalo bit his lip while he worked this out.

'I don't see why the sun has to rise and set in different places,' said Gurder, who refused to even try to understand basic astronomy.

'Going home,' said Angalo, ignoring him. 'Right. I see it. So we go with it, yes?'

'Yes.'

Angalo ran his hands over the Ship's controls.

'Right,' he said. 'Here we go. I expect the Concorde drivers will probably be quite pleased to have some company up here.'

The Ship drew level with the plane.

'It's moving around a lot,' said Angalo. 'And it's starting to go faster, too.'

'I think they may be worried about the Ship,' said Masklin.

'Can't see why,' said Angalo. 'Can't see why at all. We're not doing anything except following 'em.'

'I wish we had some proper windows,' said Gurder, wistfully. 'We could wave.'

'Have humans ever seen a Ship like this before?' Angalo asked the Thing.

'*No. But they've made up stories about Ships coming from other worlds.*'

'Yes, they'd do that,' said Masklin, half to himself. 'That's *just* the sort of thing they'd do.'

'*Sometimes they say the Ships will contain friendly people —* '

'That's us,' said Angalo.

' *— and sometimes they say they will contain monsters with wavy tentacles and big teeth.*'

The nomes looked at one another.

Gurder cast an apprehensive eye over his shoulder. Then they all stared at the passages that radiated off the control-room.

'Like alligators?' said Masklin.

'*Worse.*'

'Er,' Gurder said, 'we *did* look in all the rooms, didn't we?'

'It's something they make up, Gurder. It's not real,' said Masklin.

'Whoever would want to make up something like that?'

'Humans would,' said Masklin.

'Huh,' said Angalo, nonchalantly trying to swivel around in the chair in case any tentacled things with teeth were trying to creep up on him. 'I can't see why.'

'I think I can. I've been thinking about humans a lot.'

'Can't the Thing send a message to the Concorde drivers?' said Gurder. 'Something like "Don't worry, we haven't got any teeth and tentacles, guaranteed"?'

'They probably wouldn't believe us,' said Angalo. 'If *I* had teeth and tentacles all over the place that's just the sort of message I'd send. Cunning.'

The Concorde screamed across the top of the sky, breaking the transatlantic record. The Ship drifted along behind it.

'I reckon,' said Angalo, looking down, 'that humans are just about intelligent enough to be crazy.'

'I think,' said Masklin, 'that maybe they're intelligent enough to be lonely.'

The plane touched down with its tyres screaming. Fire engines raced across the airport, and there were other vehicles behind them.

The great black Ship shot over them, turned across the sky like a frisbee, and slowed.

'There's the reservoir!' said Gurder. 'Right under us! And that's the railway line! And that's the quarry! It's still there!'

'Of course it's still there, idiot,' muttered Angalo, as he headed the Ship towards the hills, which were patchy with melting snow.

'Some of it,' said Masklin.

A pall of black smoke hung over the quarry. As they got closer, they saw it was rising from a burning truck. There were more trucks around it, and also several humans that started to run when they saw the shadow of the Ship.

'Lonely, eh?' snarled Angalo. 'If they've hurt a single nome, they'll wish they'd never been born!'

'If they've hurt a single nome they'll wish *I'd* never been born,' said Masklin. 'But I don't think anyone's down there. They wouldn't hang around if the humans came. And who set fire to the truck?'

'Yay!' said Angalo, waving a fist in the air.

Masklin scanned the landscape below them. Somehow he couldn't imagine people like Grimma and Dorcas sitting in holes, waiting for humans to take over. Trucks didn't just set fire to themselves. A couple of buildings looked damaged, too. Humans wouldn't have done that, would they?

He stared at the field by the quarry. The gate had been

smashed, and a pair of wide tracks led through the slush and mud.

'I think they got away in another truck,' he said.

'What do you mean, *yay?*' said Gurder, lagging a bit behind the conversation.

'Across the fields?' said Angalo. 'It'd get stuck, wouldn't it?'

Masklin shook his head. Perhaps even a nome could have instincts. 'Follow the tracks,' he said urgently. 'And quickly!'

'Quickly? *Quickly?* Do you know know difficult it is to make this thing go *slowly?*' Angalo nudged a lever. The Ship lurched up the hillside, straining at the indignity of restraint.

They'd been up here before, on foot, months ago. It was hard to believe.

The hills were quite flat on the top, forming a kind of plateau overlooking the airport. There was the field where there had been potatoes. There was the thicket where they'd hunted, and the wood where they'd killed a fox for eating nomes.

And there . . . there was something small and yellow, rolling across the fields.

Angalo craned forward.

'Looks like some kind of a machine,' he admitted, fumbling for levers without taking his eyes off the screen. 'Weird kind of one, though.'

There were other things moving on the roads down there. They had flashing lights on top.

'Those cars are chasing it, do you think?' said Angalo.

'Maybe they want to talk to it about a burning truck,' said Masklin. 'Can you get to it before they do?'

Angalo narrowed his eyes. 'Listen, I think we can get to it before they do even if we go via Floridia.' He found another lever and gave it a nudge.

There was the briefest flicker in the landscape, and the truck was now right in front of them.

'See?' he said.

'Move in more,' said Masklin.

Angalo pressed a button. 'See, the screen can show you below — ,' he began.

'There's nomes!' said Gurder.

'Yeah, and those cars are running away!' shouted Angalo. 'That's it, run away! Otherwise it's teeth-and-tentacles time!'

'So long as the nomes don't think that too,' said Gurder. 'Masklin, do you think — '

Once again, Masklin wasn't there.

I should have thought about this before, he thought.

The piece of branch was thirty times longer than a nome. They'd been keeping it under lights, and it seemed to be growing quite happily with one end in a pot of special plant water. The nomes who had once flown in the Ship had obviously grown lots of plants that way.

Pion helped him drag the pot towards the hatch. The frogs watched Masklin with interest.

When it was positioned as well as the two of them could manage, Masklin let the hatch open. It wasn't one that slid aside. The ancient nomes had used it as a kind of lift, but it didn't have wires — it went up and down by some force as mysterious as auntie's gravy or whatever it was.

It dropped away. Masklin looked down and saw the yellow truck roll to a halt. When he straightened up, Pion was giving him a puzzled look.

'Flower is a message?' said the boy.

'Yes. Kind of.'

'Not using words?'

'No,' said Masklin.

'Why not?'

Masklin shrugged.

'Don't know how to say them.'

It nearly ends there . . .

But it shouldn't end there.

Nomes swarmed all over the Ship. If there *were* any monsters with tentacles and teeth, they'd have been overwhelmed by sheer force of nome.

Young nomes filled the control-room, where they were industriously trying to press buttons. Dorcas and his trainee engineers had disappeared in search of the Ship's engines. Voices and laughter echoed along the grey corridors.

Masklin and Grimma sat by themselves, watching the frogs in their flower.

'I had to see if it was true,' said Masklin.

'The most wonderful thing in the world,' said Grimma.

'No. I think there are probably much more wonderful things in the world,' said Masklin. 'But it's pretty good, all the same.'

Grimma told him about events in the quarry — the fight with the humans, and the stealing of Jekub the earth-mover to escape. Her eyes gleamed when she talked about fighting humans. Masklin looked at her with his mouth open in admiration. She was muddy, her dress torn, her hair looked like it had been combed with a hedge, but she crackled with so much internal power that she was nearly throwing off sparks. It's a good thing we got here in time, he thought. Humans ought to thank me.

'What are we going to do now?' she said.

'I don't know,' said Masklin. 'According to the Thing, there's worlds out there with nomes on. Just nomes, I mean. Or we can find one all to ourselves.'

'You know,' said Grimma, 'I think the Store nomes would be happier just staying on the Ship. That's why they like it so much. It's like being in the Store. All the Outside is outside.'

'Then I'd better go along to make sure they remember that there *is* an Outside. It's sort of my job, I suppose,' said Masklin. 'And, when we've found somewhere, I want to bring the Ship back.'

'Why? What'll be here?' said Grimma.

'Humans,' said Masklin. 'We should talk to them.'

'Huh!'

'They really want to believe in . . . I mean, they spend all their time making up stories about things that don't exist. They think it's just themselves in the world. We never thought like that. We always *knew* there were humans. They're terribly lonely and don't know it.' He waved his hands vaguely. 'It's just that I think we might get along with them,' he finished.

'They'd turn us into pixies!'

'Not if we come back in the Ship. If there's one thing even humans can tell, it's that the Ship isn't very pixyish.'

Grimma reach out and took his hand.

'Well . . . if that's what you really want to do . . .'

'It is.'

'I'll come back with you.'

There was a sound behind them. It was Gurder. The Abbot had a bag slung around his neck and had the drawn, determined look of someone who is going to See It Through no matter what.

'Er. I've come to say goodbye,' he said.

'What do you mean?' said Masklin.

'I heard you say you're coming back in the Ship?'

'Yes, but — '

'Please don't argue.' Gurder looked around. 'I've been thinking about this ever since we got the Ship. There *are* other nomes out there. *Someone* ought to tell them about the Ship coming back. We can't take them now, but someone ought to find all the other nomes in the world and make sure that they know about the Ship. Someone ought to be telling them about what's really true. It should be me, don't you think? I've got to be useful for *something*.'

'All by *yourself?*' said Masklin.

Gurder rummaged in the bag.

'No, I'm taking the Thing,' he said, producing the black cube.

'Er –' Masklin began.

'Don't worry,' said the Thing. *'I have copied myself into the Ship's own computers. I can be here and there at the same time.'*

'It's something I really want to do,' said Gurder helplessly.

Masklin thought about arguing and then thought, why? Gurder will probably be happier like this. Anyway, it's true, this Ship belongs to all nomes. We're just borrowing it for a while. So Gurder's right. Maybe someone ought to find the rest of them, wherever they are in the world, and tell them the truth about nomes. I can't think of anyone better for the job than Gurder. It's a big world. You need someone really ready to *believe*.

'Do you want anyone to go with you?' he said.

'No. Maybe I can find some nomes out there to help me.' He leaned closer. 'To tell the truth,' he said, 'I'm looking forward to it.'

'Er. Yes. There's a lot of world, though,' said Masklin.

'I've taken that into consideration. I've been talking to Pion.'

'Oh? Well . . . if you're sure . . .'

'Yes. More than I've ever been about anything, now,' said Gurder. 'And I've been pretty sure of a lot of things in my time, as you know.'

'We'd better find somewhere suitable to set you down.'

'That's right,' said Gurder. He tried to look brave. 'Somewhere with a lot of geese,' he said.

They left him at sunset, by a lake. It was a brief parting. If the Ship stayed anywhere for more than a few minutes now, humans would flock towards it.

The last Masklin saw of him was a small waving figure on the shore. And then there was just a lake, turning into a green dot on a dwindling landscape. A world unfolded, with one invisible nome in the middle of it.

And then there was nothing.

The control-room was full of nomes, watching the landscape unroll as the Ship rose.

Grimma stared at it.

'I never realized it looked like that,' she said. 'There's so much of it!'

'It's pretty big,' said Masklin.

'You'd think one world would be big enough for all of us,' said Grimma.

'Oh, I don't know,' said Masklin. 'Maybe one world isn't big enough for anyone. Where are we heading, Angalo?'

Angalo rubbed his hands and pulled every lever right back.

'So far up,' he said, with satisfaction, 'that there is no down.'

The Ship curved up, towards the stars. Below, the world stopped unrolling because it had reached its edges, and became a black disc against the sun.

Nomes and frogs looked down on it.

And the sunlight caught it and made it glow around the rim, sending rays up into the darkness, so that it looked exactly like a flower.